THESE WICKED WATERS

EMILY LAYNE

OWL HOLLOW PRESS

Owl Hollow Press, LLC, Springville, UT 84663

These Wicked Waters

Library of Congress Cataloging-in-Publication Data
These Wicked Waters / E. Layne. — First edition.

Summary:
When Annie makes a terrifying discovery on a cursed island, she must face her biggest fears to uncover the truth and save the people she loves.

ISBN 978-1-945654-39-8 (paperback)
ISBN 978-1-945654-40-4 (e-book)
LCCN TBD

For my sister Maddie, the writing soundtrack and siren-drawing queen. This book would not be the same without you.

DAY ONE, 10:30 A.M.

F or a cursed island I'd expected dense fog and gnawed skeletons stretched across the beach. A summer packed with danger and mystery? That I could handle—even enjoy. But this? Oh, anything but *this*.

I gripped the ferry's warm railing and squinted through blinding sunlight at the approaching island. Azure water glistened as it rushed past a pier and broke against a crescent swath of shoreline. Clusters of bright pink, blue, and green shops littered the pier-turned-boardwalk farther down. Even from the boat, I heard the echo of peppy tropical music pumping through the sound system.

Definitely not cursed-looking.

Chimes rang from the speaker behind me in high-pitched tones. "Ladies and gentlemen." The deep voice cut through the thrum of conversations. Static buzzed as talking became hushed whispers and then silence. "This is your captain. We are now pulling into dock. Make your way to the ferry's front to get your first look at the world-famous resort, Mayfield Villa."

I scowled at the speaker, bending the rim of my favorite baseball hat to better block the sun. World famous? That was the overstatement of the month. The place had just opened. *Enough marketing, Mom. The guests are* here.

The scattered observers along the railing morphed into a frenzied mob. Soon-to-be guests clustered around me, smart phones and cameras clicking away. Kids screamed to be lifted because "I can't see, I can't see!"

Someone jostled me from behind with a pointy elbow, knocking me into the belly of someone who already looked sunburned. The crowd's heavy cologne, flowery perfume, and body odor mingled with the salt air.

I vacated my spot with a few well-placed shoves and squeezed through the mass of bodies, no longer able to see if Viaii Nisi's shady past matched its tropical exterior. There would be time for exploring once we docked. If Mom didn't have hours of torture lined up for me, of course. That thought made me grimace, and the difference between my mood and the eagerness of the crowd sent pinpricks of frustration across the back of my neck.

I abandoned the deck for a secluded air-conditioned corner in the ferry's lounge, ordering a grilled cheese and putting it on Mom's tab.

By the time I finished, half the guests had abandoned the ferry, exiting along the gangplank in a messy cluster. After waiting in a congested line, I handed my resort ID—a must for anyone visiting Viaii Nisi—to one of the three clerks at the ferry's exit.

The guy scanned it with a small gadget attached to his phone and passed it back to me with a warm smile. "Enjoy your stay at Mayfield Villa, Miss Annie *Mayfield*." I barely heard his Australian-accented voice over the music ahead of me and chatter behind but couldn't miss his emphasis.

"By *stay*, I think you mean participate in indentured servitude," I muttered as I took my ID. "But thanks just the same." I gave him a halfhearted salute, whipped off my hat to use as a makeshift fan—I was already sweating—and strolled down the gangplank.

While the majority of guests streamed down the pier to the waiting buses, a few guests paused to gawk at the clear blue water, take thumbs-up selfies, or readjust their bags. One guy had rested an open textbook on his head, flattening blond spikes, while his hands rifled through the pockets of a pair of blue swim trunks. I did a double take. He was actually kinda cute.

Loud thumps against the pier's wooden boards interrupted my people watching, and I turned to look behind me. An overweight man was running backward in my direction, a tablet held high above his head.

"Just need a little more space, lo—" he was calling as I said, "Watch out!" even as the man's polo-covered back slammed into me. My hands splayed reflexively as I tried to catch myself. The heels of my Sketchers skidded against the pier and caught at the raised edge. Momentum carried me forward, the ocean yawning yards below.

A bolt of panic shot through me, brief and electrifying, just as a pair of tanned arms caught my waist. I hung for a moment, suspended over the water, until I was yanked back to the safety of the pier. I sucked in a savage breath and squeezed my eyes shut to collect myself. When I opened them, I stared into the face of the cute spiky-haired textbook boy I'd noticed earlier. He gave me a breathless but earnest smile that asked, *Are you all right?*

Heat warmed my cheeks. I stepped back, wary of the pier's edge and crossed my arms. "Uh, thanks."

"No problem." He rolled his shoulders, green t-shirt declaring *I'm off like a herd of turtles*. A little but determined turtle sporting a red sweatband was plastered in the center.

"Try watching the edge next time," he continued. "You know, instead of strangers." He winked and scooped up his abandoned textbook, plopping it back on his head. Without another word, he ambled off, whistling Johnny Cash's "I Walk the Line."

I frowned at his retreating back until a gust of salty wind blew my hair into my face. I tucked the wild strands behind my ear, then slowly moved my hands from my ears to the top of my head. My mouth dropped open in horror as I clutched my mussed curly hair.

"Oh, no, oh, no." I fell to my knees at the pier's edge. The wood bit into my skin, but the discomfort felt faraway and unimportant. My gaze swept the ocean below in frantic sweeps before it landed on the object I sought.

My favorite baseball hat bobbed in the waves fifteen feet below. The bold white *Climb Like a Girl* stitched onto the front seemed to beg for me to claim it with each surge of water. Dad custom ordered the hat for me when rock climbing first sparked my interest, and now my arch nemesis, the ocean, had whisked it away.

Maybe a cursed island wasn't so far off the mark.

A long human-sized shadow flitted beneath the surface, and the faintest hum of a melody twisted through the buzz of conversations and music. I leaned over the pier as far as I dared. A sparkling orange fin pierced the blue for the briefest instant…

Before it twisted around my hat and both disappeared.

My eyes bulged in their sockets. *No. Way.*

I whirled around to see if there were other witnesses. Couples smiled into cameras, kids were tugged away from the pier's edge, groups hurried toward food and souvenir shops—everyone continued about their business as if some enormous fish hadn't just *eaten* my hat.

"Miss!" someone called with a distinct British accent to my right. I glanced over and recognized the striped polo that had almost killed me. The man wearing the blue-and-pink abomination hurried over, sunglasses in one hand, forehead creased with apology.

"I am *so* sorry." The man clasped his palms together, possibly on the verge of falling to his knees for the sake of forgiveness. "I wasn't paying attention while taking pictures and…" He snuck a look back at a woman waiting yards off. She glared at us with a suspicious twist to her lips. "My wife didn't want me to come, thinking you'd want to sue, but I had to make sure you were all right." He paused and leaned forward, waiting for me to confirm that I was okay.

I blinked and tried to get my mouth to speak—or at least shut! All I saw was that lithe shadow and a flash of scales as my...

"Hat," I croaked, pointing over the side of the pier. "I lost my hat." Thank goodness my mouth turned on its filter for once. *An enormous fish ate my hat* had a crazed ring to it. I pushed myself to my feet, brushing imaginary dust from my knees.

He peered into the water and, though my hat was long gone, winced in what seemed genuine sympathy. "I'm such an idiot." He looked behind me, toward the shops on the much safer boardwalk. "Could I buy you a new one?"

A new hat? With a front that had *Mayfield Villa* written on it? Thanks, but no thanks.

I shook my head. "Don't worry. It's just a... hat." That I wore everywhere, all the time. Even in winter. My shock at the orange fin waned, frustration surging forward to replace it. Oh, my poor hat!

"Please? I'd feel loads better."

"Adam!" The disgruntled wife stomped up to us, her patience withered—if not dead. "The first resort bus is almost full." She gestured toward the boardwalk with a manicured hand. "We should go."

I considered telling *Adam* no again but abandoned that idea as I held a hand up against the sunlight streaming down on us. Why not? The guy owed me for that scare. A Mayfield Villa hat was better than no hat.

My gaze flickered to the ocean below where that scaled thing lurked. "Okay," I said and turned to Adam. "I'll go for the hat. Thanks."

"That's brilliant," Adam said, shaking my hand in his enthusiasm then glancing at his wife. "Do you mind waiting for the next bus, love?"

She grunted a noncommittal answer and stormed toward a bar sporting swirly glasses and fruity drinks.

Adam cleared his throat, pink splotching his cheeks as he watched his wife go. Then he turned back to me with a resigned sigh. "So what's your name?"

"Annie," I said, leading the way down the pier toward a gaudy souvenir shop. The florescent hats hanging from a rack outside made me cringe.

"Nice to meet you. I'm Adam, if you haven't gathered already."

We abandoned the pier for the cement of the boardwalk-style shops, passing beneath a sign that blazed "Welcome Center" in block letters. The crowd had thinned, those not clustered around food stands in line for the buses bound for Mayfield Villa.

A quick look at my watch made me groan. I was supposed to meet Benny, Mom's assistant, by that bus stop—ten minutes ago. Benny might wait in Mom's private limo for a while, but not forever.

"Which one suits your fancy?" Adam asked, wallet in hand. I caught sight of quite a few fifties nestled inside.

"Hmm." I spun the rack and looked over each hat with a critical eye.

To my relief, only half the hats said *Mayfield Villa*. I settled on a florescent blue one with *Viaii Nisi*, the name of the island, stitched across the front. I wondered if Mom knew what Viaii Nisi meant in Greek. If so, I doubted she'd want to advertise the name on Mayfield merchandise.

While Adam went inside, I pulled a map of the island off a nearby shelf. Viaii Nisi was shaped like a giant lima bean with Mayfield Villa smack dab in the center, butting against the shore of the natural lagoon. A few trails snaked out from the villa into the jungle behind it, though none seemed to lead anyplace in particular. On the south tip of the island, near the pier where I stood, there was also an Aquatic Adventures building for "marine interaction." Perched on the north tip was a lighthouse advertised by "romantic, five course dinner, free childcare!" The back half of the island, dotted with jagged cliffs, was unmarked by tourist attractions. I frowned. Mom had spent a pretty penny on this place. Why hadn't she used every square foot to rake in more profit?

Adam emerged from the shop and I returned the map to the shelf.

"It's not your original," he said, handing over the hat. "But I hope you get good use out of it."

I rolled the stiff bill in my hands and forced a smile. "Don't worry." I tugged on the hat and popped my hands out to either side like a picture frame. "It's perfect."

"Wonderful! Now I better join my wife." He wiped sweat from his brow with a handkerchief he slipped from a pants pocket. "Hope to see you again, Annie." With a final smile, he turned and ambled away.

I shifted the new hat on my head, missing my old one but grudgingly thankful for a replacement. Praying Benny hadn't abandoned me, I jogged toward the bus stop at the boardwalk's end.

As I approached, a packed bus drove off, revealing a parked limo behind it. Leaning against the trunk, a trim figure in a dark gray suit, was the one and only Benson Parson.

"Benny!" I cried, excited for the first time since boarding the ferry for Viaii Nisi.

Benny looked up from his phone as I sprinted toward him. "Hey, kiddo!" he cried, arms going out wide.

I hurled myself into his embrace and squeezed him in a tight hug. He gripped me twice as hard, a deep laugh echoing through his chest, breath smelling of fruity gum.

"Let me get a look at you." Benny held me at arm's length. "It's been what, a year?" He pursed his lips, playacting the critical art collector. "Hair still short and messy as ever. Eyes their *very* mischievous blue. And what's this?" He rapped his knuckles on the bill of my hat.

"An enormous fish ate my other one. Right after I nearly fell to my death."

"An enormous fish, huh?"

I stepped back, hands on my hips. "That's what you're concerned about?"

"Well, you did say *nearly*. Hop in." His white teeth flashed in a smile as he swung open the limo door. "You're fifteen minutes late."

With that charming smile and those warm eyes, Benny could pass for Will Smith's younger brother—a fact I wrote stories about back when my tween crush on Benny was in full swing. Embarrassing tropes like *Benson & Annie's Forbidden Fantasy*, *The Truth Behind the Smiths*, and *Breakfast with Benson*.

Ugh.

A chirp came from Benny's suit jacket. He held up a finger in the universal *hold on* and slid out a Blackberry. Despite Mom's best efforts, he refused to make the switch to Apple. Or at least Android. Benny argued that a Blackberry made a man appear more trustworthy.

"It's your mom asking if I've gotten you," he explained, not looking up as he typed a reply.

My excitement at seeing him died a quick death. I swallowed against a snappy retort along the lines of *Oh, now she cares?*

"This is the third message from her. We better get moving. Ready?" he asked with a gesture toward the open limo.

"Do I have a choice?"

"Not really." He shot me his evil eye, summoning memories of twelve-year-old me refusing to obey bedtime. Yeah, Benny's duties also doubled as a babysitter when he first joined the company after college. Though I doubted most babysitters made $200,000 a year.

I held my hands up in surrender. "Fine, fine."

After we settled inside the limo, the driver took off down the road, soon catching up to the bus that had left before it. I leaned back against the leather and eyed Benny in his seat across from me, still tapping on his Blackberry.

"So," I began. "Remember the enormous fish that ate my hat?"

"Don't even try it." His gaze stayed fixed on the Blackberry's screen.

I huffed. "What do you mean?"

"Your mom told me about Viaii Nisi's past owners." Now he did meet my eyes. "And your interest in them." He sighed. "Kiddo, they're silly stories people made up. The waters are safe, and there are tons of precautions that have been put in place. You should go easy on your mom. She's been under a lot of stress with the construction and that late occupancy permit." He raised one eyebrow. "Your little stunt at school didn't help either."

"That's just what she wants you to think. Stories have to come from somewhere!" I rubbed at my face in exasperation. "Instead of being here, I should be—"

"And the truth comes out!" Benny abandoned his Blackberry to a pocket. "Now I know why you're so fixed on those crazy theories."

I shook my head, annoyed. "That's not the only reason. There *was* a huge fish. And it *did* eat my hat."

"I believe you," he said, tone serious—though the twinkle in his eye made me doubt his sincerity. "A fish got your favorite hat. I'm sure it's happened to people before."

"Yeah, but Viaii Nisi is different," I grumbled and glared out the tinted limousine window as Mom's sprawling resort appeared. The dumb island had already stolen my summer, and now my hat.

What would it take next?

DAY ONE, 11:12 A.M.

An enormous statue of Poseidon studied me as I stepped through the villa's automatic doors. He made a somber observer, brow creased in a stern yet curious wrinkle. In one mammoth hand he clutched his signature three-point trident, their tips sharpened to gleaming points. I sucked in a gasp at the sheer magnitude of the Greek god.

"Annie?" Benny's voice reached my ears, towing me back to reality.

The lobby of the villa behind Poseidon swam into focus, packed with guests hurrying across the marble floor, leaning against enormous columns, or waiting in line at the busy Guest Services' desk.

"He's amazing," I murmured over the echoing chatter.

Beside me Benny nodded at Poseidon. "Your mom commissioned an artist to design and carve him." He cleared his throat and peered behind us through the front doors. "We better get moving. The next bus just pulled up, and I want to give you a tour before things get hectic."

That snapped me out of my daze. "And after the tour?"

Benny hummed the *Jaws* theme song, sliding his hands into his pant pockets. "You'll face your mom." His elbow nudged my shoulder in a playful tap. "If you think this statue is cool, wait until you see the theater."

Torn, my mouth settled somewhere between a grimace and a grin. "Okay," I said on a sigh. "Tour away."

The rest of the villa didn't disappoint. Benny ushered me from an enormous two-story theater into a dining hall, buffet room, indoor and outdoor pool areas, exercise room, and spa. The place's luxury reminded me of a cruise ship.

Unfortunately, the tour only took a whopping thirty minutes. Despite my best efforts to extend it, I soon found myself inside a mirrored elevator headed to the villa's top floor.

The doors slid open noiselessly. Benny leaned out and pointed down a hall with ornate sconces fixed to teal-painted walls. Two double doors, outlined in silver filigree, waited at the end.

"Your mom's office is in there." He opened his mouth as if to continue speaking but shook his head instead. "Don't mention the rumors. She'll only get mad, trust me. Good luck, kiddo." He shooed me into the corridor. My sneakers squeaked on the hardwood floor that was polished and buffed to look like drift-wood.

Before I could flee back into the elevator, the doors closed, Benny's amused yet sympathetic smile disappearing behind them.

"Come on, Annie," I muttered to my sneakers. "It's just Mom."

I crept along the silent hall to the double doors at the end. The plaque fixed on the left side, perfectly centered, made my palms dampen.

Florence Mayfield
Owner & Manager

I lifted my hand to knock but paused. Through the wood, familiar shouting reached my ears. Part of me wanted to flee down the hallway rather than face Rampaging Mom. But that would only postpone the inevitable.

I straightened my shoulders, breathed deep, and knocked.

The muffled conversation continued. No "Come in!" or "Who is it?"

I knocked again. And again no response.

That settled it. Mom knew I was coming. I swung open the door and called out, "Mom?"

"No, I'm not pleased!" Mom's raised voice made me flinch. "I barely got the permit in time."

Directly ahead of me, she perched on the back of a couch at the far end of her office, glaring out one of three bay windows, cell phone clutched to her ear. She glanced over her shoulder and wiggled her fingers in a wave. "One second," she mouthed.

I rolled my eyes and wandered to the floor-to-ceiling book-shelf behind her desk. Books filled every row, all the same size and brown hues. I walked along, fingers trailing over the worn covers. My eyes caught on familiar lines and curves that popped out on the spines. I leaned closer.

Greek. All *Greek* books. Mom couldn't even read Greek!

I slid out a copy of Homer's *The Odyssey* and flipped through the pages covered in English words. *English* words. Not Greek. The books' spines were just for show.

Mom had gone way overboard with Mayfield Villa's theme. Despite how beautiful everything was, the decor felt like a slap in the face, like Mom was rubbing it in that I was stuck here in-stead of...

I jammed the book back into its spot with more force than necessary. Two years laboring over the Greek language merely to read fake book bindings—not how this summer was supposed to go.

I collapsed into Mom's swivel chair, propping my feet up on the clear glass of her desk.

"Look, I don't have time for this," she declared into the phone. "I have a resort to run. If you have any more questions, contact my assistant." She hung up and took a slow breath be-fore turning to face me. "Annie Mayfield, get your feet off of there." She flicked my sneakers with French manicured nails.

I smacked them to the floor and crossed my arms. "Nice dé-cor, Mom. It's like *I'm in Greece.*"

"Don't start." Mom planted a distracted kiss atop my head. "How was the ferry ride?" She slid a book from the shelf and opened it, revealing it as just an iPad cover. Another façade. "I worried about you all alone but couldn't get clearance for the chopper." She tapped on the screen, a frown pulling at the corners of her mouth.

"The ferry ride was fine," I said, losing hold on my bitter-ness at the momentary concern in her eyes. "Who were you talking to?"

"The contractor. I complained about how late the occupan-cy permit got to us. I'm never dealing with that company again." She tucked an escaped curl of blond hair behind her ear. "The workers were the most superstitious group I've ever seen. They refused to stay here overnight! The building almost wasn't fin-ished in time. Can you believe that?"

Don't mention the rumors, Benny's warning echoed in my head. *She'll only get mad, trust me.* Words like "drownings," "enormous fish," and "unexplained gashes"—from articles I'd found online when I learned I'd be stuck here this summer—kicked against my teeth. I swallowed them back. Instead, I said, "Oh?"

"Anyway, back to you." She slid her finger across the iPad's screen, all business. "Every job is filled, so it was hard to place you. You'll be on a rotation instead."

"Or," I ventured, leaning forward in the chair, hands balled into fists. "We could skip the rotation, and you could send me to Meteora to rock climb like I've been planning for, oh, you know, *two years.*"

Mom rubbed her temples as if massaging away a headache. "We've been over this, Annie. You're only sixteen—"

"Almost seventeen."

"You're still underage, too young to travel so far by your-self."

"I traveled here alone! This island is part of Greece! Going to Greece—to *Meteora*—shouldn't be—"

"Viaii Nisi is a *territory* of Greece. It's off the coast of Florida and a quick ferry ride from the US. This island is safe—I can guarantee that. But a foreign country? I have no control there. What kind of mother would I be if I let you traipse around the world alone? Once your sister backed out, that was it. And climbing that big rock?" She shivered.

I sunk into the chair, my chest burning afresh at Lynn's betrayal. "Mom, you could've hired someone to go with me. Easy!"

"I would've considered it," she began, "before you became a juvenile delinquent at your boarding school."

I fought the urge to roll my eyes. "Juvenile delinquent? That's a little dramatic."

Her mouth fell open to form a small pink O. "A little *dramatic*?" She slammed the iPad cover shut. "You climbed up on your school's roof—six stories high—and put a pink tutu around the statue of Saint Thomas Aquinas! *The saint of education.* That's vandalism, a misdemeanor! And you might've been hurt." Her voice wavered, and she cleared her throat. "Your headmistress would've expelled you if I hadn't intervened."

"It was just a joke," I muttered. "The statue is so ugly, the tutu was an improvement. Besides, you shouldn't be mad at me. The birds did way worse to poor Thomas."

Mom let out a breath. "Enough arguing, okay? You're working here this summer as punishment. That's it."

I sighed and tugged off my hat. This wasn't how I wanted the conversation to go, though I suppose Mom changing her mind and booking me the first flight to Meteora was too much to hope for. I ran my fingers across the threads composing *Viaii Nisi* on my hat.

"You might not want to advertise this," I said, holding it up for her to see, a final jab. "Viaii Nisi basically means *violent isle* in Greek."

"Violent…?" Mom's forehead creased in confusion before her gaze flicked to my face. She threw her head back as if asking the crystal chandeliers for help. "Oh, you're worse than your father with those sad eyes! Please don't make me feel guilty, Annie. This will be a fun summer." Mom grabbed my hands and tugged me to my feet.

A sharp pang went through me. She didn't even notice my missing *Climb Like a Girl* hat.

"You'll work, yes, but only Monday through Thursday. There will be plenty of downtime. Relax, get a tan, make friends. There are plenty of people your age."

"Tanning. How… *exciting.*"

She shot me a *that's enough* look. "I have a meeting with the maintenance staff…" Her eyes darted to her dainty gold watch. "Yikes. Three minutes ago. New plan. I want you to go to floor two and report to the head of housekeepers. Her name's Iona. She'll get you settled with your first job."

I crinkled my nose. "Mom, being a maid is so boring. At least give me something interesting to do."

Mom's lips curved in a playful smirk. "Honey, you won't be a housekeeper all the time. You're doing a bit of everything! Maid in the mornings and towel clerk in the afternoon. You'll rotate to daycare duty and waitressing in a couple weeks. Or whenever we're short-staffed. Fun, huh?"

I crossed my arms and groaned. "Loads." This summer officially stunk.

Mom fixed her hands on my shoulders and guided me to the doors. "Everyone is busy with the first day, so don't cause trouble." She checked her watch again. "Remember, second floor. Look for Iona's office. It's got a sign on the door. She'll give you your room assignment and uniforms."

A summer spent wearing plastic gloves and wielding a toilet brush—instead of chalk-covered fingers and my skin pressed against sun-kissed rock…

"Forget about a cursed island," I muttered and swung open the door. "*I'm* cursed."

Mom's cry reached me before I escaped into the elevator. "And brush your hair, sweetheart. It looks like a tumble of seaweed!"

Lorelei's Song, Verse One
"Of all creatures that breathe and move upon the earth,
nothing is bred that is weaker than man."
~ *The Odyssey, Book 18*

Power rippled through Lorelei's scaled limbs as she swam. Sand flitted about in the dark ocean as she rushed past, catching fragmented moonlight. Victory would be hers in just a few whale-lengths. She risked a look back.

A sapphire-hued blur spiraled past her in a whirlwind of bubbles. Lorelei snapped her teeth in despair. Echo would win again. The rampaging thrill in Lorelei's blood dulled to a mere whisper. Her eyes swept the sea for the other competitors and fixed on a foreign glow. Orange and red flickered against the surface in a merry dance. Her excitement faded as curiosity hummed an undeniable song in her veins.

Acantha and Niamh shot through the water on either side of Lorelei, heartbeats behind Echo. Their tails and webbed hands turned the placid water into froth. Lorelei spun away from the sirens. Let the others race. She would explore that strange light.

The orange scales on her belly brushed soft sand as she entered the enclosure of a small inlet. She broke the surface without a sound, sliding behind a boulder. Gentle waves rippled around the rock, foaming with glee as they hurried by to roll onto the shore.

Lorelei peered around the boulder, slim webbed fingers spread for balance. Her pupils widened and dilated as her night vision adjusted.

Cattails lined the inlet on every side. They swayed back and forth in the moon's light as they danced to the wind's silent tune. Four figures stood silhouetted on a slender curve of sand. They clustered together, hands held out to a roaring mass of light, speaking a familiar language. Of course, any spoken language heard often enough soon became familiar to Lorelei.

Words were like music for Lorelei and her sisters; learning another language came as easily as singing a newly taught melody.

But the words of the figures were unimportant. Lorelei stared transfixed at the foreign flickers of red, orange, and yellow.

Fire.

The word hit her like a slap, and oozing dread slithered through her. Fire meant one thing. Those figures on shore with their two legs, so much like her dual tails... They were lung-breathers.

An icy hand squeezed one of Lorelei's fins. She gasped and looked down, relieved to see Echo's angular face emerge from the water, jet black curls floating around her shoulders. The siren's blue eyes and hairless brow crinkled with concern.

"Why did you abandon the game?" Echo asked in hushed Greek, the same language as the lung-breathers. Her sharp teeth sparkled in the moonlight.

Lorelei held a finger to her lips and gestured toward the water. They slipped below. Acantha and Niamh waited on the sandy floor. They watched with slitted eyes as Echo and Lorelei joined them.

"What is it?" Echo asked, her question coming out as a series of clicks that carried underwater.

Acantha answered, her eyes on the fiery light above them. "Lung-breathers." Her scaled face twisted in a sneer. "Vile creatures."

"Lung-breathers?" Echo trembled and looked over her shoulder, as if a phantom escaped from Hades lurked there. "Queen Thessalonike forbade us from going near them."

"She's not here now," Acantha mused. She circled Echo with the predatory grace of a shark. "Unless the Favorite, the Theía Kóri, wishes to tell our queen? You would be punished as well. You're not that highly favored." Acantha's dual tails brushed against Echo's single one. "Five lashes? Ten? No, too soft a punishment for such a transgression. Perhaps she will toss you into the caverns where the sharks hunger—"

"Enough, Acantha," Lorelei snapped. Acantha rarely provoked Echo so openly; Lorelei was the siren's usual target. As thankful as Lorelei was to the Sea God for a reprieve, she wouldn't allow her Echo to be tormented.

Acantha flexed the corded muscles in her arms, threatening to snap the gold band around her right bicep. Swirls decorated the metal, marking her as one of Queen Thessalonike's elite guard. "Do you wish to challenge me, Lorelei?"

Lorelei's jaw popped as she ground her teeth together, catching her cheek. Copper burst in her mouth. "If *you* are brave enough to challenge *me*."

A forked tongue shot out between Echo's teeth in clear disapproval. "Lorelei, don't—"

"What will this challenge be?" Niamh asked as she slid her webbed fingers over a fleeing starfish. "Please make it entertaining. You know I despise races." Her placid face brightened as an idea alighted in her mind. "We should sing and lure them into the water." She clacked her teeth, gray tangles of hair floating around her head like a thunderous cloud. "I hear their flavor is akin to squid." She held the starfish by a point. "Except less salty."

Lorelei's taste buds tingled.

"That is no challenge," Acantha scoffed. "Though…" She glided closer to Lorelei, hooking an arm through hers. "Luring one lung-breather, the handsomest one, into the water might be worthy of Lorelei's especial talent."

Lorelei's lips spread wide in a toothy grin despite the flutter of fear should the queen discover their disobedience. The scars across her back burned with remembered agony.

But she would never cower before Acantha.

"Show me the handsome lung-breather." Lorelei raised her chin in defiance, eager to show Acantha's inferiority. Acantha was a guard. Echo, the fastest swimmer. Niamh, the most beautiful. But Lorelei—Lorelei possessed the most alluring voice of all the sirens. She would not fail.

"Lorelei, please. Queen Thessalonike ordered—" Echo attempted to repeat their queen's warning, but Acantha silenced her with a snarl.

"If you're so concerned, stand watch, Echo."

Echo's gaze slid to Lorelei. In their blue depths, Lorelei read fear and hope. Hope that Lorelei would change her mind. Fear she wouldn't.

Lorelei shook her head. "Do as Acantha says."

"But—" The rest of Echo's sentence was lost to the deep as Acantha and Lorelei broke the surface.

Acantha surveyed the lung-breathers. Above water, she whispered in Greek. "See that one?" She pointed with a taloned finger.

Lorelei leaned around the weathered rock and peered through the darkness.

The creatures still sat around the writhing fire. Acantha's "handsome" one took a swig from a large glass bottle before passing it to the lung-breather on his right. Handsome's hair hung at the nape of his neck, tied into a tail with a cord. Moonrises' worth of stubble colored his jawline, drawing attention to a perfect Roman nose above too-thin lips.

"So?" Acantha asked, reeling Lorelei's attention back to the siren's challenge.

"He's the most handsome, truly?" Lorelei tilted her head, enjoying the feel of her tangled blond braids sliding across her back. "Did you see his lips? That huge forehead and scraggly frame?"

"Maybe not handsome, but he is royalty. That is a far better prize."

"Oh?" Lorelei gave a quiet snort. "How do you know his bloodline?"

"The way he carries himself. They all bend to him, even with that bottle. He sipped first." She caught Lorelei's chin, talons scraping along the scales there. "Do you accept my challenge, or are you afraid?"

Lorelei tore her face from Acantha's grip. "I accept your challenge," she hissed. "I will lure the ugly lung-breather into the water."

"In *under* five heartbeats."

"Very well."

"Perfect." Acantha's sneer turned venomous in the slivers of moonlight. "I shall inform our sisters." She sunk below with the smallest of ripples.

Lorelei tilted her face toward the sky as dense clouds hid the moon's glow. She sucked a slow, yet unnecessary, breath to steady herself. Acantha would regret her challenge. All creatures adored Lorelei's voice. An ugly lung-breather would be no exception.

She mentally composed the melody she would sing, a melody that would ensnare and captivate. A smile curled her lips.

Acantha and Niamh emerged from the water and clustered around Lorelei, each finding handholds on the rock.

"Echo agreed to be sentry. Are you ready?" Acantha murmured, two fingers pressed against her neck to keep time.

Lorelei didn't reply, enthralled with her imagined song. She hoisted herself above the rock, hidden only by the clouds covering the moon, and tilted her face to the sky. She sang to the stars, though her voice was for the ugly lung-breather, and him alone. A melody rolled from between her lips, nonsensical words with no meaning yet full of depth, desire, and welcome.

The lung-breathers around the fire stilled as if holding their breath, appearing much like the lifeless rock where Lorelei perched. The royal one staggered to his feet. He seemed unaware of his body, even when the tip of his boot submerged beneath a wave.

A choked cry and splash tugged Lorelei's attention from her melody.

"The queen comes!" Echo's panicked Greek sent a wave of ice through Lorelei's veins.

Moonlight burst through the wisps of clouds as Lorelei's song staggered and stopped. The royal lung-breather's head swiveled in Lorelei's direction, and his gaze locked with hers. In their murky depths Lorelei perceived awe, surprise… and admiration.

Quiet splashes echoed through the night as Acantha and Niamh heeded Echo's warning.

"Now, Lorelei!" Echo pleaded.

A sharp tug on one of Lorelei's tails forced her back to reality, freeing her from the lung-breather's wonder. She dove from the rock into the safe embrace of the sea.

3

DAY TWO, 7:45 A.M.

I studied the mass of scrambled yellow on my plate, sneaking glances around the room. At the opposite end of the cafeteria table, men and women in polos and khaki shorts gathered with their breakfasts. Even though they couldn't have been here more than a couple weeks, everyone seemed to be laughing together like old friends.

Villa employees in an array of different uniforms shuffled into the cafeteria and through the buffet bar, their conversations blurring into a collective buzz while the scent of bacon, waffles, and syrup permeated the air. Instead of heading for my empty side of the table, the new arrivals shot me a wary glance and squeezed in somewhere else.

I swallowed hard and turned back to my eggs. Even my attempted "Can I sit here?" earlier had been met with a "Sorry, we're saving a seat for someone."

Where did I belong on this island? The boss's daughter and girl of all positions, but master of none. The packed plate that made my mouth water minutes ago now tightened my throat.

"You must be Annie."

My head jerked up at the lilting voice. A girl stood before me with tan skin, thick black hair, and blue eyes crinkled in a smile. With her willowy frame and easy grace, she made our old-fashioned maid uniforms look couture.

I smoothed my apron, a front for removing palm sweat, before sticking out my hand. "That's me. You are…?"

Her palm met mine in a firm shake, surprising me with hard calluses. "Tamara. Mind if I sit?" She gestured to the empty seat across from me.

"*Please.*" I nodded so eagerly, Tamara might've confused me with a bobblehead.

She slid onto the cafeteria bench, and the citrusy spark of her perfume overwhelmed the breakfast aroma. I wondered if the crinoline underneath her maid uniform itched as bad as mine did.

After a beat of awkward silence while Tamara peeled her orange, I blurted, "So these uniforms? Pretty uncomfortable, huh?"

"I like the vintage vibe." Tamara swiped her sticky fingers on a napkin and shrugged. "Not everyone can pull it off though."

"I can't even pull off naked." Hello, mouth. Meet foot. I wanted to melt into the floor.

Tamara's mascaraed eyelashes did a few quick flutters in surprise.

I cleared my throat and let out a too-loud laugh. "Awkward. Sorry. Just forget I said that."

After a shake of her head, Tamara smiled again. "I meant to pick you up at your room for breakfast. If I hadn't overslept, you could've avoided this." She gestured to our vacant end of the table. "A lot of people are too nervous to sit with Mrs. Mayfield's daughter. Try not to take it personally. Your mom told me to watch out for you. We'll be teaming up."

"Oh, really?" I raised my brows. The lack of trust Mom placed in me bordered embarrassing. Didn't she realize I could handle things myself?

Then again, who cared what she thought? At least I wasn't sitting by myself anymore.

"We'll be cleaning—Oh!" Tamara gasped and waved her hands in the air like an airport runway director. "Heather, Suze, Maisie! Ladies, *venid aquí!*"

Three maids paused at the end of the food line, a few yards from my table. Their heads swiveled in unison as they sought Tamara. When they found her, matching grins shone from very different faces.

Within moments my empty corner of the table was full and lively. A woman with fiery red hair and a Marilyn Monroe figure squeezed beside me. I scooted further down the bench to make room.

"Did you get your schedule, Tamara?" asked a maid with wrinkles around her eyes. A bowl of oatmeal and a steaming mug of tea sat on the tray in front of her.

Tamara crunched on a piece of bacon. "Annie and I've got twelve rooms on platinum level."

"Annie, you say?" The maid beside me turned to look at me anew. She pursed her ruby lips and cocked her head, framed by a few red curls that had escaped her bun. "So you're the girl everyone's buzzing about. Mrs. Mayfield's daughter?"

I nodded. "I'm surprised you didn't guess. Everyone else has avoided me."

"They're just cautious." A blond girl across from me shook her head. Her words were thick with a German accent. "They'll warm up to you. Though..." She nibbled on the crust of a piece of peanut butter toast. "We better warn her."

Tamara and the others nodded their agreement.

The blond girl lowered her toast. "On the first day I ever worked as I maid, I knocked on a door. A man opened it completely naked. I was like, *zur hölle!*" She laughed. "Let's just say I never knew it was possible for a human to be so hairy."

My mouth fell open. "People do that? Open the door without... clothes?"

"Oh, it gets worse." The red-haired maid waved off my shock. "I once got stuck cleaning a room after the guests had a bout with food poisoning."

Each maid let out a groan of sympathy. I fought to keep my breakfast down. *Mom, what did you get me into?*

The older maid sipped her tea. "No naked men or food poisoning, but a mattress fell on me once. No one found me for two hours!"

Tamara cleared her throat when I met her eyes with a panicked look. She silenced the others with a pointed glare and shake of her head. "Don't worry, Annie. We've got platinum level. The suites shouldn't be too messy. Plus, it's the first day. How bad could it get?"

As I forced the remains of hash browns down my throat with a swig of orange juice, I prayed Tamara was right.

Three knocks of Tamara's knuckles echoed through Room 1146's door. She paused and tucked a stray hair behind her ear. I rolled my aching shoulders. Never had I imagined that a maid's job involved so much procedure and, worst of all, *work*. I considered myself an in-shape girl, but at the end of today I'd have serious sore muscles.

After a few seconds, Tamara swung open the door while calling, "Housekeeping!"

The room, like the eleven prior, was spacious. The main area showcased a couch, flat-screen TV, and fireplace. What use a fireplace served on an island resort, I wasn't sure. On the left waited a closed bathroom door, and on the right, an open doorway leading to the bedroom. Enormous windows let in warm sunlight, plus a perfect view of the crowded beach. I couldn't help but wonder how much Mom charged for these platinum level suites.

As I entered the room after Tamara, the front door clicked closed, trapping my dress.

"Annie, keep that door open," Tamara called from the bedroom. "The guests need to see we're in here. Plus, we need the supplies on the cart."

"I know, I know," I grumbled. I'd already gotten her speech three times today—every time the door shut on my dress.

I tugged the door open, propped it with a jamb, and then started toward the bedroom where Tamara was fluffing pillows the size of my torso.

She wagged a finger at me. "Nuh-uh. Bathroom duty." She jerked a thumb at the closed door across the hallway.

"But I'm so tired—"

"If I can be a full-time maid by day and a guest services worker by night," Tamara raised perfectly plucked brows at me, "you can clean the last bathroom."

Who could argue with that work ethic? With a sigh, I shuffled out of the room and fished inside our rolling cart for a pair of plastic gloves.

"This is not acceptable!" a British-accented voice snapped.

I glanced down the hall to see a woman clad in a wispy swimsuit cover-up, oversized sunglasses, and a floppy straw hat. She stabbed a finger at a man dressed in a guest services uniform: khaki pants, gray vest, and green tie.

Though the pair stood at the far end of the hallway, their voices carried.

"I want to know where my husband is." The woman slid her sunglasses off, and I gasped. That surly expression, expertly applied makeup, and blond hair…

She was the grumpy woman from the pier yesterday—Adam's wife.

Despite her harsh tone, the woman's grip on her glasses trembled. "He went for a walk on the beach last night and never returned." Her head turned toward me. I ducked behind the cart, jostling it. A towel tumbled off the top stack and smacked onto my head. For a moment the world turned dark and very floral before I tugged the thing off and tossed it to the carpet.

"Mrs. Finley, I promise we're doing the best we can. Every spare employee has searched the grounds." The guest services man kept his voice even and slow.

"What about security footage? Have you checked that?"

At Mrs. Finley's question, I peeked around the side of the cart.

The man nodded. "Unfortunately, we don't have full coverage of the beach. Our cameras are limited to Mayfield Villa's buildings. Is it possible...?" He cleared his throat and adjusted his tie, man-code for obvious discomfort. "I don't want to assume, but could he have become friendly with another guest? Or, uh, an employee? Possibly?"

Mrs. Finley blinked in surprise and then scoffed. "What an idiotic accusation. It's the first day. How friendly can one man get?" She jammed her sunglasses back into place. "Find my husband," she spat, "or I'll go straight to the authorities." With that, she marched away from the shocked employee toward the elevators. And me.

I popped out of my hiding spot, heart thundering a deafening cadence. "Mrs. Finley!" I called, rushing over.

She turned to me. Her brow wrinkled as she shoved her sunglasses into her hair. "Yes?" she asked in a how-dare-you-talk-to-me kind of way.

Up close I could see how red her eyes were in the hallway's warm lighting. My annoyance at her high-and-mighty attitude lessened. Slightly.

"You probably don't recognize me." I tugged at the maid uniform. "But I met you and your husband yesterday. He bought me a hat."

Recognition swept across her face, and her haughty expression softened. "Have you seen him?" she whispered, glancing around as if paranoid someone might witness her concern.

I shook my head. "Sorry, no. But I overheard you saying Adam went for a walk last night on the beach. Was it dark out by then?"

She nodded. "It was a few hours after sunset. Maybe ten o'clock. We argued, and he'd had a few drinks—" She caught herself, clearing her throat, mouth a thin line. "I haven't seen him since."

A chill rippled along my skin. Unknown to guests, Mayfield Villa, with its spas and fancy all-inclusive restaurants, perched atop decades of nighttime murders. Or, according to the Greek police reports, "a string of mysterious deaths."

"Hello, girl?" Mrs. Finley's voice intruded on my thoughts. Her face hovered inches from mine, eyes wide. "Why do you look so panicked? Tell me."

I shook my head and stepped back. "It's nothing. Really." If I went around telling guests about the rumored sharks and cannibal natives the Internet had touted as theories, Mom would be enraged. Instead of working here, she might force me to intern with Dad at corporate—a fate worse than scrubbing toilets.

"I'm sure Adam will turn up," I continued when her expression didn't relax. The memory of Adam's flushed cheeks as he watched his wife stomp away rose in my mind. I felt a pang of guilt at hiding what I knew but covered it up with, "He loves you."

Her lips parted in surprise. "What did you say?"

"Adam loves you. He'd never cheat like that guest services guy implied."

Mrs. Finley let out a forced laugh that rang shrill. "You're just a child. What do you know?"

I thought of Mom and Dad. Their nightly arguments—when they were both home—and the secret, yearning looks they cast each other. They claimed the demands of Mayfield Corp forced Dad to find an apartment in New York City, closer to headquarters, but I suspected there was a deeper meaning. A possibility that I couldn't bear to give a name to. Not yet.

The elevator dinged, and the doors whooshed open. Mrs. Finley readjusted her sunglasses and stepped inside without another word.

I turned back toward Room 1146 as the doors closed and jumped in surprise. Tamara leaned against the doorframe, color drained from her tanned face. One hand was clasped over her mouth, the other splayed across her chest. "*Dios mío,*" she breathed.

"Tamara?" I asked, hurrying to her side. She looked ready to faint. "Are you okay?"

She let out a shaky breath and lowered her hands. "I'm fine." Her gaze lingered on the elevator before it settled on me. "Something from breakfast must've disagreed with me."

"It looks like more than an upset stomach."

"I'm *fine.*" She spun away, black dress swinging around her knees. "But the bathroom isn't. We're on the clock here, Annie."

"Right. Sorry." I eyed Tamara's rigid posture and the delicate way she carried herself, like traversing a sea of shattered glass. Had she heard about Adam going missing? Sure, it was weird, but I didn't think her reaction was solely about that. What else was going on?

I snatched the towel I'd knocked off earlier, returned it to the pile, and grabbed my cleaning supplies. Facing the bathroom, I murmured a quick prayer for no food poisoning before I opened the door.

White and gray tile stretched along the floor to a glass shower at the opposite end of the room. A toilet and two-person sink were positioned along the right wall. The enormous Jacuzzi bathtub took up half the room's left side, and in the bathroom's center waited a pile of used white towels. Just what I'd always wanted.

As I moved through the bathroom, restocking toilet paper, wiping the mirror and sinks, I replayed my conversation with Mrs. Finley. As I'd told her, I didn't believe the easy explanation of Adam running off. His tentative smile, genuine apology, and eagerness to please contradicted the suave personality of a cheater.

Something must've happened to him. Something Viaii Nisi related. An after-work chat with Mom was in order. As the Queen of Micromanagement, she probably knew every inch of the island. If anyone could figure out where Adam had disappeared to, she could.

By the time I reached this conclusion, I'd completed everything on my bathroom checklist. Except the shower and the toilet.

With horror stories stalking through my imagination, I straightened my shoulders and lifted the toilet's lid. A small brown stain screamed a hearty hello.

"Oh, this is vile." I gagged and dumped half a bottle of Lysol into the bowl. Next time Mom forced me to work for her, I was totally running away.

4

DAY TWO, 2:58 P.M.

"Think you've got it?" Nandan asked for what felt like the hundredth time.

I squinted up at his dark skin and narrowed brown eyes. The guy was more than a little overprotective of his towels, though I suppose having Mom as a boss would keep anyone on their toes. And, to be fair, I hadn't exactly been paying attention.

"Towels." I pointed to a bin where a pile of dark blue towels were folded. "Maximum of two per guest. Card scanner." I tapped the machine set up on the table in front of me. "We already did a test run with that kid earlier. The tech's easy to work. So… yeah. I think I got it."

Nandan gave me a forced smile that indented a particularly endearing dimple on his left cheek. "Okay. I'll be in my office if you have *any* questions." Somehow he managed to put the weight of the world on the three-lettered word.

"Aye, aye." I gave him a determined salute to which he shook his head.

I watched him walk up the stone path back toward the villa. Even in the hideous dark green shorts and *Mayfield Villa: Yes, you MAY!* t-shirt required of towel assistants, he cut a nice figure. Too bad he took paranoid to the next level.

I lowered myself onto a stool, dropped my chin into my hand and blew out a sigh. Instead of passing out towels, I should be talking to Mom. Except when I tried to confront her during my two-hour lunch break—one of my few perks—she'd shooed me out of her office. Apparently a conference call with some talk show host was more important than a missing man. Or her own daughter.

A tropical scene stretched out before me: sun bathers slick with tanning oil, kids splashing in the crystalline water, and twenty-one and overs sipping glasses with cute little umbrellas. I wondered if any of them ever climbed up on their school's roof and tutu-ed a statue. Or, more importantly, if they would believe the bloody secret lurking beneath Viaii Nisi's sun-kissed waves.

That every owner who had purchased the island drowned.

Which explained why Mom snagged the island so cheap; it was part of a hasty estate sale. How or *why* so many people drowned themselves... that part remained a mystery. A mystery no one seemed to question. Well, no one except me.

A lifeguard blew his whistle and pointed at a little girl sprinting down the beach with an inflated crab floatie above her head.

"No running!" he shouted.

I leaned forward, eyeing the lifeguard's profile. Blond hair, tanned skin, biceps that flexed with each movement, and a patch of sunscreen on his nose. Unfortunately, the angle of the stand hid the rest of him from view.

"Ahem."

I started to my feet. A large man in swim trunks, showing more hair than skin, held out his ID card.

"One towel," he ordered.

"Uh, sure." I gave him a smile and swiped his card through the reader. On the small touch screen, an unflattering picture of him popped up. I pressed "1" on the keypad and then enter. "You're all set." I handed him a towel and returned his card. "Remember to bring the towel back before the end of the day. Otherwise we'll have to charge a fee."

"Yeah, yeah." The man swung the towel over his shoulder, giving me a glimpse of his hairy Amazon armpit before ambling away.

I would be forever scarred by the things I'd seen today.

An elderly woman glided up as the hairy guy shuffled off. Her gray hair was permed and short in the typical older lady style, yet the hot pink lipstick hinted at a fun side.

"Hi, how many towels can I get you?" I asked.

"One, *Rybka*," she answered in a heavy Russian accent.

I squinted. "Rybka? What does that mean?"

A skinny arm darted for the clean towel bin on my left. I smacked it away before it snatched anything.

"Ow!"

I glared at a little boy with a spattering of freckles across his nose and a mop of carrot-colored hair. "Back off, kid. I already gave you a towel." He'd been my test run with Nandan, in fact. "Bring your ID, and I'll give you another."

He stuck out his tongue and ran off.

I rolled my eyes. "Sorry about that." I turned back to the woman who had watched the exchange with a wry smile.

"Rybka," she said. "Russian for little fish." She raised her brows in a knowing way. "My nickname to you."

"Um, thanks." I resisted the urge to step back. This woman was kind of creepy in a socially awkward kind of way. Who went around and nicknamed strangers *little fish*?

"You can call me…" She trailed off, eyes studying me with such an intensity that goose bumps prickled up my arms. "Mrs. Samson." She nodded as if pleased with herself. "Yes, Mrs. Samson will do." She passed me her ID card. "One towel, please."

"Yes, ma'am." I swiped her card. Sure enough, "Elvira Samson" showed up on the screen. I passed her a towel. "Enjoy your stay."

"I intend to." She smiled, eyes twinkling. "Have good day, Rybka." She waved before walking away down the beach.

What a weird old lady.

A muffled giggle made me turn. With a victorious grin, the freckled boy snagged a towel and scurried off.

"Hey!" I lunged from my perch. The stool fell and clattered against the concrete. "Get back here!" Arms pumping, I sprinted after the kid.

If I lost even one towel, Nandan would have an aneurism. I could see the headline: "Attractive India Native Killed by Irresponsible American."

That thought propelled my legs faster. The kid abandoned the sidewalk and took off toward the beach. Sand flew up in waves behind his feet. Sunbathers cried out as he passed, then swore as I pursued.

The kid zigzagged down the beach and sprinted along the shoreline. He'd tied the towel around his neck, Superman style. It flapped behind him, just out of reach. Sweat rolled down my forehead, and sand sucked at my every step as we ran along the water's edge.

A piercing whistle blew, followed by a familiar shout. "No running!"

Just as the kid turned to dart away from the ocean, my fingers caught the end of the towel. It came loose, and I skidded to a stop. The kid whirled around and grabbed the other side. He tugged, and I tugged back.

"Drop it," I panted. "*Now!*"

He gritted his teeth and tugged harder, his bony chest heaving. "I need it… to play… *Superman!*"

"Then ask your parents to get you another towel!"

"But…" His gazed shifted to stare over my shoulder. Suddenly his eyes widened, and he let go.

I cried out and stumbled backward, towel still gripped in my hand. The ocean exploded around me as I fell. Salt and foam rushed up my nose and burned my eyes. Terror cinched around my lungs, stealing my breath. I jerked upright, sputtering and gagging. A blurry man-shape hovered before me. I swiped at my watering eyes and blinked.

Behind the towel thief stood the guy from the pier. Red swim shorts, tan skin, familiar blond hair, and, yes, his crossed arms showcased the biceps I'd admired minutes before. That guy and the hot lifeguard were one and the same.

Oh, lovely.

"Come on." He held out a hand. A penny hanging from a thin cord around his neck swung forward.

My gaze shot to the stupid freckled kid watching me, a finger jammed up his nose, before I took the lifeguard's hand and stood. "Thank you," I grumbled. "Again."

"You know, I'm starting to consider this a part-time job."

"Part-time job?" I shifted and mentally grimaced at the grit of sand in my shorts.

"Rescuing you all the time." He grinned. "You looked pretty scared just now." His expression shifted to mime someone screaming, eyes wide.

Was my fear that obvious? And was he really making fun of it? I gritted my teeth.

"I don't need to be rescued." I shoved the sandy wet towel into his chest and stomped up the beach.

The lifeguard called, "Hey, don't get mad. I was just kidding!"

I didn't bother turning around. Ahead, I could see Nandan striding toward me. The dimple in his left cheek stood out against his dark skin. This time, he wasn't smiling.

Lorelei's Song, Verse Two
"Whoever unwittingly goes past them and hears the
sirens' call never gets back."
~The Odyssey, Book 12

The coral and surrounding sea were quiet as if Poseidon had ordered it so. Lorelei's golden gaze swept the open ocean a third time before she slid between dancing curtains of kelp.

Her siren sisters would no doubt be awake, racing with dolphins in the waves, hunting for food. While Lorelei's queen and mother—

"Lorelei." A commanding chirp cleaved through the silence.

Lorelei froze mid-stroke. Her body hummed with the desire to flee, but she suppressed the urge and faced the speaker.

Queen Thessalonike lurked in a crevice of coral, her gray eyes sharp despite the milky-white film covering them. "Where do you wander, child of my sorrow?"

Lorelei swallowed. She pitched her voice low to hide her fear, wrapping her lie in a kiss of truth. "To explore the deep, my queen."

"Explore?" Queen Thessalonike raised her webbed hand. A red fish darted out from her curls to weave between each finger. "You recall my warning of the lung-breathers, do you not?" Her tone was gentle, but an undercurrent of warning slithered inside each word. "I care for you, Lorelei."

Lorelei clamped her jaw shut to keep a derisive laugh from escaping.

The queen slid through the water until she floated a handspan away. She patted Lorelei's cheek in a motherly gesture. "I wouldn't want you to transgress another of my laws. This time the punishment may be more… severe."

The scars across Lorelei's back twitched with a phantom pain. "Never, Queen Thessalonike." She bowed her head in submission while her hands tightened to fists. "I want to please you."

Though her head was still lowered, Lorelei could hear the smile in her queen's voice. "It seems my Echo has calmed your wild heart."

Lorelei gritted her teeth. *My Echo.* The one thing Queen Thessalonike and Lorelei shared was their tenderness for the youngest siren. Lorelei despised even that one similarity.

"She is loyal to you," Lorelei said once her wave of fury receded.

"This I know." Queen Thessalonike moved back. Lorelei met her eyes. Softness warmed the queen's icy blue irises for a moment. "Enjoy the night, Lorelei. I will be watching to ensure none of my daughters come to harm."

Rather than safety, Lorelei felt the threat in Queen Thessalonike's words. "We are blessed by Aegaeon to have you, my queen."

A flicker of pain moved across Queen Thessalonike's placid face. One of her hands curled into a fist. "Carry on, Lorelei." Her teeth clacked together as she spun around, single tail propelling her through the ocean, back toward the sirens' coral home.

Lorelei bit the inside of her cheek to fight off a satisfied smirk. Mentioning the god Aegaeon never failed to distract the queen. Lorelei didn't understand why. Nor did she care. The queen was gone and it was time to go.

Her tense muscles demanded haste, but she didn't want to rouse the suspicions of anyone who may be watching. She kept her strokes slow as she swam until she created enough distance between herself and the coral. Then her two tails worked the water, seamlessly pushing her through the darkness faster and faster. As she approached her destination, the sea floor rose to create a shallow pool.

Lorelei's head pierced the surface, and she emerged behind a large boulder—the same boulder she had sung from last night while Niamh and Acantha watched. The very place where the lung-breather witnessed her form and her song.

She wanted that sensation again. The power she felt upon seeing the need in the ugly creature's eyes. Being desired, wanted, cherished. She'd vowed to ensnare him again.

But would he be back at the inlet?

Lorelei slid around the rock, no longer afraid she might be seen. She'd already broken that taboo.

The lung-breather sat huddled on the sand, forearms braced on his knees, head bowed.

Lorelei cocked her head. What a strange position he held. She slapped her webbed fingers against the water with a crack. The lung-breather did not stir.

Stupid creatures, lung-breathers were. How they survived century after century remained a mystery. Lorelei could rip out his heart and feast on his flesh, and he would be unaware until she struck.

But Lorelei didn't want that revelry. She longed for his look again. The look Queen Thessalonike gifted to Echo and her other one-tailed daughters.

Lorelei drifted through the water toward the hunched lung-breather. Her stomach brushed against satiny sand and the top half of her scaled body glowed in the moonlight. Waves pulled against her waist almost in warning, begging her to return to the deep. She would not.

Lorelei stopped a tail-length away and began to hum.

The gentle croon of her voice melded with the swish of the sea waves and the wind stirring the cattails. At first the man didn't wake, his chest rising and falling with the steady rhythm of sleep.

Then his eyes drifted open. He raised his head, the motion slow, as if he believed himself in a dream. Lorelei continued her song, her mouth turning up in a toothy smile. He was hers.

The lung-breather's stare washed over Lorelei with a sleepy fuzziness. Her voice faded—she didn't want him completely entranced. He would only be a puppet then. A plaything. The whistling wind replaced her crooning. Awareness crept into the lung-breather's face. He now watched her with clear brown eyes, mouth slightly parted.

When Lorelei didn't move to flee, the man shifted to his hands and knees. He kept his motions gentle and fluid as if she were an eel about to strike. He held out a trembling hand that hovered inches from her face.

Lorelei tilted her head, braids sliding off her shoulders.

The lung-breather spoke in an awe-filled gasp, breathing life to words that would forever seal his fate and those of his people.

"What are you?"

5

DAY TWO, 3:34 P.M.

All afternoon I'd imagined talking with Mom. My mind concocted numerous scenarios that ended with her realizing the island's danger and buying me a one-way ticket to Greece. But I'd never thought our talk would start like *this.*

"Annie Marie Mayfield," Mom said, voice firm. "Look at me when I'm speaking."

I flattened my hands on my thighs and looked up from the upholstery of her office couch, clenching my jaw. Mom's hair was swept behind her head, her bright blue eyes lined with brown kohl. "Yes?"

"Tell me why," she leaned back on her glass desk, arms crossed, "I come back from a meeting to find an exasperated message from Nandan and my soaking wet daughter waiting outside my office?"

I picked at the damp material of my shorts with my thumbnail. Looking back, maybe I'd been too gung-ho about getting that kid. "Someone stole a towel."

Mom shook her head. A curl sprung loose from her chignon and danced around her face. "An *eight-year-old boy* stole a towel." She brushed the wayward hair behind her ear. "Oh, Annie. What am I going to do with you? How many times do I have to tell you to think before you act?"

The disappointed expression on Mom's face slashed at my heart. Why couldn't I be more like Lynn? Cautious, plan-oriented. She was the daughter Mom preferred.

"What was I supposed to do then?" I asked, suddenly feeling very useless.

Mom softened and sat beside me on the couch. "You should've told Nandan. It's in the guidelines, all part of procedure and protocol. Didn't he tell you?"

I cleared my throat. "Uh, he might've. I wasn't exactly paying attention."

A knowing smirk tickled the corner of Mom's mouth. She knocked my shoulder with hers. "Got distracted by how attractive he is, didn't you?"

I whirled on Mom, horrified. "*What?*"

Mom waved me off. "I'm a woman too, Annie." She patted her chignon with a hand, tucking the loose curl back in. "That dimple of his is very distracting."

Someone kill me. Mom and I had checked out *the same dimple.*

"I'm sorry for yelling at you," she continued. "In the grand scheme of things, your towel incident isn't the end of Mayfield Villa." Mom paused for a moment, looking me over. "Are you doing okay?"

I blinked, thrown by the change in topic. "What?"

She placed a cool palm to my forehead. The sweet pea scent of her lotion drifted down to me. "I didn't mean to kick you out of my office earlier. You looked upset, but it was *Ellen*, and I couldn't say no. I need the positive publicity."

I took a breath, ready to launch into my Adam Finley crusade when a telltale buzzing sounded from Mom's desk.

"One second, sweetheart." She patted my knee in a dismissive gesture and hurried to answer the call. "Florence Mayfield."

I watched as her face transformed from smiling to neutral to serious, her mouth pinched at the corners and her penciled-in brows furrowed. Whatever she was hearing, it couldn't be good.

"And the security footage?" Mom asked as she collapsed into her desk chair, the fingertips of her free hand massaging her temple. "No, it seems so unlikely. It's only the second day." A heavy sigh. "Okay, well, bring her in. She was the last one to see the man."

My heart jolted. She had to be talking about Adam.

"Okay." Mom nodded. "Yes. Have Iona reach out as manager first." She paused then rolled her eyes. "Not now, Greg. After her shift this afternoon. I don't want an uproar over this, understand?" She eyed me, aware I was listening. "I've got to go. Keep me updated." Mom hung up and resumed rubbing her temples, now with both hands.

I gripped the lip of the couch, knuckles going white as my imagination entered hyper speed, cruising right along with Chewie and Han Solo. The guest services man, Mom, and whoever Greg was had all mentioned security tapes. Now something suspicious had surfaced. Something involving a *her*.

"Sorry about that," Mom said. I looked up to see her groan and shove out of her chair. "Also, you didn't hear that conversation," she added.

"Mom, I know the guy who's missing."

"You what? How did you know someone was missing?"

I stood, pacing along the floor from one end of the couch to the other. "What if there really *is* something in the water? Something that could've gotten Adam Finley." *Like the fish that stole my hat.* "Some Internet forums claimed giant creatures—"

"Annie, those are just stories." Mom's tone took on a hard edge. I clamped my mouth shut, hard-won Google facts still dangling from my tongue. In the past, I hadn't believed most of the crazy theories. Instead, I had attempted to use them to convince her to let me go rock-climbing. The theories hadn't worked then—why did I think they would work now? But with Adam's disappearance...

"Mr. Finley hasn't disappeared," she continued. "In fact, the security staff has a strong lead on his whereabouts. And it's not at the bottom of the ocean. I don't want you worrying *or* getting into trouble, okay?"

"You're basically asking me to become someone else. Mom, I've got a really bad feeling about this."

"And what about when you put a tutu on Saint Thomas Aquinas? Or broke your leg free-climbing those rocks in California?"

"It's bouldering, Mom. And it wasn't just rocks, it was the Buttermilks."

"Yes, well, what did your intuition say then? That they were good ideas?"

I groaned, throwing my head back. "Mom, come on! You and I both know Viaii Nisi has a dark past. Shouldn't you check into that, at least a little?"

"Well, last time *I* checked, the Greek police didn't see this 'dark past' as a problem. And last time *I* checked, I own Mayfield Villa and Viaii Nisi. So I'm in charge. Besides, there's an industrial-grade net in the water by the beach. Nothing dangerous, not even a shark, could get through that." Mom kissed the top of my head, the signal that my case was dismissed.

I brushed her off and stomped toward the doors. A net wouldn't do much good against something intelligent with sharp teeth and a hungry determination to get to the beach. If Mom wouldn't look for hands-on evidence of Viaii Nisi's past and the sea creatures the Internet mentioned, I would. My three-day weekend was fast approaching, and I knew exactly how I would spend it.

"Oh, Annie!" Mom called, and I paused, one hand on the doorknob.

I turned. "Yes?"

"You're coming to the staff party the day after tomorrow. I'll have a dress sent to your room."

"Do I really—?"

"Yes. Now you better get showered and cleaned up. Nandan expects you back at the towel stand."

"Fantastic." I tugged Mom's office doors open and stepped into the hallway. Benny sat on one of the cushioned benches lining the wall. When I'd schlepped into Mom's office, still sopping wet, Benny was unceremoniously kicked out.

He looked up when he saw me, slipping his DS into a pocket. "Hey, kiddo." He pushed himself upright.

"Playing Pokémon?" I asked.

"Man." He snapped his fingers. "You caught me."

"Still trying to beat the Elite Four?"

Benny's face screwed up in a grimace. He patted the spot where his DS was concealed. "Pokémon Black and White is killing me."

I laughed. "And you call me *kiddo*." I did air quotes.

"Quiet, you." He ruffled my tangled hair. Surprise crossed his face, and he pulled his hand back, rubbing his fingers together. "Uh, you've got some sand."

"Ask me where I *don't* have sand," I countered.

"Touché."

I fiddled with the hem of my *Mayfield Villa: Yes, you MAY!* shirt. Sprinkle-sized pebbles tumbled to the floor. If I couldn't wheedle anything out of Mom, maybe Benny would make an easier target.

"So…" I ventured. "Do you know anything about the man who disappeared?" Though my gaze was lowered, I felt Benny's shock on his sharp intake of breath. I looked up.

"How did you…?" He shook his head. "Look, never mind. It's nothing for you to worry about anyway. The last thing we need are rumors spreading." He adjusted his suit jacket and smoothed his tie. "How did it go with your mom?"

Changing the topic, just like Mom. Didn't they realize *not* telling me made me more curious and worried?

But as much as I loathed admitting it, Mom was smart. If something bad was going down, she'd pull out of the resort business. Nothing would be allowed to stain the Mayfield name.

Not even me.

"Annie?" Benny asked, cocking his head. "How'd it go?"

My focus shifted. "Oh, it was *great*." I slid a finger across my throat.

He clamped a hand on my head and wiggled. Sand fell from my hair. "Looks like it's still attached to me."

I brushed him off. "Well, it feels like I've been decapitated." I crossed my arms. "And no matter what you or Mom say to change the subject, I know something weird is going on with Adam's disappearance. And I'm going to find out what."

"Look." Benny's gaze darted from me to the closed office doors. "If you stop worrying about this man, you can rock climb some cursed ruins your mom found."

I leaned forward, interest piqued first by "rock climb" and then by "cursed." The unmarked cliffs on the map of Viaii Nisi flashed through my mind. They would make a great place for a haunted fortress or something equally creepy. My toes curled in excitement. Then I frowned.

"Wait. I don't have my gear. Mom refused to let me bring it. She said there wasn't anything on the island to climb." *The liar.*

"*You* don't, but I do." At my growing smile, he shrugged. "I had your stuff shipped over as a surprise to make being stuck here suck a little less. How am I doing?"

"Honestly? I think I'm in love with you."

He grinned. "I'll take that. So what do you say? Do you agree to drop this whole investigation business and get to go climbing?"

"Well…" My fingers itched for chalk and sun-warmed rock. I nibbled my lower lip, weighing the options. Maybe Mom and Benny were right and Adam had slipped under the radar somehow.

I let out a breath. The siren call of rock-climbing was too irresistible. "Okay. I'll nix the investigating. Just tell me where my gear is."

"Shake on it." Benny held out a hand.

I reached forward to clasp my palm into his, but he *tsked* me.

"Have you really forgotten?"

"Oh, *that* handshake." I wiggled my fingers against his, the first step in the secret handshake we'd made up when I was thirteen and that sort of thing had been cool.

"Benny," I said after we'd spun, hip bumped, and whispered the magic rhyme in proper order. Worries crowded my preliminary excitement. "You know how Mom feels about rock climbing. I don't want you getting in trouble."

"I trust that you can keep a secret. Besides," Benny crouched to whisper in my ear, "since Lynn's accident your mom's been a little uptight. She's just scared something will happen to you. Don't be so mad at her, okay?"

I crinkled my nose. "Easier said than done."

"By the way, those ruins atop the cliffs? I was kidding. They're just—"

Benny was cut off as one of Mom's doors swung open and her head poked out. "Hey, Benson, can you come in here? We've got an emergency Skype call with the board members. I need you to take down the minutes."

Benny nodded. "Sure."

"Thanks." Mom arched a brow at me. "Aren't you supposed to be showering?"

"I was actually going for a new look, but if you insist, Mother." I started to walk away, but Benny caught my arm.

"Your stuff is in my room," Benny hissed into my ear. His hot breath tickled my skin. "I'll get you an extra key and give it to you after the big staff dinner." He gave my arm a squeeze before he joined Mom in her office.

Once inside the elevator, I allowed myself to squeal. My reflection looked back at me, a mess of salt-crusted hair and a giddy smile. But who cared? I was going to go climbing!

I paused mid happy dance when the doors slid open on floor five.

The towel thief squelched inside the elevator, his flip-flops squeaking with each step. By the time he looked up at me, the doors were already closing. A futile escape plan flashed across his face.

I sighed and stuck out a hand. "Truce?"

His eyes narrowed, gaze going from my open hand to my face and back again. "Is this a trick?" A slight lisp colored his words, courtesy of two missing front teeth.

The elevator doors swung open on the second floor where I needed to get off. I stuck my foot between them. "It could be. Are you brave enough to risk it?"

At my challenge, he puffed out his chest in his imitation of a man or a blowfish, I wasn't sure. "Okay then. Truce." He shook my hand.

I smiled. Hopefully this would keep the kid from stealing any future towels. "See you later," I called as I stepped off the elevator.

He waved at me before the doors closed with a click. I whistled as I headed to my room to pick up my shower caddy. Funny how a promised day of rock climbing made everything seem so much brighter.

DAY FOUR, 6:26 P.M.

"**O**uch!" I scowled at the bobby pin secured between my thumb and forefinger. The rubber tip had fallen off, and I'd just punctured my scalp.

In the full-length mirror, my disheveled reflection glared at me, eyes mutinous. My short hair stood up in a curly cloud and bobby pins stuck out at awkward angles, doing little to tame the Medusa-like beast. I looked terrible, and I hadn't even gotten to the makeup part yet.

"This is pointless." I spun around and leaned against the mirror. The glass cooled the flushed skin on my shoulders, bare except for the thin pink straps of the dress Mom sent.

Across the room, my blue Viaii Nisi hat hung from a bed post. I swallowed hard as I looked at it. Two days had passed, and Adam was still missing. Mom's security footage theory, whatever it was, had been wrong. Just this morning she reported Adam's disappearance to the authorities. Tonight, at the employee party, she planned to tell the staff.

I only knew this because Benny warned me at lunch when he slipped me the key to his room. Apparently he worried I might get upset and wanted to give me a heads up before the staff party.

Upset wasn't the right word for it.

I was furious.

Mom should've reported Adam missing from the beginning. At the very least she should've investigated the rumors I mentioned.

I picked up the hat, running my thumbs over the threaded lettering. "Adam," I murmured. "Where are you?"

My imagination summoned a bloated, half-eaten body trailing along the ocean bottom. Ravenous sharks circled Adam's corpse. One darted forward with its jaws extended—

"Stop it!" I told myself, returning the hat to its bedpost shrine. "Adam is fine. He has to be." The words did little to convince me. My skin felt rubbery and too tight at the same time. The room was thick with the half a bottle of hairspray I'd used. It hadn't bothered me before, but now...

I stumbled toward my bedroom door, flung it open, and screamed in surprise.

The girl standing outside my door screamed as well.

And I'm pretty sure I heard a third scream come from someone somewhere in the hallway. I cocked my head and glanced to the left and right, trying to pinpoint the third screamer. They were obviously a kindred spirit.

A burst of colorful Spanish had me looking back at my unexpected visitor. It took me a moment to recognize the runway model before me as Tamara, full-time maid and part-time guest services assistant.

"Wow," I murmured in awe.

"Wow," Tamara echoed with a wince at my hair, followed by a yawn. "What happened to you?"

I patted my head and grimaced as a bobby pin stabbed the tender skin of my palm. "Bad hair day?"

Tamara smiled. Unlike me, her dark hair was styled in a sleek updo with tendrils of curls falling around her face. Somehow she'd even covered up the dark circles that'd plagued her eyes since I met her. "If you let me in, I can do damage control."

I pursed my lips. "That's okay. I can handle it."

"If by handling it you mean looking like you stuck your finger in an electrical socket," Tamara swept past me in a Hawaiian-red sari-styled dress, "then you're doing a stellar job." She froze in the center of the room and gasped. "Annie, what happened in here? Battle of the Styling Tools?" She gestured to my floor where an exploded box of bobby pins, a curler and straightener, and bottles of product littered the hardwood.

I sighed. "Lynn used to help. I don't have much experience with... this." I motioned to all of me.

"Lynn?" Tamara scooped the curler off the floor and plugged it into the outlet near my desk.

"My older sister," I murmured, avoiding Tamara's questioning gaze. To forestall further questions, I added, "We don't talk much anymore." When I looked up from the ground zero my room had become, I found Tamara staring at the poster I'd tacked on the wall above the desk.

"That's Meteora, Greece." I explained. The poster depicted a perfect sky speckled with fluffy clouds and masses of rock slashing against the blue. Green littered the cliffs and a scattering of tiny huts seemed magically balanced on the stone.

That was where I should be right now. Scaling cliffs, blood singing, hands covered in white chalk. Not trying to primp for a work party.

"Cool." Tamara tugged the desk's chair out, and I dutifully sat. "It reminds me of Spain a little." She smoothed her red nails through my hair and began plucking out bobby pins. "Something happened between you and your sister, didn't it?"

I stiffened. "I'd rather not talk about it." Even now, at the thought of Lynn, my chest burned. The pain was a well-kept secret. My pride refused to admit how much I missed my big sister, how much her silence hurt.

Tamara was quiet for a beat. "Back home I've got twelve brothers and sisters. They used to drive my mama crazy with their antics, but when Papa had a stroke, they grew up quickly." The curling iron creaked as Tamara opened it. Her sigh fluttered the small hairs near my face. "Now we work around the world to help pay for medical bills. I see some of my siblings now and then, but we haven't all been together in a while."

I fiddled with a fake flower sewn on the waist of my dress. "I'm sorry."

"Nothing to be sorry about. We're together in our labors of love." Tamara paused to tug more bobby pins from my hair. "Family is important, Annie. Whatever happened between you and Lynn, remember that bitterness only makes the heartache fester. The wound will never heal that way. You should talk to her about it."

"Thanks," I said while thinking, *You don't understand at all.* I wanted to talk things out, but all I managed to do was get Lynn's voicemail each time I called. I probably had gangrene of the heart by now.

Ten minutes later, after Tamara switched from a heart-to-heart to funny family stories, she unplugged the curler. After a few sweeps of mascara and eyeliner and dabs of lipstick, Tamara pronounced me finished.

I checked myself out in the mirror. "Where'd Medusa go?" I asked, tugging on a loose curl. Tamara had smoothed the mess on my head to a, if not as glamorous as hers, simple curled style swept to the left side of my face.

Tamara's reflection winked behind me. "I think she's still lurking in there somewhere." She studied me for a moment, finger tapping a quick rhythm on her cheek. "You just need one more thing. *Un momento.*"

Before I could protest, Tamara fled my room. She returned a minute later with a silver necklace dangling from her fingertips. "This will look perfect with your pink dress." She clasped the chain around my neck and nodded with satisfaction.

I looked at the pendant, an intricately carved origami crane. A word was carved into one wing in a cursive script.

"*De-sear?*" I sounded the word out. It tasted foreign.

"De-se-ar," Tamara corrected. "It's Spanish. It means *to make a wish*. My brother works at a restaurant in Japan. He sent me this for my twenty-third birthday last month."

"I can't wear something this important!" I reached back to unhook the necklace.

Tamara moved to stop me but instead palmed a yawn and blinked back the accompanying tears. "Yes, you can. I want you to."

"Are you okay?" I asked, abandoning my efforts. "You seem tired. Maybe you should skip the party tonight. Have you been sleeping any better?"

"Not really, but I've been working a lot. I need to save up for a plane ticket home." Tamara yawned again. "Besides, I'm not missing this. I heard we're having lobster."

"Glad to see you're motivated for the right reasons." I laughed. Who knew Tamara and I were so alike? The food was why I hadn't faked sick tonight.

She looped an arm around my shoulders and gave me a squeeze. "C'mon. I want to get to Lover's Point before all the big tails are snatched up."

Lover's Point rivaled the world-famous Lindau Lighthouse—a castle-like lighthouse in Germany—with its beauty. Instead of cement, or whatever lighthouses were made of, Lover's Point glittered with floor-to-ceiling glass walls. Because of its location on the highest point of Viaii Nisi, the restaurant afforded 360-degree sweeping views of the entire island. In summary: the place was gorgeous.

Tamara scanned the crowded circular room for her maid friends. One of them—I could never remember which was which, and I was too embarrassed to ask at this point—had promised to arrive early and save seats. The loud conversations and classical music coming from the front of the room disoriented me. If Tamara hadn't been holding my arm in a death grip, I would've run for the doors.

Finally, Tamara spotted her friends and led the way to a table at the back beside a window.

"Tamara," the redhead whistled when we reached her. Heather? Who knew. "You look amazing." She'd done her red hair '50s style and was sporting a low-cut wiggle dress.

The blond German one smiled at me. "You too, Annie. You clean up wonderfully."

"Thanks to Tamara," I said, giving credit where it was due. "If not for her, I probably wouldn't have made it out of my room."

Tamara didn't even bother disagreeing. She laughed. "You were quite a mess."

"You wouldn't even be able to tell," the older maid said, dressed in a simple sparkling gray dress with quarter sleeves. "You look lovely, Annie."

"Thank you," I said, wishing I could remember what her name was.

Pleasantries and compliments out of the way, we made a rush for the packed buffet table, gathering delicacies onto our plates, before relaxing back into our cushioned chairs.

While the others chatted, I surveyed the room, fingering the lobster tail Tamara made me get. People wore their fanciest clothes: women in gowns or little black dresses, men in tuxedos or suits. The chandeliers sparkled with a romantic light that bathed everyone in a flattering glow. Musicians played one of Beethoven's more popular compositions while couples danced in slow waltzes nearby, a few with glasses of champagne in hand. Their glamorous dresses and adult beverages made me feel like a kid in my little pink dress and ballet flats.

I caught sight of Mom near the stage, talking to Benny. She wore a beautiful midnight-blue gown that, if Dad saw, would make him abandon his New York apartment. For a fleeting moment, I wished he was here. Then reality sunk in. They'd just fight, regardless of Mom's fancy clothes.

Across the room, my gaze locked with a pair of brown eyes. The lifeguard. He wore black pants, a striped dress shirt with sleeves rolled to the elbows, and a blue tie. He looked away from the girl he was talking to and gave me a subtle wave. I ignored him—cuteness didn't make up for laughing at someone's fear of the ocean—and turned to stare out the window.

The darkness beyond was so complete, my reflection watched me in the glass. I pressed my fingers against the window, cool from the air conditioning. Somewhere below, the ocean roared.

"Good evening, ladies and gentlemen." Mom's microphone-enhanced voice drew my attention to the platform where the musicians sat. They had stopped playing. Mom spoke into a wireless microphone, center stage with a smile on her pink lips. "Thank you for coming this evening and for choosing to share your many talents with Mayfield Villa. We survived the first week. Woo-hoo!" She did a fist pump. Scattered laughter echoed through the room.

I slouched in my seat. Public speaking always made Mom do weird things. I prayed she didn't resort to baby stories like at that White House tea.

She continued, oblivious to my embarrassment. "I hope you enjoy yourselves tonight. We've got tons of fun ice-breaker events to introduce you to the different teams that keep Mayfield Villa running."

"Are you going to eat that?" Tamara whispered to me. She pointed at my untouched lobster tail.

I eyed the discarded remains of six on her plate. "Here." I scooted my meal toward her.

"Thanks!" She swapped plates with me and cut into the tail with vigor.

"But before we get to the fun, I have an unfortunate announcement." Mom's gaze swept the crowd and fixed on our table. I frowned. Why was she looking at me?

"Many of you know that a British guest named Adam Finley has been absent from our villa for a few days now." My eyes widened as I realized that Mom wasn't staring at me, but at Tamara. "Earlier this evening due to his wife's concern and my own, I reported Mr. Finley's disappearance to authorities in the UK."

Beside me Tamara gasped, and her silverware clattered against her plate. People turned with curious stares. "No," she wheezed, gripping the table with white-knuckles.

"Are you okay?" I hissed, reaching for her while glaring at the curious onlookers.

"Tamara?" the maid with the German accent asked. "What's going on?"

"Ladies, gentlemen." Mom cleared her throat, oblivious to Tamara's distress, or trying to cover it. Attention flickered back to the front of the room.

Mom shot her renewed audience a bear-with-me smile and continued, "There was a complication due to country jurisdiction, but investigators will likely arrive in a day or two. I will hold staff meetings tomorrow to discuss this further and give you the opportunity to ask questions. But enough serious talk." Her smile widened. "It's time for the fun to begin…"

As Mom launched into the evening's schedule, Tamara scooted out of her chair and stood on wobbly legs. She weaved through the tables toward the stairwell exit.

"*Wait!*" I whisper-shouted after her, leaping up to follow. Once the stairwell door slammed shut behind me, I called, "Tamara! Stop!" My voiced echoed along the white-washed walls.

Tamara, stop! Tamara, stop! Tamara, stop!

Tamara, deaf to my protests, hiked up her dress as she rushed down the stairs. Her labored breaths and clacking heels bounced back to me in the enclosed space.

Thanks to my flats, I caught up to her in front of the ground floor exit. "What are you doing?" My hand snaked around her wrist and tugged. "Tamara!" She whirled to face me, eyes wide and panicked.

"Annie," she gasped, chest heaving. "Oh, Annie." The delicate makeup around her eyes had smeared with sweat and tears. "I thought they would find him. I never…"

"Tamara? What is it? What did you do?" My heart thrummed like a plucked rubber band. "Does this have something to do with Adam?" When she just stared at me, terrified, I gritted my teeth. All the facts were pounding around in my head, connecting into dangerous theories. "What do you know?"

"I…" She swallowed hard, lips parted as if about to speak. Fear flashed in her eyes and the hope in them twisted into hard resolve. "Agh! *No importa.* You're just like your mom." She ripped her arm free of my hold. "Breaking the rules is fine when you're rich." Her gaze burned into me, accusatory. Like I was to blame for whatever had happened. "I can't lose this job. I need to work. I need to support my family. That's not something the Annie Mayfields of this world can grasp. Now let. Me. *Go!*"

I staggered back, Tamara's words a physical blow. She spun away from me and flung the door open. I watched her run down a barely lit side path toward the ocean before the door closed.

"What happened to her?" I asked the red exit sign above. The memory of Tamara's reaction two days ago, when I was talking to Mrs. Finley, rose before me. And Mom watching Tamara as she announced Adam's disappearance…

Was Tamara responsible somehow? Maybe she and Adam—

No way. Even after her cruel words to me, I knew Tamara wouldn't do that. Adam wouldn't do that.

The drive to find answers faltered under the sting of Tamara's words. I had no idea she considered me an entitled rich girl. Everything in me wanted to turn around and march up the steps. I wanted to bury the hurt Tamara caused right next to the half-healed scars from Lynn.

But no. Something was wrong. Tamara shouldn't be alone while this upset. I could prove to her that I cared, that I was nothing like my mom.

I shoved open the door and hurried along the stepping-stone path leading toward the beach. The salty wind tugged at my hair, whipping it about my face.

"Tamara!" I shouted, hands cupped around my mouth. I squinted through the star-speckled darkness for her, but the full moon above only illuminated the empty path.

I slid my hand into a pocket of my dress, toying with my cellphone. More than anything I wanted to call Lynn. She always sorted my tumbleweed of thoughts into order. Lynn would know what to do about Tamara.

Lynn fixed everything.

One call. If she didn't pick up, fine. Though I knew, deep inside, being ignored again wouldn't be "fine" at all.

I swallowed and pressed the green phone icon by her name. My heart thudded harder with each ring. The hand holding the phone to my ear trembled. I took a slow, steadying breath and kept walking.

Answer, I begged her. *Please,* please *answer.*

"Hello."

I gasped, nearly dropping my phone. "Lynn, hey—!"

"You've reached Lynn Mayfield's voicemail. I'm busy, but I'll give you a call when I can." Her staticky voice paused. "And if this is Annie, I'm still mad at you for… Well, you know." Lynn's voicemail ended, followed by the automated "Leave your message after the beep."

Then I got the "Sorry, the mailbox is full."

I blinked back disappointment and ended the call. Lynn still hadn't changed her voicemail greeting. She'd set it for my own personal guilt trip two years ago before she entered basic to be a nurse in the Army. Then she'd deployed. I couldn't even remember what I'd done to make her mad.

I abandoned my phone to the depths of a pocket and clenched my hands into fists, striding onto the beach. Who needed stupid Lynn? I kicked off my flats and left them by a "No Lifeguard on Duty" sign.

The beach waited, empty and inviting. Faint music and laughter from the boardwalk near the villa reached me on a sigh of wind. Abandoned lounge chairs and closed umbrellas took on the forms of broken ghosts in the faint light.

As soon as my feet touched sand, I let out a sigh. The sun's blush of heat still lingered. I squished the coarseness with my toes, wandering closer to the water's edge. A wave brushed against my skin, and I flinched in surprise. I hadn't meant to come this close to the water, but it felt warm, and I ventured a few steps deeper until it lapped against my ankles, my jaw clenched from both fear and pleasure.

The ocean seemed endless and minute at the same time. Freedom and wonder swirled inside of me, merging into a bubbly happiness that overpowered my usual water-related terror. My hurt over Lynn, Tamara's confusing behavior, and worry about Adam drifted away on the foam. The man in the moon kept a careful watch over me, his face perplexed, maybe even concerned.

A soft hum leapt across the waves, similar to the melody from the pier, yet different somehow, more pronounced. The sound magnified and transformed into a gentle crooning, a haunting tune. I closed my eyes, transfixed. A chasm of longing ripped through me, a chasm only the song could fill...

Cold splashed against my stomach, and my eyes snapped open with a grunt. A wave rolled toward me, crashing against my chest. The sand under my feet undulated then disappeared. I let out a gurgled scream and stumbled back. Open water met my floundering feet. I tried to cry out, but fear cinched my throat, only letting out a breathy squeak.

Then the wave retreated, and I found purchase on the ocean floor. Eyes and throat burning, I whirled around, stumbling for the lights of Lover's Point.

When my feet hit hard-packed sand, I fell to my knees, wheezing. What was I thinking going out that far? I glanced back toward the inky ocean. The emptiness I felt earlier lingered. Part of me longed to return to the water and surrender myself to its dark embrace. My foot twitched.

"No!" I gave my head a sharp shake to fight off the urge. Half-damp curls slapped against my cheeks. Still, I looked out across the dark water, searching for something that hovered at the edges of memory. A flash of scales in the moonlight flitted just under the surface. It darted toward me, only to vanish under the foam of a crashing wave.

I slid backward in the sand. The grains scraped against the back of my thighs and embedded in my ruined dress, but I didn't care. The stories about Viaii Nisi flickered through my mind like a black-and-white movie, chilling me more than the ocean water running down my legs.

For the thousandth time this week, I wondered what happened to Adam—and my hat. The sea creature "articles" I'd read online at school had been too incredible even for me to believe, but after hearing that song, seeing that flash of scales… The thought that, even now, Adam's body decayed beneath the ocean's surface, joining so many mysterious disappearances before him, caused a shudder to scuttle down my spine.

I staggered to my feet and hurried away from the surf, toward light and safety. As I entered Lover's Point, shivering in the air conditioning, I wondered if Mom remembered I couldn't swim before she dragged me to her island.

Lorelei's Song, Verse Three
"The gods are working now in strange new ways."
~ The Odyssey, Book 7

Pearls rolled through Lorelei's cupped palms, their surface cool and smooth. A thrill shot through her as she imagined Acantha's jealous rage. Despite all her oyster beds, even Acantha didn't possess this many pearls.

Lorelei lowered her hands to the crude bag and scooped up more. The pearls fell through her webbed fingers like rain, clinking against one another.

"You are so beautiful."

She shifted, the dry sand tickling her tails and stomach, to look up at the man who spoke, the one who had gifted her with the pearls. He sat next to her, fingers entwined in her hair as he braided. The royal one was still an ugly thing, but he made up for his looks with gifts. Each time they saw each other, he brought something new. In the beginning, they met every seven moonrises, but now he insisted on seeing her every night.

"I am very beautiful." Lorelei chuckled, enjoying the hum against her scalp as he toyed with her hair.

"I wish others, my people, could see you." His eyes loomed closer, mouth moving for hers.

Lorelei jerked her face away from the man's. He had a name, Lorelei knew, but she could never remember it. Nor did she care. "Others must not see me," she hissed, teeth bared.

The man jumped at the siren's sudden harshness. "Of course, of course. Forgive me."

Lorelei pondered his words, rolling onto her back. Her fingers swirled in the sand. Each pass left behind a nonsensical shape. "Where are the diamonds you promised?" She tilted her head to stare at the man.

His eyelashes fluttered as if he might faint. A hideous splotch of color crept up his neck and over the tips of his ears. "I had to trade those on the mainland. My people needed more supplies and food."

Lorelei turned onto her side, showing him her back. "Unfortunate."

She heard the man's boots slip on the sand as he crawled around to her face. "I-I will get them for you. I promise." He reached out a tentative hand to stroke her scaled cheek. "I will get you everything, my love."

Lorelei snarled. "I am not yours!"

He cowered, reminding Lorelei of a guppy, a weak fish when separated from the protection of its kind. "You are right," he whispered. "You are not mine… yet." A hint of something dark flashed in his eyes, but Lorelei's attention returned to her pearls. A weak lung-breather was no threat to one such as her.

Lorelei shifted onto her stomach and nestled her head in her arms. Her scales felt dry and parched, but she was too tired to slip into the sea. In a few heartbeats she would. But for now, sleep…

Burning pain ripped Lorelei awake. She cried out and flailed. A ray of sunlight poked through the foliage and blistered the skin of her upper arm. The scales swelled and rippled, blackening around the edges.

Lorelei wriggled, but the sleeping man had his pudgy hands entwined around her, holding her close. Lorelei hissed and bucked, breaking free from his hold and jerking her body into the shade's protection.

The man groaned and pushed himself up with one arm. His eyes landed on Lorelei's injury. "What is it? What happened?" He reached for her, but she skittered back.

The shadows covering the inlet were leached away by the rising sun. Even now, a strip of sunlight barricaded Lorelei from the safety of the sea.

Panic bubbled in her veins, and instinct seized control. She surged forward, muscles in her tails and arms taut. She tore across the sand. Hot pain electrified her nerves as she hit the wall of sun, but then her body splashed into the water.

7

Day Five, 9:13 a.m.

Early mornings, sunshine, and salt air never felt so good. I increased my pace, eager to leave Mayfield Villa, the gravel of the jogging trail behind the resort crunching under my feet. Fragmented sunlight drifted through the palm trees above, creating leafy spotlights throughout the path. I was thankful for the shade. Nine in the morning, and it was already eighty degrees.

The jogging track curved to the right, and I skidded to a stop. The enormous bouldering pad strapped to my back threw me off balance. I staggered to the left then grunted as I righted myself. A forest of palm trees, fronds, and a bunch of other tropical plants waited ahead, perfumed with the scent of hibiscus. I jammed a hand into my backpack, slung over the front of my body, and grabbed a folded piece of paper.

Viaii Nisi stretched out on the map I'd "borrowed." I fingered the spot where I stood. From here it was a straight path to the cliffs Benny mentioned.

A spark of silver caught my eye, and I glanced down at Tamara's necklace where it rested against my chest. I sighed with frustration. I'd wanted to give the necklace back before I left, but Tamara hadn't answered my knocks on her bedroom door this morning. Maybe she was already up and working. Or maybe she was avoiding me.

"Enough of that," I chided myself, determined to forget last night and live in the moment. "Happiness depends on ourselves," I quoted Aristotle in murmured Greek.

I slipped the map back into my pack and started off at a jog, eager to reach the cliffs before the sun got any higher.

The vegetation grew denser as I traveled toward the back of the island. Sand slowly turned into hard-packed dirt littered with bits of shells and rotting coconuts. I stopped once to grab a swig of water and then again to wipe beads of sweat from my face. As I peered through the curtain of trees, I caught sight of a wall of stone. I grinned and picked up my pace.

Within moments I stood before a wall of rock that extended to either side. Its surface bore vertical ridges, created, I assumed, by the steady trickling of water over time. Almost as if the island had flooded long ago. The grooves would make for perfect handholds. I walked along both ways, the humidity and heat of the day forgotten in my excitement. Just like the map had shown, the cliffs spanned the back half of the island, ending in a small inlet on one side and a rocky beach on the other. The top would have a beautiful view of the Atlantic Ocean. I curled my toes, barely resisting the urge to squeal.

After I chose my ascension spot, I plastered my sweaty cheek against the still-cool rock. "Oh, I love you," I cooed, rubbing a hand across its rough surface.

I pulled back, guilt nipping at my conscience. Maybe it was selfish to promise Benny I'd stop investigating Adam's disappearance. But with my body pressed against stone, I felt useful, strong, invincible. Mom would find Adam. She never failed at anything she did.

I looked up, hands on hips. The cliff appeared to be about thirty feet high, too high for my boulder pad to be effective. I chewed my lip. I'd have to use ropes then.

Or...

I slid my sunglasses up into my hair and squinted at the sky. The watch on my wrist read 9:30. By the time I had my ropes set up, it'd be almost 10:15. I needed to be back at the villa by noon, or I'd miss the staff meeting with Mom. It wasn't mandatory, but I knew she wouldn't be pleased if I didn't show. That didn't leave much time for climbing or exploring.

The bouldering pad would have to do, and I would just be extra careful at the top.

I slung my backpack to the ground and freed my arms of the bouldering pad with a relieved groan. As the big blue square hit the earth, sand plumed up around it. I coughed and stepped back. Great, more sand to coat my lungs. No doubt I could create another island with what had found its way into my Sketchers.

I tugged the bouldering pad and my backpack under the cliff's shade. A quick yank and turn of my sneakers revealed two piles of sand. I slid off my socks and shoved them into the sneakers before strapping on my rock-climbing shoes. As I secured the Velcro, a sense of completeness buzzed along my skin.

I studied the cliff wall in front of me. The lack of chalk to mark the path of previous climbers meant I'd be plotting my own route. A little more dangerous, but also a lot of fun.

I took a moment to map out potential hand and footholds. Then, after pulling my bouldering pad underneath where I planned to climb, I strapped my smaller pack filled with snacks to my back and cinched my bag of chalk around my waist. Finally, I was ready to go.

Well, almost. This morning, once I texted Benny that I'd gotten my gear from his room on the twelfth floor—which was way nicer than the employee rooms on floor two—he made me promise to text him at each point of my climb. "Not that I don't trust your skills," he'd written. "Just let me know when you start, get to the top, and then get back down."

Dutifully, I sent off a quick text with a mountain emoji.

A second later Benny replied, "Have fun!"

I grinned and dropped the phone into my backpack.

I dipped my hands into the chalk powder, rolling the whiteness between my fingers. Nerves sent my heart fluttering. It was always the same before a climb. The rush of adrenaline, the jumpy excitement. I stretched, loosening my arms and legs.

With a sharp breath, I grabbed my first handhold, feet finding purchase in the rock below. I swung my left hand up to the next indent in the rock. Imaginary action music played in my mind, accompanied by the occasional real-life bird call.

I glanced up, searching for my next handhold. This cliff was harder than my most recent climbs. Maybe I should've put on my helmet…

Sweat trickled along the sides of my face, melting into my hair. The surrounding island and its mysteries and terrors vanished from my mind. My focus narrowed to my fast breaths and the rock above and against me.

I fell into the easy motion of reaching, sliding, pulling. The bulge of muscles under my skin sent a jolt of power through me. My left leg protested now and then, not completely up to strength since my accident in California a year ago. But soon even that slight discomfort faded. Without the swishing or tug of ropes and harnesses, I felt dangerous and alive.

My fingers swung up for a piece of rock jutting out of the cliff. As soon as I touched it, I knew.

The rock's connection to the cliff crumbled. Pebbles scattered down as my hand slipped. My palm sliced across sharp rock. I let out a ragged gasp and shifted my weight, fighting to stay upright. The muscles on the left side of my body burned as my right arm hung, useless. A lazy drop of blood rolled off my middle finger.

I gritted my teeth and stretched my injured hand up again. My left leg threatened to buckle. That indent there, just out of reach, might save me.

My fingernails scrabbled and tore at the rock. *Curse you, Grandma Mayfield, and your short genetics!*

I cried out in frustration, shoving myself up on my tiptoes. My injured hand slid into the groove and held firm.

For a moment, I rested my forehead against the cliff. Damp brown curls framed my face, casting me in darkness. The burning sensation in my left side eased to a dull ache that solidified in my leg.

I continued the last few feet of my climb. First my right hand found the top of the cliff, then my left. I swung up with my stronger right leg and rolled over the top, letting out an "oomph."

Air whooshed in and out of my lungs. I laid my injured hand over my eyes to block out the sun's rays, too lazy to get my sunglasses out of my backpack.

I'd made it. All on my own. A new burst of energy shot through me. I pushed to my feet and jumped into the sky, fist pointed toward the bluebird hues. "Yes!" I cried.

A warm breeze brushed my skin, cooling the sweat on my face and neck. I yanked my hair into a loose ponytail. In the distance, the red roofs of Mayfield Villa rose out of waves of green. A flock of birds leapt from a cluster of trees and took to the sky with noisy chatter. I smiled.

Typing another text to Benny, I turned to check out the plateau behind me. In the distance stood the crumbled remains of some massive structure. My curiosity stirred. Could those be the cursed ruins Benny mentioned?

I took a minute to catch my breath and bandage my hand, grateful for the travel first-aid kit in my pack. The rock had only scratched off the first layer of skin, but I'd need my hands in perfect condition to navigate down the rock face. The next time I came up it'd be easier, now that a path was mapped out. I closed my eyes and committed my trek up to memory.

After a sip of water, I dusted off my hands and swung my pack over a shoulder. The solitary *scritch-scratch* of my climbing shoes on the rocky cliff resounded around me as I walked. I tried to keep my tread soft, somehow apprehensive of being too loud. Not to mention my climbing shoes pinched my toes and made heel-toe walking almost impossible.

As I got closer, the weather-worn skeleton of a castle or fort of some kind came into focus. The ruins were almost as expansive as the villa, the highest point a crumbling turret that disappeared halfway up. On the other side of the ruins, a line of dark blue contrasted with the sky where the cliffs ended—the ocean.

I drew closer as foreboding prickled the nape of my neck. I stopped to run my fingers against the rocks of one wall. They were worn smooth and flat by the relentless barrage of ocean winds. To my left, a section had crumbled away to reveal a narrow entrance.

After a quick glance over my shoulder, I stepped through the gap. I squinted as my eyes adjusted to the dimness of the ruins, the sun filtered into patchwork shadows by what remained of the roof. I swept my gaze upward as I walked, marveling at crumbling pillars and archways. A collapsed doorway to my right, partially blocked by rubble, drew my attention. I veered toward it. On the ground in front lay long splinters of rotten wood.

Two clay women draped in flowing robes decorated both sides of the doorframe, raised arms cut off at the elbow. Deep claw marks gouged angry lines into both of their chests while their faces were punched-in divots, hairline cracks running through the gray rock. I suppressed a shiver and climbed over the rubble blocking the entrance. I hopped down into the large chamber beyond.

A soft crunch sounded underneath my foot. I glanced down and froze.

The tip of my climbing shoe was shoved into the remnants of a human skull.

A high-pitched, hysterical laugh creaked from my throat. "Oh, excuse me." I wiggled my foot back. The rest of the skull shattered into a pile of shards. "Whoops."

I looked up and staggered backward, hitting the wall. Unlike the rest of the ruins, this room's walls were intact, save for the ceiling where rotted timber, riddled with gaping holes, served as a roof. And in place of a stone floor were hundreds of bones.

Human bones.

I tiptoed into the room, careful to avoid trodding on the skeletons.

The bones were piled on top of each other, skulls resting against femurs and ribcages. The largest grouping was in a far corner of the room, as if people had cowered against some foe and then been slaughtered where they stood. A weight tugged on my heart, a sorrow I didn't understand.

I clambered back out of the room and knelt at the doorway. Now that I looked closer, the shattered bits of wood looked as if they had once been a door and some force had burst them apart—not that I was an expert archaeologist.

My gaze caught and fixed on the scarred statues. The weight tugging on my heart doubled in size. I ran my fingers over the gashes on their chests. A sharp piece of stone nicked my skin, and I pulled back.

Whatever happened to these people, it wasn't good. How could Mom know about this place and still open the resort? If my hours of online research didn't reveal a massive burial ground, it must be very hush-hush. Could the ruins be related to the string of deaths that haunted the island's owners? This place felt ominous and forbidden, like whatever had killed these people might come after me next. That last thought had me backtracking out of the ruins and fleeing through the makeshift entrance.

Chalk it up to my imagination, but as soon as I stepped into open air, the tightness in my shoulders eased. Curiosity thrummed at the back of my mind, ordering me to find out what happened to these people. But I had no real way of looking into it. Mom refused to give me the Internet password that the employees used. Guests had to pay for the Wi-Fi with their resort ID, linked to their credit cards, and guess who didn't have a payment account set up? Yeah. Me. This trip was supposed to be a punishment, and part of that punishment was being forced to disconnect.

I strolled parallel to the structure for a few feet until I reached the end. Before me, the cliff plummeted in a steep fall before meeting the crashing waters of the Atlantic Ocean. I eased away from the edge, not wanting to risk a clumsy misstep or a loose rock.

My watch chirped twice: a preset warning that eleven o'clock just struck. I had to eat a quick lunch, get off this cliff, and get ready for Mom's staff meeting if I wanted to keep my little excursion a secret.

I turned to trek back to my ascension spot, half eager and half disappointed to go, but hesitated. To my right, a flight of crude stairs had been cut into the cliff.

Hmm... Interesting.

I approached and placed a cautious foot on the first step. Sturdy and unmoving. The stairs below split the cliff face in a deep sloping angle. At the end waited a large flat surface that jutted into the ocean for at least fifteen feet. Maybe that's where the people in the ruins tied their boats?

Either way, it was worth checking out. I also wouldn't mind dipping my sweaty feet into some cool water.

"One, two, three..." I kept count as I inched down the staircase. Though I longed to marvel at the ocean and surrounding cliffs, my eyes focused on the tips of my shoes to avoid tripping.

Yet, somehow, I still missed the thick cracks gouging the second-to-last step. The rock broke off in a huge chunk when I rested my foot on it, and I cried out.

My feet dropped from under me, and my butt smacked onto the flat rock. Pain reverberated up my spine, nestling at the base of my skull. I groaned, opened my eyes...

And let out an ear-piercing shriek. Centered between my thighs rested another human skull.

I scurried to my feet, wiping at my athletic shorts. My eyes traveled down the links of the skeleton's spinal cord. Where it should've stopped at the hips, it kept going, forming a pointed tip beyond where legs would have ended.

"I should've paid more attention in biology," I muttered. Then my gaze settled on the rusted manacles. They were drilled into the rock on either side of the skull with a few bleached bones scattered around them. I tiptoed over an arm bone and crouched near the skeleton's hips. At the ends of the extended spinal cord, a few long, thin bones stretched out on either side. Almost like a... a fish tail.

I swallowed hard as déjà vu tingled at the dark corners of my mind. A mixture of revulsion and excitement warred inside me.

The words left my mouth in a whisper. "I've just found a mermaid."

DAY FIVE, 11:49 A.M.

Sweat trickled down my forehead and dripped into my eyes.
I wiped it away with an impatient hand.

I had less than ten minutes until the staff meeting started,
and I still needed to store my gear. But that was only part of the
motivation for my mad dash. Fear of Mom's wrath didn't spur
my feet to move faster and faster despite the awkward bouldering mat strapped to my back.

Something horrible happened on those cliffs. Not just the
mass grave in the ruins, but the strange skeleton at the bottom of
the steps. That creature had been chained to the rock and abandoned. I prayed it died before the locks clicked around its wrists,
but somehow I knew that hadn't been the case. I mean, why
would someone chain up something already dead?

Part of me wanted to play the bones off as a joke—a weird,
pointless joke—but that flash of scales in the ocean last night
and on my first day kept me from doubting. What if the online
rumors were right? Anyone could mistake a mermaid for a giant
fish.

I needed to talk to Mom.

My feet left the sand and crunched onto the gravel jogging
trail. A massive body slammed into my left side. I squealed in
surprise and toppled backward. The bouldering mat smacked
onto the ground, yanking me down with it.

Air rushed out of my lungs. I heaved in a gurgling breath
and erupted into a fit of coughing.

"Hey! I'm so sorry. Are you okay?"

That voice. *You've got to be kidding me!*

I gritted my teeth and strained to sit up. I only rose a few inches before I slammed back down.

The lifeguard's face filled my vision, replacing the palm trees and blue sky. He blinked a pair of misleadingly innocent chocolate brown eyes. His penny necklace swung around his neck in a strangely hypnotic rhythm, catching the sunlight and almost blinding me.

"Hey." The lifeguard's mouth quirked up in a smile. "It's you. We've got to stop meeting like this."

I ignored him and tried to roll over. The straps of the mat dug into my shoulders. With a grunt I swung myself the other way. The mat lifted up for a few victorious seconds before slapping back to the sand.

"It's funny." He tapped the side of his cheek. "You remind me of something."

I kept my gaze fixed on his white sleeveless shirt. *Happy as a clam* in curly yellow writing sat below a clam with a ridiculous, too-big smile. I glared at the mollusk and its stupid grin.

After watching me struggle for a few beats more, the lifeguard snapped his fingers. "That's it! A turtle! You know when they get stuck on their back and—"

"Just help me!" I shouted.

He gave me a lopsided smile that was way too cute for the situation. He stood and held both hands down to me. I reached out and locked my fingers with his. With one tug, he hauled me to my feet. Only then did I realize that taking off the mat before trying to stand would've made me look less turtle-like.

Curse you, hindsight!

I brushed off the back of my legs. Sand fell away in a glittering cloud. One thing I wouldn't miss about this island come September. No. More. Sand.

I readjusted the straps of my bouldering mat and started off down the jogging path, strides long and fast. Well, as fast and long as any five-foot girl's strides could be.

"Hey!" The lifeguard jogged to catch up. "Where are you going?"

I kept my gaze fixed on the gravel trail. No doubt my face looked as red as it felt. The hair plastered to the back of my sweaty neck and forehead probably added to the whole ensemble. Chalk smudges on my butt were also a definite possibility.

A tan shoulder hovered at the corner of my eye, but I didn't turn to look at him.

"Don't be embarrassed," the lifeguard said, moving to block my path. His blond hair stuck up in all directions thanks to humidity. Ear buds hung around his neck and dangled over one shoulder. "Yesterday I—"

I stepped around him to keep walking. His hand closed over my wrist and tugged me back. This time I met his eyes, inhaling his scent of sunscreen and salt. My heart did a little oh-he's-really-cute skip before I gave it a mental sumo punch.

"What is it?" I snapped, tugging at my arm.

He watched me for a few seconds before holding out his other hand. "Can I call for a truce?"

I glanced at his offered palm then back up at his face. I raised my brows. They likely had sand in them too. "You know, a coerced truce doesn't count." I waggled the arm he held captive.

He waited a beat before releasing his grip around my wrist. "So? What do you say?"

I shoved damp hair off my forehead and contemplated. "Why should I agree to a truce with you? You're a jerk."

His mouth fell open. He recovered a second later. "You mean on the beach?" When I didn't respond, he continued, "Look, I'm sorry about that. When I meet a pretty girl, I say the first thing that comes to mind. Usually it's stupid."

Did he just say *pretty girl*? As in me? The snappy retort on the tip of my tongue dissolved.

A woman with a thick ponytail jogged around and past us. The heavy bass beat of whatever song she listened to lingered behind before fading away.

"Complimenting me isn't going to work," I finally said, arms crossed.

"It's not a play," the lifeguard promised. "It's true. Being scared of the ocean isn't a big deal. I shouldn't have made fun of it. What else can I do to show you how sorry I am?"

I considered the earnest expression in his eyes, aware of time ticking by. My watch let out a rapid set of beeps as if to confirm my worry. I silenced it. Five minutes.

"Okay, I'll agree to your *truce*," I did air quotes, "on one condition."

A slow smile slipped across his lips. "Okay."

"An ice cream cone."

He blinked. "What?"

"I want you to buy me an ice cream cone. It's crazy hot out here."

He raked a hand through his hair, the sharp scent of him tickling my nose, and scratched the back of his head. The muscles in his arm twitched. He sighed. "Fine. An ice cream cone it is."

"With a chocolate shell."

"With a... that adds like two dollars to the cost!"

I raised my brows again.

He groaned. "Okay. An ice cream cone with a chocolate shell."

"Great!" I snagged his hand, which had fallen back to his side, and gave it a firm shake. "I've got a staff meeting, so I'll meet you around the front in thirty minutes or so." Before he could reply, I jogged off toward the pool and the villa's back entrance.

After storing my stuff in my room and blotting my tomato-red face with a towel, I raced to the employee cafeteria. The doors were already shut so I stood on tiptoe and peeked through the rectangular glass windows.

Maids clustered at two long tables while Mom stood in front of the room talking. The meeting had already started. *Oh, great!*

I'd only eased the door open a crack when Mom called out, "Hurry along, Annie. We can't wait forever." Muffled chuckles followed her words.

"Sorry," I mumbled and hurried toward an empty seat next to a gray-haired woman in a sundress. The scent of lunch still lingered in the cafeteria. Possibly burgers and French fries.

As Mom praised our hard work, I surreptitiously scanned the room. The familiar faces of Tamara's friends caught my eye, but Tamara herself was nowhere to be seen. Worry sucked at my stomach. No way would she miss a staff meeting just to avoid me.

"Now that the day-to-day commentary is finished," Mom continued. "Let's discuss what I know you're waiting for: an update on Adam Finley's case."

Though no one had been talking, the room seemed to grow quieter with an intense focus. Mom took a slow breath. "At this point it's only speculation, but to keep gossip from spreading, I want to give you the facts. Not only has Mr. Finley disappeared, but so has Tamara Espanza."

My heart plummeted into my dirty sneakers. Hushed whispers broke out across the room. This couldn't be happening. Tamara's tear-streaked face flashed through my mind, the raw panic in her eyes.

Mom fought to regain the audience's attention. Her words reached me from far away. "Adam's case was passed to the NIS, the Greek National Intelligence Service. I learned just this morning that they won't be coming to investigate. Circumstances point to Mr. Finley and Miss Espanza leaving the island together. But if you have any information or suspicions, please speak to Iona. Even the tiniest detail may help determine what happened. Any questions?"

Hands shot into the air. One man asked about security footage being looked at, as if Mom was an idiot and hadn't already checked it out. Someone else wondered if the guests would be informed. Mom affirmed that yes, they would. Soon all the questions began to sound the same, though Mom answered them with a smile, repeating herself over and over.

I gritted my teeth, my knee bobbing up and down while I waited for everyone to finish. "Come on, come on," I muttered when someone asked, "Are we safe?" for the third time. The woman beside me *tsked*.

Finally, the meeting ended. People broke off in small groups, chatting among themselves. It didn't take a mind reader to guess what they gossiped about.

Tamara and Adam. Sneaking off together.

Mom stood in a corner of the cafeteria, phone clutched in one hand, chatting with Iona. I crept toward them, ducking behind a tower of folded tables.

Iona flicked her 80's-style blonde hair over a shoulder. "To be honest, I don't know, Florence. Tamara never seemed the type to do something like that. She was very devoted. I think we should pressure the NIS to come anyway."

"That doesn't change what we saw on the security feed," Mom murmured. She smoothed the front of her blazer. "It's enough proof that Adam Finley and Tamara ran off together. Even a government agency thinks so."

"It's not true!" I cried, jumping from my hiding spot. A few of the lingering maids turned to look at me.

Iona's hand fluttered over her chest. "Annie, honey. You scared the living daylights out of me." Her Southern twang honeyed every word.

Mom crossed her arms. "Eavesdropping, Annie?"

I ignored her disapproving stare. "Mom, Tamara wouldn't do that. She has a family to support."

"And Adam had a lot of money." Mom raised her wrist, eyeing the time on her watch. "The next meeting starts in a few minutes." She turned to Iona. "Keep an eye on your employees, okay? Let me know if any of them approach you with information. You've been a great help so far." She squeezed Iona's sweater-covered shoulder and gave her a sincere smile.

"This will sort itself out. In a few days, we'll be laughing over some spiked pink lemonade." Iona winked at me as she walked by.

Through the now open cafeteria doors, other employees entered. Some wore casual clothes and others sported the ugly towel assistant uniforms. Mom moved to greet them, heels clacking on the marble floor.

"Wait," I said, blocking her path. "I need to talk to you about Tamara and something that I found."

Mom shook her head. "Sorry, Annie. I can't fall behind schedule with these meetings or tomorrow will be a mess." Her gaze slid away from me as she analyzed the fresh audience waiting for her. "Come to my office after dinner. We'll talk then." She strolled away, plastering on a smile. "Thank you all for coming. Especially since it's a day off for some of you..."

I huffed. Had I really expected her to listen?

With no other choice, I shuffled out of the cafeteria and onto an elevator, bound for my meeting with the lifeguard. Even the thought of an ice cream cone wasn't enough to cheer me up. Outside the villa, guests wandered about, taking pictures and toting beach bags. The sound of crashing waves acted as a harmony to contented chatter. I toyed with Tamara's necklace, biting my lip. The wingtips of the crane dug into my skin, I held it so tight.

"Hey."

I looked up, squinting against the sun. The lifeguard lounged in a chair by the door. He pushed himself to his feet, grinning.

I gave him a weak smile. "Hey."

"Uh oh." He looked me over. "Seems you need that ice cream cone, stat. C'mon."

He led me to the boardwalk that ran across the right side of the beach. People walked past us in swimsuits, carrying tubs of caramel popcorn, cups of French fries, and sizzling hot dogs wrapped in doughy buns.

"How'd your meeting go?" he asked as our feet pounded out a rhythm on the boardwalk's wooden beams. "I had mine earlier. Crazy about that maid and Mr. Finley, huh?"

"It's not true," I snapped. "Tamara didn't run off with Mr. Finley. They're just making it sound that way."

The lifeguard's hands went up in surrender. "Sorry, sorry. I didn't mean to make you angry. Sheesh."

I shoved dark curls out of my face with a sigh. "It's just… Tamara and I worked together. She wouldn't do what everyone is saying, I know it."

"I understand. Let's just change the subject. I'd like our truce to hold for at least an hour."

I smiled at that. "Good idea."

We stopped in front of an ice cream stand. The man behind the counter waited, scoop in one freckle-covered hand. "What can I get you?" he asked.

"Small vanilla cone," I told him. "Dipped in chocolate, please." Originally I'd been gunning for a large, but after the meeting with Mom, my appetite wasn't up to par.

"What kind of cone would that be, Ms. Mayfield?"

I glanced sideways at the lifeguard to see if my last name made an impression on him. He stared into his wallet, brows furrowed. When he caught me looking at him, he shrugged and pretended he'd been wiping a smudge off the cheap imitation leather. Unlike the guests, the food wasn't all-inclusive for the villa's employees.

"Sugar," I finally answered the man.

Seconds later, I had a delicious ice cream cone in hand. The promise of its sugary sweetness eased the swirling worry in my mind. A little, at least.

"That'll be $4.68," the man told the lifeguard.

"Are you going to get anything?" I asked.

"Uh, no. I'm good." The lifeguard fished into his wallet, pulling out his identification card. The vendor swiped it, charging the lifeguard's account, before passing it back. "Wanna walk along the beach for a bit?" he suggested.

I nodded.

The lifeguard led the way down a flight of steps and onto the sand. Kids ran to and from the water with pails. Moms darted around with digital cameras, snapping pictures. I caught sight of the freckled towel thief and waved.

After a few minutes of silence passed, I asked, "So, what's your name?"

"Victor. Victor Hale. You?" His gaze stayed fixed on the path ahead.

"Annie Mayfield," I said, crunching on the chocolate shell of my ice cream. "But I think you already know that."

He chuckled. "Someone pointed you out after the incident on the beach. Said your mom made you work here because you stole some priceless statue or something."

I laughed. "Wow. That's not what happened at all."

"Oh?"

"Yeah. It was an old statue on my boarding school's roof. I put a tutu on it."

Now it was his turn to laugh. "Nice."

We walked in silence for a while. I would've ventured more conversation, but I fought a losing battle with my melting ice cream. When I'd licked the vanilla down to where it nestled safely in the cone, I looked up at Victor. He stared out at the sea, gaze faraway, lost in thought.

"What do you see that's so captivating?" I asked, nodding toward the horizon when he looked over at me. "Out there?"

He jammed his hands into the pockets of... yes, swim trunks. Was that all the guy ever wore?

"Mystery," Victor said with a shrug. "There's so much about the ocean's depths that's unknown. It's intriguing, I guess."

I let his words settle around me while I munched on the soggy cone. "So, are you in college? A marine biology major or something?"

Victor's steady steps slowed to a stop. He fiddled with the penny dangling from his neck. In the distance, I could see the Aquatic Adventures building jutting into the water. Kids and adults in life jackets were lined up on the mini boardwalk outside. Probably headed to do a dolphin swim.

"Victor?" I questioned when he didn't reply.

"No, I'm not in college yet." He abandoned the penny to his chest. "But I plan to go to Boston U and, like you said, study marine biology."

"Oh." I swallowed the last of my cone and slipped the paper covering into my pocket. "How old are you, anyway?"

"Almost nineteen."

"You said earlier that there's so much about the ocean we don't know."

He nodded. "We're making advancements every day though."

"What about, say... mermaids. Do you think they exist? Maybe in the waters around Viaii Nisi?" My words came out in a rush, and I held my breath, hoping he didn't think I was a total idiot.

Victor took a moment to process my question, then nodded with a chuckle. "Sure, why not? But sirens would be more realistic. I mean, we are on a Greek island." He winked, probably thinking I was joking.

A chill spread from my chest to the tips of my toes.

Sirens.

Lorelei's Song, Verse Four
"For a friend with a loving heart."
~The Odyssey, Book 8

Lorelei clenched her jaw against the tingling itch deep in her right arm. Something had gone wrong in her treatments of the sunburn. The itching hinted at infection. If she wasn't careful, she could lose the appendage. She had seen it happen to other sirens.

But she could not examine the injury, hidden under seaweed wrappings. Queen Thessalonike was holding court in her rocky cavern, and every siren's attendance was mandatory. The two-tailed sirens, like Lorelei, perched on boulders jutting above the water. The favored single-tailed sisters floated before the queen, all but their shoulders and faces hidden by the ocean.

Lorelei had taken her usual spot in the back of the cave, positioned on a flat shelf of stone, though everything in her screamed for the forbidden comfort of the ocean.

Her fins, ends dangling from the rock, swayed in the gentle current of water. She focused on that rhythm and the hypnotic drone of Queen Thessalonike's voice.

The staggered and flitting movements of Queen Thessalonike's pet, the red mullet fish, caught Lorelei's attention. The pathetic creature had followed the queen from her original home in the Aegean Sea. Lorelei wondered when the decrepit thing would die. While the siren queen sat on her rocky throne in the back of the cavern, the enamored fish floated in the currents at her half-submerged gray tail.

Ridiculous.

Lorelei's half-listening ears caught on one of Queen Thessalonike's words: "lung-breather."

Her gaze flicked to where the queen reclined, two-tailed siren guards stretched out in the water on either side of her throne. Lorelei found Acantha's smug face among them. She wanted to scoff at the siren's self-importance. Acantha could be replaced as easily as she had been raised up.

Queen Thessalonike's eyes darted about, icy blue and ghost-like.

"I remind you, my daughters," Thessalonike continued in her husky Greek. "Stay away from those evil creatures. Those caught mingling with them…"

Lorelei felt more than saw Queen Thessalonike's gaze sear in to her. It was as if the queen knew of the night Lorelei, Echo, Acantha, and Niamh spent on the rock singing to the strange lung-breathers. Or, worse, all the moonrises Lorelei had spent with the royal one since.

But she couldn't know, could she?

"…will face severe punishment," Queen Thessalonike finished. She turned to Echo where she floated at the queen's side, an honored position. A smile lit Queen Thessalonike's usually hard features. Echo smiled back, her face a sun in the cave's darkness.

No, the queen did not know of Lorelei's treachery with the lung-breathers. If she did, Lorelei would already have the scabbed whip marks across her back, joining her other scars.

Queen Thessalonike dismissed her court with an inclination of her head.

"May the gods bless you, queen," the sirens intoned as one. Lorelei forced the words from between her clenched teeth.

"And you, my daughters." Thessalonike swept through the cave, waves splashing their goodbyes on stone as she passed.

Even after Thessalonike departed and the siren gathering broke apart, Lorelei waited to slip back into the water. Her right arm felt like a disfigured mass of pain and fire. She feared to examine it, let alone shift position. Once the other sirens left, then she would move…

"Lorelei?"

Lorelei's eyelids slid open. She blinked, not sure when she had closed her eyes against the waves of agony. Echo floated in the water below her, the only other siren in the cave, head tilted to the side. How long had she'd been there, watching?

"Yes?" The question crawled from Lorelei's lips in a raspy growl. She swallowed and spoke again, "Yes, Echo?"

"You're keeping secrets."

Lorelei hid her surprise behind a shake of her head. "You know all the secrets I keep." She pretended to examine the walls glowing a soft green, courtesy of the creatures that clung there. She couldn't hold Echo's dark blue stare. The young siren's dilated pupils, necessary for navigating the darkness of the cave, seemed too vulnerable. Lorelei couldn't lie to the face of her treasured sister.

"I've seen you sneaking away." Echo's voice was surprisingly harsh. She appeared to catch herself for her tone softened. "I worry for you, Lorelei. You are brave. I admire it, but I also fear it."

Lorelei risked a look at Echo. She'd moved closer to the rock where Lorelei rested. Echo's thin, webbed fingers gripped the smooth stone. The sapphire scales on her skin seemed a deeper, more midnight color in the light of the glowing creatures.

If Lorelei stayed a moment longer, her resolve would crumble. She tensed her muscles and slid into the salty pool. A searing hiss spat from her mouth as soon as the ocean brushed against her arm. She forced herself to go deeper into the underwater depths of the cave. She kept her injured arm nestled against her stomach and cleaved through the water with her left. If she got away from Echo, she could tend to her wound, though the thought made her want to whimper.

A shape darted past, turning the water into froth and bubbles. Echo halted a shark-length away. She held her arms out wide as if blocking the cave's exit.

Lorelei halted with a sigh. Even if she swam with both arms, she'd never outrun Echo. Echo raced sailfish, with their lithe bodies and quick limbs. And she always won.

"Your arm," Echo's high-pitched clicks rolled through the water. "It pains you." She approached slowly. "May I see?"

Lorelei relented and held out her left arm, gaze fixed on the rocky bottom of the cave.

Echo's touch was gentle as she unwound the seaweed wrappings, her scaled fingers nimble and quick. Still, the pain made Lorelei growl. Echo's soft chirp of surprise confirmed Lorelei's fears.

"The sun?" Echo asked, voice low. The chirps they used underwater carried so easily.

Lorelei could only nod. Now that her wound was exposed to the water, the pain doubled.

"You are not treating this in the proper manner. We should... we should tell—"

"No!" Lorelei gasped. "We cannot tell her. You know what she will do."

Echo didn't back down as she normally did. Her dilated pupils constricted with anger. The time she spent with Queen Thessalonike was starting to show. Lorelei prayed their queen didn't change her precious Echo entirely.

"I won't let her whip you. Why this secrecy?"

Lorelei didn't answer.

"If you do not tell me, I cannot help you," Echo murmured. She knocked her forehead against Lorelei's, a gesture that promised protection and safety. "I want to help you, sister."

The words burbled up inside Lorelei, hungry for release. "The man—the lung-breather we saw that night. The one that saw us. I've been with him."

Echo slid back. Cold ocean rushed to fill the space where their foreheads touched. The siren's face was a perfect mask.

"He gives me gifts," Lorelei continued, struggling to explain her actions to her beloved sister. Each word felt like a knife in her chest. The taboo, the betrayal, the weakness. What would Echo think of her? "I stayed too late one night. The sun...

I don't care for him! He is hideous and stupid. I just… I just want to feel…"

"Why was my love not enough for you?"

The pain in Echo's voice ignited a coal of hidden rage in Lorelei's heart. "Because I can't choose! You're a favored one. I'm *forced* to love you."

Echo was silent for a moment as Lorelei's words rebounded in the cave. Fear flooded through Lorelei then. Had she gone too far? Been too honest? Would Echo turn on her and confess Lorelei's secret to the queen?

"True." Echo's chirp was barely audible. Lorelei strained to hear. "But the man didn't choose either."

The two sirens floated in an unbearable silence. Lorelei closed her eyes as Echo's words cocooned her in their truth. Could she be as wicked as Queen Thessalonike? Forcing love where love wasn't due?

"I will keep your secret," Echo said.

Lorelei's eyes snapped open. "Echo?"

"Your cares are my cares, sister." She moved to examine Lorelei's injured arm again. "I will tend to this. We cannot let our queen discover it."

DAY FIVE, 9:09 P.M.

Audrey Hepburn even looked good on a wrinkled, over-sized t-shirt. I tugged the hem away from me and looked down at her face, covered up with enormous sunglasses, *Breakfast at Tiffany's* style. Shame on me, I despised the movie, but I loved this shirt.

Well, maybe not the shirt as much as the sister who gave it to me. Though lately, I'd relegated Audrey to a pajama top out of spite. Stupid full voicemail and no response texts.

I shoved Lynn out of my thoughts and into a mental box labeled "Not Worth Thinking About."

The door to Mom's office clicked open, and I looked up. Mom stood in the doorway, brows drawn together, lips pursed. The eyeliner on her left lid had smudged, and she hadn't fixed it. Worse still, I detected nibble marks on the tips of her French manicured nails—a habit she'd kicked years ago. Or so I thought.

"Hey, Mom." I stood, linen pajama pants brushing the hardwood floor.

"Annie, you can't walk around in—"

"You told me to come after dinner," I cut in. "I've been waiting out here for over an hour. Benny said that you were on an important call and to go to bed. But I need to talk to you."

She sighed. "Walk with me back to my room, hmm?"

"Sure." I glanced behind her at the dark office, abandoned for the night. "Can I borrow a book first?"

Her eyes widened in a silent question: *You read?*

I took that for a yes and hurried past her. The automatic lights flicked on as I moved toward the bookshelf. Within seconds I had *The Odyssey* clutched under one arm and met Mom back in the hall.

She tilted her head at my choice. "Why that book? I thought you read it last year for school."

If by "read it" she meant "SparkNotes," then sure. "Yeah," I said, tapping my fingers on its fake Greek spine. "But there's a passage I want to reread."

"Okay then. Just remember to bring it back."

"I will." I fell in step beside her as we moved along the hall. My smacking flip-flops sounded like cherry bombs in the quiet.

We passed empty conference rooms and a few closed doors before we stopped in front of hers. 1207 hung from the frame in gold numbers.

"You said you had dinner?" Mom asked as she slid the cardkey inside. The door opened to darkness and quiet, and I wondered if Mom was lonely. Yeah, I had my own room too. But I couldn't go down the hallway without getting blown kisses by cheeky busboys or asked about my day by the maids. Mom walked through an empty corridor to an empty room—a room without Dad or Lynn. I doubted I was a good substitute for either of them.

"Annie?" Mom asked. "Are you coming?" She stepped inside and flipped a switch. The room flooded with light.

Okay, never mind. Who cared about loneliness when Mom had a room like *this*. Tamara and I cleaned platinum level rooms, which were high on the extravagant scale, but those were on floor eleven. Even Benny's room, a few doors down from Mom's, didn't compare to this.

The front hall stretched out, ending in a large room with hardwood floors. A chandelier hung over a large oak table with a vase of blooming roses. Above the fireplace rested a flat-

screen TV, the centerpiece of a large sitting area complete with
an antique-looking couch and two arm chairs.

"Uh, Mom?" I asked, doing a slow spin in the middle of the
room.

Mom slipped off her heels and kicked them behind her.
"Yeah, sweetheart?" She wandered through an archway into the
sprawling stainless steel kitchen.

"This room!" I cried as I followed her. "It's amazing."

Her back faced me as she reached into the fridge. "Thank
you. I designed it personally." She closed the fridge with a hip
bump. In one hand was a bottle of white wine and in the other...

My mouth fell open. "Yoo-hoo? You remembered." I
smirked. "Or is the wine for me and the Yoo-hoo for you?"

She rolled her eyes. "Very funny. You're not old enough
yet."

I wanted to ask what she thought happened on the weekends
at the boarding school she'd banished me to, but instead I said,
"I know, I know. I was just kidding."

Mom passed me the Yoo-hoo and inclined her head toward
a high table in the corner of the kitchen. She grabbed a wine
glass and glided onto a stool with the graceful ease tall people
possessed.

I eyed the stool. The thing stood half as tall as me. I placed
the precious Yoo-hoo bottle on the table and swung a leg up. I
proceeded to do a combination of hops and wriggles until I slid
on. Who needed kickboxing when I could do this?

I gave my drink a good shake then popped off the top. It let
out a soft and oh-so-satisfying hiss.

"Just so you know," Mom began as she poured her wine, "I
stuck you in the employee rooms because I love you." She took
a dainty sip of her glass and let out a contented sigh before leaning closer to me. "I figured it'd be easier for you to make friends
and keep you humble."

"I think you and Dad have already taught me humility."
Years of menial summer jobs were proof enough of that. "And

with my stellar personality, I would've made friends anyway."
Despite my words, deep down, I knew Mom was right. The employees had been suspicious on day one in the cafeteria. Without Tamara introducing me to people...

She toyed with the stem of her glass, watching the golden liquid swirl around and around. "You'll understand when you're a mother, Annie. Now, what did you want to discuss?"

I sipped at the Yoo-hoo to calm my sudden nerves. While I centered my scattered thoughts, I offered, "So what was that call about, the one Benny mentioned?"

"Nothing important. Just your dad. We had a slight disagreement..." She seemed to search for the right words, taking a longer than necessary sip of wine. One might even call it a swig if Mom wasn't so elegant. "About how I handled an issue with the villa. Guest related."

"Oh."

She shrugged off the topic like it wasn't a big deal, though it was. I could see anxiety in the set of her jaw. And the way she refilled her glass. "I don't really want to talk about your dad, and I doubt that's your real question."

Here it goes. I opened my mouth to answer, but she spoke first.

"So we're clear, you're not getting out of maid duty."

I glowered at her. "That's not it."

She waved for me to continue.

Might as well be blunt. "The NIS need to come to the island. Tamara and Adam didn't run off together."

Mom sighed as if she'd been expecting this. "Annie..."

"Everyone is talking about it like Tamara is the villain."

"Put the pieces together, Annie." She slid her wine glass out of the way, hands flat on the table. Her wedding ring caught the light and winked at me. "Adam Finley was in an unhappy marriage—his wife even said so."

"I still don't—"

"The night he disappeared, Tamara was there."

"She... Wait. *What?* What do you mean?"

A flicker of indecision moved across Mom's face.

"Tell me," I ordered. My body hummed as my defense, ironclad minutes ago, weakened with doubt.

"I'd rather show you." She slipped off the stool and returned moments later with an iPad. A few taps to the screen pulled up an HD video. Mom laid the tablet on the table and pressed play.

The camera focused on the empty lobby of Mayfield Villa. At the bottom right corner, the timestamp read 23:16. Tamara stood in her guest services uniform at the front desk, chin in hand, an open book before her.

"The nightshift can be pretty slow," Mom commented.

At that moment Adam Finley staggered out of an elevator. He wore another striped polo and cargo shorts, but no shoes.

Tamara looked up as Adam shuffled toward the front doors, his bare feet squeaking on the floor.

"Excuse me," her voice called out in perfect quality. My throat tightened. Looking at her on the screen made me realize how much I missed my fellow maid. "Excuse me, sir. Are you all right?"

Tamara moved from behind the desk to Adam's side. The camera provided a perfect aerial view of the pair.

"I just want to walk on the beach," Adam slurred.

"I'm sorry." She shook her head, reaching to support Adam when he stumbled, though he was almost twice the size she was and probably would've crushed her if he fell. "It's not safe for you to be out on the beach... in your condition. How about a massage? The masseuse is still available."

Mom interjected again as the video played, "Intoxicated guests aren't allowed to leave the villa once it gets dark. It's for their own safety. We lock the front doors after eleven. Tamara knew this, but watch."

I was watching. And I could see how Mom arrived at her theory. Adam sidled closer to Tamara and murmured something in her ear that the camera didn't catch. Her dark cheeks colored, and she glanced over her shoulder.

"It's been a lousy night," Adam said at regular volume. "A jaunt on the beach would clear my thoughts. Please, love?"

"See that? He called her *love*." Mom jabbed the tablet screen, accidentally pausing the video.

I swatted her hand away. "He's *British,* Mom. They call everyone that." I hit play and the footage resumed.

My stomach sunk as I watched Adam reach into his pocket and pull out a wad of cash. He pressed it into Tamara's hands.

"There's more where that came from," he promised. "What do you say?"

Tamara stared at the money resting in her cupped palms. I could practically hear the thoughts racing through her mind. *My family. My papa. I could see them again.* All *of them.*

"Oh... *okay.*" Tamara stepped out of Adam's way, slid behind the desk, and pressed a button. "The doors are unlocked. Be careful."

"Thank you." The sincerity in Adam's voice made my eyes burn. With a cheery wave, he turned and ambled unsteadily out of the villa.

Mom sighed and picked up the tablet. "He makes it past the towel stand. That's the last time we catch him on our feed. Tamara never reappeared after the party at Lover's Point. With the ferries and helicopters coming and going, they could've snuck off the island. Easily."

I stared at the tabletop, feeling empty and deflated. In my peripheral vision, I saw Mom put the tablet away and return to her stool.

"What do you think now?" she asked.

I shook my head and looked up. "I still don't believe she ran off with him. You barely knew Tamara! She was working two shifts to—"

"Help support her family," Mom finished. "I know more about my employees than you think. During questioning, Tamara was very evasive. She denied receiving money from Mr. Finley, even though I promised I wouldn't terminate her. What else could she have been hiding? I'm sure Mr. Finley is paying Tamara for—"

"No!" I resisted the urge to jump to my feet. Or, rather, fall off the stool. "Tamara would never stoop so low. And Adam loves his wife—I could tell when he bought me a hat."

"The man buying you a hat hardly—"

"Something happened to them," I interjected, refusing to be swayed by Mom's logic. "No matter how you disregard the stories online, people died on this island. And not just recently. The cliffs—"

Mom went rigid. It was her turn to cut me off. "How do you know about the cliffs?" She didn't give me a chance to reply. Emotions warred on her face, too fast for me to identify. She finally settled on anger. "If Benson had something to do with this…"

Miniature fireworks of terror popped inside my veins. I clenched my jaw against the reply bursting to my lips. Benny's voice echoed in my mind when he told me about my climbing gear: *I trust that you can keep a secret.*

I wouldn't get Benny in trouble. Judging by Mom's expression, this might be worthy of a pink slip.

I shook my head though I wanted to scream about the bones. Benny was more important. I needed him, and he needed this job. And they didn't have anything to do with Tamara and Adam—whatever happened in the fort had happened long ago.

"No. No, of course not. I saw some cliffs while I was wandering around the island today. I just… I wanted to know if they'd be safe to climb."

"They're not, and you shouldn't wander around the island alone."

Too late. "Why won't you just believe me?" I asked. "What harm could looking into the island do?"

"I don't have time for your theories, Annie. I know I haven't given you much attention since you got here—"

Anger surged up inside me. "You think this is about *attention?*"

"You've done things like this before. Running away from school. Ditching your field trip group to climb those rocks in Cali. The tutu..."

I clenched my jaw. "I see." So this really had been pointless after all. Mom would never believe me. I swallowed hard, burrowing my hurt deep inside my chest. "I should get to bed. It's late."

At the door, Mom fiddled with the knob. "I've got an extra bedroom. You could stay here tonight, if you want. I didn't mean to make you upset."

I shook my head. "No thanks."

She reached out to give me a hug, but I stepped back, *The Odyssey* clutched to my chest.

Pain flashed in her eyes, but she didn't comment on my rejection. "Good night then."

"Good night." I didn't even bother grabbing my Yoo-hoo before I fled into the hall.

Once inside the elevator I took a deep breath. Anger, hurt, and frustration brewed under my skin. I couldn't believe Mom really thought I was doing all of this for attention.

Whatever. No matter what she said, I refused to believe Tamara and Adam ran off together.

So what really happened to them?

As the elevator moved toward floor two, I flipped open *The Odyssey*, turning until I found the appropriate passage. I read how Odysseus relayed Circe's warning to his men, saying, "We should guard against the wondrous voices of the sirens in their flowery meadows."

Many considered *The Odyssey* to be a work of fiction. But what if... *What if...*

The book clattered from my hands, falling page-down on the elevator floor. My mind replayed that night I stood on the beach and the moments before I almost drowned. The irresistible song. The need I felt. The longing.

I staggered back against the mirrored wall.

There were *sirens* on Viaii Nisi.

It sounded too strange to be real. But the manacled skeleton by the cliff...

"Tamara," I vowed, voice strained. "Adam. I'll get proof of what's going on. Something other than old bones. And then... then I'm going to find you."

DAY SIX, 1:59 P.M.

"Thanks for making this!" I called to Chef Almanzo as I swiped my bagged lunch off the stainless steel counter. He looked up from a steaming pot of alfredo noodles, face blotchy.

After spending the morning actually reading *The Odyssey*, which hadn't done much except give me a splitting headache, I was headed out to do some on-the-ground investigating. I'd missed lunch at the employee cafeteria, so I'd played the I'm-Florence-Mayfield's-daughter card and ordered something yummy from Lover's Point to bolster my spirits.

"Wait, wait!" Chef Almanzo scooped up a circular tray covered in plates piled with steaming food and shoved it toward me. His black handlebar mustache quivered as he spoke. "Take this to table seven, quickly, quickly."

I grabbed the tray by reflex. "I'm not here to work, I just wanted—"

Chef Almanzo tugged off his tall white hat and used it to fan himself. People bustled behind him—waiters balancing trays, other cooks chopping ingredients. The kitchen existed in a state of organized chaos and smelled strongly of oregano. And this was just Floor Six's kitchen in Lover's Point. One existed on every level, run by different chefs from different countries.

"Who made that for you?" Chef Almanzo poked my bagged lunch, the plastic dangling from the crook of my elbow. "For free?"

"You know my mom owns the villa, right?" When that didn't convince him, I sighed. Luckily I'd spent a summer when I was fourteen waitressing at one of my parents' restaurants. "You Italians are good at guilt trips."

Chef Almanzo chuckled and then turned to snap at one cook furiously stirring a bubbling pot of linguini. I abandoned the bagged lunch and shoved through the double doors toward the sunlit dining room.

I navigated crowded tables, bound for one at the back with a number seven centerpiece. Mrs. Samson and the freckled-towel thief sat across from each other, five other guests filling the chairs between. Assumedly, the two next to the kid were his parents. Part of the fun of coming to Lover's Point without a reservation—depending on your personality—was sitting with random people.

"Hello," I said, spinning the tray around to grab the first plate, a delicious-looking chicken slathered in herbs and a lemon sauce.

Mrs. Samson raised a hand. "That be mine. Nice to see you, Rybka."

I placed it front of her, moving around the table as the others indicated their orders.

"You're not wearing a uniform," the freckled kid called, finger pointed at me and then at my hair. "You look funny."

"Tommy," his father hissed, clamping one hand on his son's shoulder. "Enough."

I resisted the urge to stick my tongue out at him or touch the hair I'd rushed to pin away from my face this morning. Stupid kid. "They're busy back in the kitchen. I'm Florence Mayfield's daughter. I fill in when I can." *Or when I'm forced to in order to get free food.*

Favor for Chef Almanzo complete, I turned back toward the kitchen to retrieve the bagged lunch, only to stop mid-stride.

Mrs. Finley huddled at a two-person table by a window. Sunlight filtered through, casting her ponytail in a halo glow.

Two plates of lasagna sat on the table, one in front of her and the other before the empty seat.

I pushed aside my sudden nervousness and moved toward her, serving tray flat against my side. "Hey," I murmured.

She looked up, and I tried not to gasp. Days-old makeup smeared her face, black kohl a smudgy line at the corners of her eyes. In fact, it looked like she hadn't showered in a long time. Or slept.

"It's you," her voice creaked. She visibly swallowed. "We had reservations here today... I couldn't stand to break them."

I struggled to find the right words. Days ago I'd promised her that Adam would come back, that he still loved her. "Mrs. Finley—"

"Don't!" A spark of her old superiority flickered to life. Heads turned at her shout, and she lowered her voice. "Don't you dare call me that. Not after Ad—that *man*—ran off with that maid."

I opened my mouth to contradict her but decided it would make things worse. Even the NIS with their "experts" had come to the same conclusion. Adam Finley ran off with Tamara Espanza. An open and closed case.

The reminder of their conclusion made my grip on the serving tray tighten. I would prove the NIS, Mom, and Mrs. Finley wrong. I'd keep the promise I made. Today I was going to find out what *really* happened to Tamara and Adam.

No. Matter. What.

The rock skittered forward a few feet. In a couple steps, I caught up and brought my foot back again. This time the rock arced high before bouncing back onto the asphalt. With a sigh, I jammed my hands into my pockets and abandoned the halfhearted soccer game. No point taking out my frustrations on an inanimate object.

Three hours into the search for more evidence of sirens and my gusto had dwindled to an unrecognizable nub. My feet had traced the shoreline from Lover's Point to Mayfield Villa, Aquatic Adventures, and now almost to the Welcome Center pier. What had I found?

Nothing. Absolutely, positively *nothing.*

No signs of sirens or sea creature versus human struggle. Not even footprints of cannibal natives! The last place on my list of places to investigate—and pretty much every other list in my mind—was the ocean. I doubted I could even make myself get in. Maybe this was all pointless and I should just go back to the ruins.

The Welcome Center and its bright colored buildings loomed ahead. I let out a relieved breath. It was an understatement to say my feet were killing me. At least the sun hid behind a patch of clouds, for now.

A few square buildings, splashed with yellows, pinks, and turquoise, lined either side of the small street. My footsteps sounded loud in the quiet, and I slowed my pace. Saturday was the only day ferries didn't arrive and depart from the villa. I would've almost preferred for the space to be bursting with people. It was too empty. Even a little lonely.

I paused outside a familiar souvenir shop. Naked hat racks stood like determined sentries outside the door. I turned one rack with a finger. It let out a loud, almost melancholy, creak. Adam and I had stood here the first day. Less than a week ago. I could almost sense his presence hovering behind me, ghost-like.

Which one suits your fancy? His voice curled through my memory. I closed my eyes, wishing for the power of time travel, to warn him and Tamara. If only…

Loud splashing shattered the quiet. My eyes snapped open and my head swiveled, ears pricked for the sound's source. As I moved toward the pier, the splashes got louder and more frantic. Water-muffled screeches reached my ears.

I broke into a run.

"Hello!" I called, weaving from side to side along the platform. "Is someone there? Hello!"

The cries of terror ceased, but the splashing didn't. On the left side of the pier, the farthest end from shore, where wood met water, I discovered a figure thrashing inside a prison of orange construction netting.

"Hold on!" I scanned the pier and let out a huff of relief. On the short railing opposite, five life preservers dangled from hooks.

I snagged a bright red disk and slid it over my hips. The distance between the pier and the ocean below yawned out. My heart gave a panicked double thud.

"Come on, Annie," I wheezed. Before I could think, I hurled myself over the edge.

The preserver slammed into my armpits, nearly dislocating my shoulders as I hit cold water. I spun around, bobbing on waves, and kicked toward the struggling person.

"Hold on!" I shouted. The netting had twisted tight around one of the pier's thick poles. The person inside kept jerking forward as if sheer momentum would free them. With each movement, the knotted netting seemed to tighten.

What I really needed was a knife, but improvisation would have to do. I tugged a bobby pin from my hair, bit off the rubber tip, and anchored my legs around the pole for leverage.

"Try to stay still," I shouted over the person's splashing. They lurched right and then left. Sunlight pierced through the clouds, illuminating the underbelly of the pier. The person screeched and darted backward, knocking into the pole and pinning my leg. Zings of pain streaked from my knee to hip. I clenched my jaw and glared at whoever thrashed in the net.

Through the orange I caught sight of textured skin and a flash of bright eyes. My stomach dropped in panic. *Who is this?*

"Just relax, okay?" My voice came out as a panicked squeak. I tugged on the construction netting and stabbed the sharp end of the bobby pin into it, ripping it across the plastic. It wasn't easy, but strand by strand fell away as I stabbed and tore.

The creature inside hissed as the netting loosened, then snapped its mouth around a part of the netting, slashing through it. Razor-sharp teeth glinted in the muted light, and I tried to swim back just as a wave carried me up, knocking me against the creature. Claws struck out and slashed four grooves down my arm. I flung my hand back with a cry. The bobby pin fell from my fingertips and disappeared into the water. Above, the sun's light dimmed, lost behind another cloud.

I gritted my teeth. "Stop being foolish!" The words tasted salty and familiar in my mouth as if I'd spoken them before. Red seeped from my arm, the salt water stinging the fresh wounds. "I am trying to help you!"

The creature stilled as if I'd struck it.

With my good arm, I pulled away the strands of plastic webbing we'd both cut apart. After a few tugs, it broke open. The creature plummeted underwater in a tight spiral dive. The construction netting unfurled on the frothy surface. Waves knocked against my preserver, rocking me back and forth. I grabbed the pier support pole to keep from going out to sea.

The creature broke the surface and shot into the air like a dolphin. Instead of skin, scales lined its—no, her—body. Two long tails extended where legs and feet should've been. She dove toward me.

I shrieked and toppled backward. The preserver slipped over my butt and off my legs. The ocean closed over my head.

Choking on salt, I fought to the surface for a gasp of air. I gained a quick breath before the current towed me back under. The racing of my heart drummed in my ears. I swung my legs and arms, fighting for sun, for oxygen, for life.

Please, no!

My eyelids tore open despite the sting of salt, desperate. Light rippled on the water, revealing a looming shape a few feet away: the strange scaled creature with huge luminous eyes. She rushed toward me, claws outstretched.

I screamed in a burst of bubbles.

DAY SIX, 5:52 P.M.

My sneakers squished and squeaked as I limped into the lobby. The heat of curious gazes burned into my back, but I didn't look up from the marble floor. The scaled creature rose in my mind's eye, killer-like grace and terrifyingly beautiful. Her large eyes, bright scales, a mess of blond hair more knots than braids. And those legs—no, tails. Long tails with fins that resembled a scuba diver's flippers.

"She was a siren," I heard myself murmur, my voice far away.

Even now, I felt the cold ridges of her scales against my skin, the sinewy muscles of her arms as she dragged me to a ladder attached to the pier. She had helped me. *Saved* me.

Then why was a similar creature chained to a rock and left to rot? Were there others? Where were they hiding? Did they know what happened to Adam and Tamara?

Momentarily I pictured teaming up with a pack of sirens to solve Viaii Nisi's mysteries. Except this wasn't a kid's cartoon. I hadn't missed the creature's razor-sharp talons and serrated teeth—and neither had my arm.

"Annie Mayfield!" The hysteria in Iona's voice made me start. "Oh, lands' sakes!" She intercepted me a few feet from the elevators, gaze on my arm, mouth open, a chewed piece of blue gum balanced on one of her back molars. "What happened to you?"

"Hmm?" I blinked as the fog in my mind cleared. "I…" My eyes followed Iona's stare. Sopping wet clothes and four bloody gashes on my right arm. I stood in a pink puddle and… Uh oh.

A glance behind me revealed a watery pink trail snaking through the lobby. I turned back to Iona, face warm. "I kind of fell off the pier at the Welcome Center."

"You *fell off the pier?*" Iona's voice rose to an ear-piercing pitch. Her hands snagged my face and turned it every which way, ignoring my cut arm. "Oh, honey, are you okay? Wait, your mama told me you can't swim. How did you—"

My face burned a darker red. "My mom told you I can't swim?"

"Well, obviously you can! Unless some mermaid rescued you!" She let out a loud chortling laugh. I joined in, though mine sounded forced. Possibly borderline hysterical.

Yeah, like anyone would believe the truth. Saved by a mermaid—*siren*. Right. I'd end up on the cover of one of those magazines that ran fake stories: "Daughter of Island Owner Rescued by Two-Tailed Lifeguard."

Yuck. If only I could prove myself with the skeleton near the cliff. But then Benny would suffer Mom's wrath.

"I, uh," I began. "I fell over with a life preserver on, that's all."

Iona raised her brows. "You had a life preserver on when you fell? I bet that's some tale." She finally looked down at my arm and winced. "Poor baby. We better get you to the medic. This might need stitches." She spun me around and towed me into a waiting elevator, grabbing a towel from a cart as it passed. I took it gratefully and cradled my arm in it, halting the bloody mess I was making but still dripping on the clean floor.

"Matthias," Iona called to a guest services man behind the lobby desk, "make sure Annie's mess gets cleaned up." She jammed the button for floor two and faced me. "Things are an adventure with you around, aren't they?"

Doctor Denton straightened and examined my bandaged arm with an expert's eye. "You got lucky, mon," he said in a heavy Jamaican accent. "I'll give you some extra supplies to care for this. You need to redo the dressing every morning with Neosporin." He smoothed the gauze and checked the medical tape.

I kept my gaze fixed on his smooth-shaven face. The hues and patterns of his Hawaiian shirt made me dizzy. "Got it."

"So, mind telling the truth on how you managed these?" He pointed to my gauze-wrapped arm and iced knee. "Falling off a pier, really?"

I mimed locking my lips with an invisible key.

"Keep your secrets, then," he said, tone dry. "Inquiring minds will want to know." He gave me a pointed stare.

My locked jaw hinged open. "You haven't called my mom, have you?" The *have you* came out in a plaintive squeak. He'd jabbed a button on his desk phone earlier. I hoped he was silencing the ringer or something.

He shrugged.

That's when I heard it. The telltale clacking of heels on tile.

I bolted across the room, swiped a lollipop from a jar with a big sticker that read "Thanks for being a great patient!", and fell back into my seat. The door slammed open as I popped the candy into my mouth. I tried not to gag. Gross, peach flavor.

Mom stood in the doorway, mouth set in a grim pink line. She stomped to where I huddled in a cushioned seat. This felt very much like when I broke my leg in California last year. A trip where I'd forged Mom's signature on my school's permission slip after she said no. Then subsequently snuck away from the chaperones to climb.

Except Dad received the brunt of Mom's anger that time. He was the one who told me about the Buttermilks in California.

Mom argued that if Lynn still went to school with me, none of it would've happened.

Lynn, the perfect, responsible one.

I watched Mom suck in a breath. The five stages of Mom-to-Annie Fury played out in my head.

Step one, *The Look*.

Mom fixed me with her blue eyes and leaned down for full effect. Her lips pursed in a disappointed-yet-I-expected-this way.

Step two, *The Sigh*.

Mom shook her head and straightened, letting out a breath. "Oh, Annie."

Step three, *Stockpiling Her Arsenal of Facts*.

Mom turned toward Doctor Denton. "So, what happened? I got your page, and Iona texted me that Annie got hurt."

Doctor Denton, unlike many past doctors Mom had fixed with her squinty look, didn't cringe or shrink back. He stood and washed his hands in a nearby sink. After patting them dry with a paper towel, he leaned against the counter and clasped his fingers atop his oversized tummy.

"Nothing serious." He gave me a reassuring smile before looking back to Mom. "She had a tumble off the Welcome Center pier. It should probably have a railing. I heard your daughter can't swim?" This time Doctor Denton was the one to fix Mom with a withering gaze as if to say, *And you brought her to an island.*

"Annie struggled to pay attention during swim lessons." Mom's eyes flicked to me. "Her older sister planned to teach her last summer when we first bought Viaii Nisi, but..." She cleared her throat. "Anyway, I see there's some gauze. Any stitches?"

"No, thankfully." He watched Mom and me, brows drawn together as if solving a complex puzzle. "Just some gashes. They should heal in about a week. She'll want to rest her knee tomorrow too, but otherwise, no permanent damage."

"Wonderful." Mom faced me again.

Stage Four, *Question the Kid.* Here we go.

"You fell off a pier?" Mom's left eyebrow quirked up.

I nodded.

"And scratched your arm?" The other eyebrow joined its arched twin.

I nodded again.

"Iona said you fell with a life preserver. How... *fortuitous.*"

I shrugged. She didn't believe me. That much was obvious. But would she believe the truth? *Sirens* were real? Not likely.

"So," Mom said in a huff, finally tiring of my wordless answers. "How did you fall?"

Instead of answering, I pointed to the lollipop in my mouth and gave her a sympathetic shrug.

"You and that lollipop trick," she muttered. If it weren't for Doctor Denton's presence, that statement would've been yelled, not whispered.

Time for Step Five, *Acceptance and/or Punishment.*

Mom turned to the doctor. "Thank you for your attentive care." She started for the door without a glance in my direction.

I bit down hard on the lollipop stick to keep a smile at bay. A punishment didn't seem imminent this time. After all, I'd already been dished the maximum sentence: indentured servitude.

Then Mom turned, one hand on the doorknob. She eyed the lollipop stick still poking from my mouth. "Though, after a scare like that, no doubt you're begging for swim lessons."

I furrowed my brows, not brave enough to extricate the candy. What was she getting at?

She shrugged in an overdramatic helpless motion. "I guess I'll take that lifeguard up on his offer."

Wait a second...

"Once you are feeling better, you'll be having swim lessons with Mr. Victor Hale."

The lollipop toppled out of my open mouth and hit the floor, cracking into bright orange pieces.

Lorelei's Song, Verse Five
"A son of pain, a name he'll earn in full."
~The Odyssey, Book 19

Five moons rose and set, and Lorelei did not visit the royal man. Each night Echo applied a grimy herbal mixture to her burn, forcing Lorelei to sit above the water for her scales to absorb the nutrients. Though Lorelei knew Echo's ministrations were effective, she became aware of a dual purpose: Echo's watchful eyes kept Lorelei from the inlet.

Lorelei longed for the diamonds the man promised. He'd told tales of how the glimmering rocks sparkled in the light, how female lung-breathers shoved them through tender ear skin or set them in gold bands for rings. He said they were a gift of promise and love, proof of a man's devotion.

She needed to see them, hold the jewels in her palms.

On the sixth night, Lorelei abandoned Echo. She swam for the inlet and the royal man.

Lorelei stayed submerged as she approached, skirting around the sea boulder and moving closer to shore. The sand tickled her stomach as it swayed on the currents. Through the ocean's rippling surface, she caught sight of him. The water's distortion of his face made it all the more hideous, but Lorelei could make out a lumpy shape in his hand. Her diamonds!

A cruel smile toyed at the corners of her scaly lips. The ugly creature probably visited the shore every night. Her absence would teach him a lesson. In the future, he would obey all she ordered.

Lorelei's head emerged from the water. She swam to shore, waves lapping around her hips, and waited for him to notice.

It took him eons. His kind were so slow and unobservant. When he did catch her shape in the darkness, he gasped and fell to his knees in the foamy surf. Dark stubble colored his cheeks

and purple smudged the skin under his eyes. Salt water dampened his leather pants, but he didn't seem to notice. Or care.

"You've returned to me." The words were barely discerni-
ble through his sobs. He pressed his head against the muscled
plain of Lorelei's chest. His unkempt face felt disgustingly
warm on her scales.

Lorelei crinkled her nose at the man's tears. She longed to
hurl him away, but she wanted the diamonds more. "Yes, I
have."

"Are you well?" The man shifted, and his gaze flicked to
her arm, still bandaged in seaweed. "You disappeared so suddenly. I feared…"

Lorelei brushed a braid out of her face with a webbed finger. "The sun is dangerous to my kind. We cannot stay
underneath its rays or we will perish." She eyed the bag the man
still held in one hand. Her patience for his emotions wore thin.
"My diamonds?"

"Yes, yes." He fumbled with the string on the bag. He
tugged it open, and moonlight sent rainbows darting across Lorelei's face. She gasped and reached to stroke the jewels with
her fingers. They were cool and unbelievably smooth, smoother
even than pearls. She felt as if she pressed her scales against a
crystallized tear. Like the tears and sea foam Queen Thessalonike used to create Lorelei and her sisters.

"Do they please you?" asked the royal one.

"Yes," she breathed. "They please me."

The man's smooth hands wrapped around Lorelei's wrists
and tugged her closer to him. She hissed in surprise. The bag
splashed into the water between them, diamonds spilling out to
sparkle against the sandy bottom.

"What is the meaning of this?" Lorelei snapped, jerking her
head up to glare into the man's face. How dare he? She would
remind him who—

He forced her webbed hands to press against his chest. She
sensed a foreign, rapid *thump thump* under her fingertips. A

deep-rooted fear screamed for her to escape, but something stronger held her transfixed. It was that steady beat, so similar to the one in the same place in her chest, though hers beat much slower.

"I was caught with the diamonds," the royal one panted into Lorelei's ear. "My advisors think me possessed." The grip around her wrists tightened. His voice took on a fevered pitch, words flying from his lips in a torrent of emotion and saliva. "You will marry me, become mine and mine alone. I will be your king and you my queen. We will rule both land and sea, more powerful than the gods! Than Zeus himself!"

Lorelei tugged on her ensnared wrists. "Never! I will never give myself to so vile a creature as you."

"Vile? But you are confused, my love. Passion...." He trailed off, fumbling for words. "Passion has addled your mind. Yes, yes!" The man let out a broken cackle of laughter.

"Passion? You disgust me," she spat.

"Oh? Very well." He released one of Lorelei's wrists and yanked a long dagger from the sheath hanging at his back. "If you won't belong to me in life, then together we will travel to the Underworld where you will be eternally mine." He slid the flat part of the blade across Lorelei's shoulder, the metal clinking against her scales.

Lorelei stared transfixed at the light reflecting off the weapon's surface, the elongated pointed tip. It reminded her so much of the swordfish who fought one another with their long noses.

The man jerked Lorelei around, her back pressing against his stomach. "I will make it quick. Then I will join you." His fevered breaths tickled her neck. He raised the knife high.

A howl, part rage and part fear, tore from Lorelei's throat. She wriggled and bucked. Her head slammed backward, crashing into the lung-breather's nose. She felt something crunch, and hot liquid slid down her back. He cried out, his grip around her loosening.

She dove into the water and swam as fast as she could, not ceasing until dawn broke.

DAY EIGHT, 6:23 P.M.

The beginnings of a bloody sunset streaked across the sky in a violent explosion of color. The hues tinted the siren bones before me, deepening the shadows beneath.

I knelt on the rock, phone in hand, poised to take a picture. Unable to leave the villa yesterday, stuck being "chaperoned" under Benny's watchful eye, I'd scarfed down dinner after work today and rushed out to climb the cliffs. A seed of doubt had wriggled through my mind last night. That all of this had been a made-up fantasy. That Mom was right and all I really wanted was attention.

But no, the bones were still here, and a *siren* rescued me two days ago. It hadn't been a dream. Or a delusion. I wasn't crazy.

…Right?

I studied the chained skeleton through my phone, thumb hovering over the capture button. Guilt pricked the tips of my fingers. Taking a picture felt wrong, like somehow I cheapened the creature's death. Besides, Mom would only think I'd found the picture on the Internet. Which I wasn't even allowed to use. I'd just end up in more trouble. With a sigh, I gave up and shoved the phone into a pocket. Memory would have to do.

I wanted to stay and explore the ruins for more clues, but I had swim lessons tonight.

Oh, that Victor Hale. He had to be the most aggravating guy on the island, butting in where he didn't belong. I pushed to my feet with a groan.

"Hey, Benny!" I called as I hurried along the gravel jogging trail. Benny looked up from his quad stretch and smiled. Sweat glistened on his dark skin and made a damp impression on his white t-shirt.

"Hey, kiddo," he panted. "What're you doing out here?" He lowered his leg and grabbed the other. "I thought you had swim lessons." Benny wiped at his sweaty forehead with a shoulder.

I eyed my watch. Five minutes late. "Yeah, well, I..." I wanted to tell Benny about my discoveries, but if I told him I knew he'd go straight to Mom, regardless of the cost. That was how Benny worked. "I wanted to get a good jog in beforehand," I finished, miming someone running in place. "You know, cardio."

"Lucky you, you've barely broken a sweat, even after hurting your knee." Benny laughed. "This tropical climate is killing me. Or I'm just getting old."

"Twenty-nine isn't old!"

"Thanks." He took a swig from his water bottle. "To be honest, I haven't gone running in a long time. The resort's kept me busy. Anyway, I'm hitting the showers. And you are hitting the beach. You better go change into a bathing suit." He eyed my t-shirt and shorts.

"It's all underneath!" I promised and hurried away from him before I admitted something I shouldn't. "Bye!"

A few minutes later, after shucking my clothes in the bathroom, I found Victor at our designated meeting spot. He stood alone on the eastern outskirts of the beach, clad in a pair of swim trunks. His gaze on the sunset-streaked ocean was so intense, I didn't think he noticed me.

Until a life jacket hurtled at my face. I caught it on reflex. "Hey!"

He glanced over his shoulder. "You're late, and we're running out of light. Put that thing on and meet me in the water."

I grumbled under my breath but obeyed, fiddling with the life jacket. Instead of looking cute in my pineapple-print tankini, I resembled an enormous lumpy orange with stubby arms and legs.

The final buckle clicked with a fate-sealing snap. I grimaced and tugged at the strap. The life jacket's grip bordered on too tight, but no matter how hard I pulled, it wouldn't loosen. I added a growl to my efforts; maybe I could scare the thing into submission.

Or not.

"Annie, hurry up! What are you doing?" Victor called from where he stood waist deep in dark blue water.

I held a hand above my eyes and squinted into the streaks of red and violet that painted the sky. "The life jacket's too tight and won't loosen." I flapped the excess strap dangling at my knees for emphasis. "A little help?"

He splashed out of the water. "If you weren't so tiny, I might've found one that fit better. This is a children's large."

"I'm not dignifying that with a response."

The side of his mouth quirked in a bemused smile. "Move your arms." Without giving me a chance to do as he asked, Victor shoved my hands upward. "Sheesh, you really tangled this." He leaned closer, bending to examine my life jacket. The scent of his hair tickled my nose. I leaned back, palms suddenly damp.

"Stay still." Victor tugged on the life jacket, and I would've stumbled forward if he didn't raise a hand to catch me. "Sorry. It's being a little... Ah, got it."

The tightness around my chest loosened. I let out a breath and looked down to examine his handiwork. He flashed a grin at me, face inches away. "Better?"

My breath caught. "Uh, yeah." *Thanks* hovered on the tip of my tongue, but I swallowed it back out of spite for the "children's large" comment.

"All right." Victor stepped back and inspected me head to feet. The excess strap looped around my back, knotted in place. He smacked the side of my life jacket. "You're good to go. Follow me." He marched into the surf. The setting sun sent streaks of golden light dancing off his muscled back.

I kept my feet planted on the sand. Maybe it wasn't the best moment to join him in the water. Not when he looked like *that*.

Victor turned and rolled his eyes. "Annie, you won't learn to swim landlocked."

I yanked on my ugly florescent life jacket and moved a few steps forward, eyeing the sapphire waves sloshing over my feet. The setting sun sparkled off the surface and darkened the water to a midnight black. How would it feel to cleave through the water like that siren had when she rescued me? To have that confidence in the ocean? It would—

Cold water splashed across my face. "Victor!" I cried, spitting salt from my mouth and pushing soggy hair out of my eyes. I probably looked more like a wet dog than a sixteen-year-old girl at this point.

"Annie, get in the water!" Victor's hand slapped the surface of the ocean. Droplets splashed up around him. "Or would you rather do this in the pool with witnesses? Your mom and I were trying to save you from embarrassment, but—"

"Oh, shut up," I growled and stomped in deeper, aware of a few couples walking the beach yards away. "I'm coming."

Victor watched as I approached, a bemused smile on his face. I stopped in front of him, goose bumps pricking up along my arms. The ocean brushed against my stomach, not high enough for the life jacket to take over.

Even still, a weight pressed on my chest. Each breath became a struggle. I tugged at the life jacket again, lowering my head to hide the fear I knew blazed on my face. "Victor, I-I can't. I need to head back."

Warm fingers wrapped around my arms. I jolted my head up in surprise. It slammed into Victor's with an audible *thunk*. We both cried out, him clapping a hand over his forehead, me the top of my head.

"Darn it, Annie," Victor groaned. "Your skull is rock-hard."

I didn't answer, too focused on trying to breathe.

Victor looked at me, a red oval burned on his forehead. His hands found my shoulders again and squeezed. "You are *safe*."

I closed my eyes and focused on the warm skin of his fingertips against my arms. "I'm scared," I whispered.

"Why?" Victor's tone matched my own. "What happened to make you scared of water?"

I swallowed. "When I was ten I fell into a pool at our vacation house. No one was outside." The memory flooded over me. My panicked attempts to get to a wall, arms and legs weakening, sinking down, down, down... "My sister saved me. I'd been under for four minutes. The paramedics didn't think I'd make it. Ever since..." I shrugged. "It's just a childhood phobia. I'll get over it. These lessons will help, right?" I forced myself to smile at him.

Victor eyed me for a moment as if he could see through the grin on my lips before he nodded in agreement. "Knowledge is the first step to conquering any fear." He turned his hands, palms up, just above the water. "If you would?"

I hesitated a beat before placing my hands in his. "Now what?"

He stared at the bandage wrapped around my left arm as if just seeing it. "Can you get that wet?"

My gaze fell to the gauze and tape around it, and the siren's sharp teeth flashing as she cut through the netting filled my mind. I tensed, then pushed away the memory. The last thing I wanted to contemplate were the creatures lurking underwater. "I think so."

"Lift your legs so we can go through some kicks."

I glowered at him. "I already know how to kick. Do I look like a five-year-old?"

His gaze swept me up and down in a mocking stare.

I opened my mouth, snappy retort ready, but his words beat mine.

"You're annoyed I mentioned swim lessons to your mom. I get it, okay? But you're on an island. You need to learn how to swim so you can be safe." His voice softened. "I need to see how much you already know, which means we've got to start at the beginning."

I swallowed, taken off guard by the genuine concern in his dark eyes. "Okay," I murmured. I tightened my grip on Victor's hands and slowly let my legs go out beneath me. The life jacket caught my weight, and I bobbed like a cork with each gentle wave.

The wide grin on Victor's face made me feel embarrassingly proud of myself. "Great job, Annie. Now let's start easy and traditional with the flutter kick."

Victor moved me through two different kicks, taking at least ten minutes on each to make sure I understood.

The sun's middle brushed the horizon when Victor told me to stand, the kicking part of the lesson finished. He raked a hand through his hair, water rolling down his temples. "We'll move on to treading water, if you think you can go out further."

I hesitated. The challenging look in his eyes sparked my pride. Besides, I had a life jacket on. What could happen? I jutted out my chin. "Yeah. I can go out further."

Before I could change my mind, he snagged my elbow and dragged me deeper into the ocean. Sand went out underneath my feet and the life jacket jolted me upward. "Victor!" I cried.

"Are you okay?" The ocean water reached the top of his shoulders. Ugh, tall people. They didn't realize how good they had it. "Do you want to go back?"

Yes, I did. But I refused to tell him that. I just scowled at him.

"Your face is going to get stuck that way." He tugged at a damp curl in my hair. "Don't worry. You're safe. I'm right here."

He moved his arms in lazy circles and his head bobbed up and down in the water. "You can't tell, but I'm moving my feet too. They should rotate opposite from each other, like egg beaters. Try and mimic me, with just your arms first." His hands found my shoulders as he anchored me in place.

I started with my arms, moving them how Victor instructed. Victor corrected me a few times, showing how to cup my hands. When I got the arm part right, I swung my legs out. A cold, slippery object knocked into the side of my foot.

I yanked my leg up, eyes bulging. "There's something in the water," I hissed through clenched teeth while my mind screamed, *Sirens, sharks, giant fish!*

His brow furrowed. "What did you say?"

"Something. Brushed. My. Foot."

He jerked a thumb behind him toward a row of buoys fifty feet out. "Don't you know about the net? It's under those buoys. It stops us from going out too far and keeps any animals from getting in here. Nothing bigger than a minnow touched your foot."

"I know about the net, but... Are you sure something couldn't get through?" I eyed the spot where I'd felt that hard, cold thing. I'd almost forgotten about the net Mom told me about.

"Yes," he assured me. "Now start again. You were getting the hang of it."

I grimaced and resumed moving my arms. I brushed my left foot out in a tentative kick. When nothing touched it, I relaxed and slid my leg in the full egg beater motion.

"Good, good," Victor said under his breath.

Then my foot knocked into something again. I cried out. "Victor, I swear, there's something in the water."

He sighed. "Okay. Fine. Where is it?"

I probed the water with my foot, jaw clenched. When I ran into the object I let out a gasp and pointed. "There, there!"

"Hold on." He dove under and resurfaced a few seconds later, shaking water from his hair. "Annie, it's just a stick." He pulled his hand up with a grunt. Clutched in his pruney fingers was a pale human arm. Dark hair curled around the bleached skin, ragged and torn where a shoulder should connect.

I screamed. Victor glanced down. Color drained from his face. He cried out and flailed backward, splashing under the ocean's surface. The arm began to bob away on the ripples.

"Victor!" I shouted, snagging the arm with two fingers and a grimace, searching the water for him. "Victor!"

He popped up again, spluttering. "That was an arm," he wheezed. "A freaking arm!"

Shock streamed through me, leaving my nerves jittery but my mind clear. My tentative grip tightened, fingers closing around rubbery flesh. I forced air in and out of my lungs. *Calm down, Annie. Relax.*

"W-we need to find the rest of the body," I stuttered. Foreboding clamped around my heart despite the calmness in my voice. "We need to see who it is."

Victor looked ready to protest, gaze locked on the severed arm. "Annie, we should get someone for this." His face had taken on a greenish hue in the disappearing light. Already his gaze scanned the almost-empty shore for help.

I shook my head. "We won't find this exact spot again. Plus the tide will change. *Please,* Victor. It might be…" I couldn't bring myself to say the words.

"I know. I know. You're right." His voice was high-pitched with borderline hysteria. "The... *arm*... was caught under a rock or something. The body should still be nearby. I'll... I'll look." A slow inhale and exhale. Then he dove.

I waited with bated breath, gaze fixed on the spot where Victor disappeared. At the edges of my vision, the arm floated in my limp grip. Its fingers were swollen and curled. A gold ring encircled a digit, the band barely visible beneath the expanded flesh. Goose bumps swept across my skin. My stomach heaved.

Victor resurfaced with a cry, arms hooked under a bloated corpse. The man's dark hair splayed across his forehead, covering half of an engorged face. I swallowed back nausea, jerking my gaze away from the body, afraid I might recognize it.

"Do you need help?" I asked, voice strained.

"No." The word sounded sharp in the heavy silence between us. Victor trudged past me, walking backward, body floating behind him. I swam to keep pace with him, unwilling to face the bloated corpse. I kicked until my feet found purchase in the sand. Fear cinched my muscles into taut lines, though my grip on the arm was feather light.

I made it to the beach before Victor and called for help. A couple nearby paused, confused. Then their gazes fell on the body as Victor hauled it ashore.

"Get someone at the front desk!" I shouted. "Doctor Denton or Florence Mayfield! Hurry!"

The man muttered something to his wife. She nodded, hiked up the hem of her maxi dress, and took off toward the villa. The man ran toward us.

"I'm a doctor," he called. "I can do CPR!"

He'd obviously missed the severed arm dangling from my fingers.

"Oh, this is bad," Victor said.

I turned to see him kneeling a few feet from the body where he'd dragged it onto the sand. Each foamy wave tickled the nibbled tips of the dead man's toes. An entire chunk of his left side was missing, broken rib bones peeking out from mottled flesh. I staggered toward the corpse.

"This is bad," Victor said again. He couldn't seem to look away. "Annie, you shouldn't—"

I ignored him, falling to my knees, dropping the arm as if it were suddenly aflame. All along, I'd known. The conclusion presented itself days ago, but I'd shoved it to the back of my mind. Hoping, praying, believing...

"What happened?" The doctor skidded in the sand next to us. "How long was he under?" He knelt, hands stretched out as if to perform CPR, only to pull back and swear.

The body's face was barely recognizable, the nose and cheeks a fleshy mass, the skin chalky white. A chilling smile curled the enlarged lips of the corpse, expression expectant, as if something glorious awaited him.

The dead man was foreign and terrifying, but achingly familiar. I didn't want to say it. I didn't want to admit it. But the damp brown hair and the tattered remains of an ugly polo shirt...

"It's Adam," I croaked. "It's Adam Finley."

DAY NINE, 9:55 A.M.

A series of taps sounded on my door. I swung it open to reveal Victor and a tall, muscled guy with thick dreads. "Oh, uh, hi." I craned my neck to meet the dreadlocked guy's eyes.

"Annie, this is Max," Victor said, gesturing at the guy. "He's a lifeguard too."

"Nice to meet you, Max."

He shook hands with me, skin smelling of coconut, but didn't speak.

"Um..." I began, glancing at Victor.

"Max is mute," he explained. Behind him, groups of Mayfield Villa employees hurried down the hall. "We better get to the cafeteria. The meeting's starting soon and I want to get a seat together."

I turned to shut my bedroom door, gaze catching on the Viaii Nisi hat still hanging from a bedpost and Tamara's necklace dangling just below. My throat tightened. I closed the door harder than necessary. The wood banged against the frame and I winced.

"You okay?" Victor whispered at my back.

No. "Okay" wasn't even in my vocabulary at the moment.

"I'm fine," I said and followed Victor and Max into the cafeteria. We squeezed onto a bench in the back.

At the front of the packed cafeteria, Mom and Benny stood together. Mom's face was paler than usual, her powder doing little to conceal it. She held a microphone in one hand and waited for the room to settle.

"Good morning, everyone." A quaver moved through Mom's voice. She paused to take a breath and clear her throat. In the silence, my cell phone, jammed into a pocket of my shorts, began to buzz. I jabbed a side button to silence the ringer.

"Tragedy has struck our villa," Mom continued. "Adam Finley's body was recovered from the ocean yesterday."

Somewhere toward the front, a girl broke into sobs. Mutters filled the cafeteria. My heart struck an extra beat.

Mom swallowed. "Tamara Espanza and another member of our staff, Gregor Vladimir, are missing."

Sweat dampened my palms as the entire room gasped in unison. Another person had disappeared? When? How?

Mom seemed to lose her gusto for a moment. "We must find these other missing individuals and ensure something of this nature doesn't happen again. Which is why Benson and I are eager to welcome Agent Floros and Agent Papadakis, members of the NIS, to Viaii Nisi."

My phone went off again, and I gritted my teeth. A few heads swiveled in my direction. I fumbled to reject the call through the material of my shorts.

A man in a suit and tie and a woman in a fitted pantsuit stood from their seats in the front row. They joined Mom on the stage, the man taking the microphone.

"This is never a pleasant topic," he said, hazel eyes warm as he watched us. "Agent Papadakis and I," the woman inclined her head with a smile, "will do everything in our power to determine the cause of the victim's death. To do that, we're dragging the water in front of the resort. We haven't discovered anything yet, but for your own safety we're locking down the beach until further notice."

Cries exploded from the gathered employees.

"Please!" Floros cried. "Ladies and gentlemen, please!" The room quieted. "We need your patience and assistance. Throughout the next few days we will be conducting interviews with all of the staff."

Hushed whispers broke out, louder than the earlier complaints. The employees at my table turned to each other, heads bowed.

"But I thought that man drowned," a guy muttered to the person next to him. "Why would they need interviews?"

"Vladimir went missing, remember," a girl a few bodies down offered. "Maybe that maid killed them both."

I started to my feet, fists clenched.

Victor's voice towed me back to my seat. "Relax, Annie."

"Ladies and gentlemen, please!" Agent Floros said again, fighting to regain control of the room. He ran a tanned hand through dark, gelled hair.

My phone vibrated for the third time. Victor glanced at me and mouthed, *Who keeps calling you?*

After a quick glance at Mom where she stood off to the side, I tugged my phone out. Lynn's name lit the screen. I nearly fell off the bench. *Lynn* was calling *me*?

"I've got to take this," I whispered to Victor and slid out of my seat. I hurried along the aisle and out the cafeteria doors as Mom stepped in to help Agent Floros calm the room.

I jogged down the hall and ducked into a vending machine alcove. I kept my gaze fixed on a dangling bag of Skittles as I tapped the phone's screen and held it up to my ear. "Hello?"

"Annie!"

Lynn's familiar voice made my knees weak. I leaned on the vending machine, forehead resting against the glass. "Hey." The word came out more like a croak.

"Sorry I've been MIA, things have been so busy with..." I found myself spacing out, eyes still glued on the Skittles bag with its bright colors and artificial flavoring. Lynn's words droned on in a nonsensical mumble. She was busy. That's the excuse she came up with?

Agent Floros's voice drifted to my alcove through the open cafeteria doors. "Interviews will begin with Mrs. Mayfield herself and then move to managers and staff."

A girl in the daycare assistant uniform hurried past me. I waited to cut Lynn off until the girl disappeared into the bathroom.

"I'm sorry, what?" I snapped.

Lynn's torrent of words screeched to a halt. She'd been saying something about her neighbor's pet cactus.

"Busy. *You're* busy?" A sarcastic laugh dripped from my mouth. "Yeah, okay, I'm busy too, but I called and sent texts. I'd leave you voicemails too, but your mailbox is full. Go figure. Bet all the messages are from me. Or are you ignoring someone else as well?"

"Annie, whoa, hold on. Listen—"

"No, *you* listen. I haven't heard from you for three months. *Three* months, Lynn. I tried to call and text you every day until two weeks ago. When I gave up." My voice broke and tears blurred the Skittles, but I couldn't stop. "You promised to go to Meteora, promised to give me swim lessons, promised after rehab you'd call. *Where have you been?*" I slammed my fist against the vending machine's glass. The Skittles trembled and slipped closer to freedom from the ring that held it.

Silence buzzed on the phone.

"I've... been busy," Lynn said again, like a stupid broken record.

"How hard is it to answer a text message?" I asked, voice rough. "Or have your fingers been amputated too?"

She gasped. Guilt bit into my stomach, but I didn't take the words back. I waited for her to speak first.

"I, uh, saw the news. The dead body."

Deflated, I dropped to my knees. No apology, no *real* explanation. She probably hadn't even called to return my messages. She noticed Viaii Nisi on TV, and her curiosity picked up the phone.

"Are you okay?" Lynn's voice sounded hesitant as if she braced herself for another tirade. Well, she didn't need to worry. I barely possessed enough strength to think, let alone yell.

"I'm fine," I rasped. My fingers brushed over the thin pink lines on my arm. The marks from that siren had healed surprisingly fast.

"Annie? You there?"

I blinked. "Yeah, I'm here."

"Are you busy or something?"

"I'm supposed to be in a meeting right now. About the dead... man." It was easier to call Adam a "man." Made his death less real, less painful. I couldn't imagine what Mrs. Finley endured even now. Rumor was she'd fled the resort via private helicopter early this morning.

Lynn cleared her throat. "Did that guy really drown?"

Adam's bloated body haunted my mind's eye. The peaceful look on his face a disturbing contrast with the nature of his death.

"Yes. He drowned." Knowing Nurse Lynn would want more information, I continued, "The NIS said—"

"NIS?"

"It's the Greek version of the FBI. NIS stands for National Intelligence Service."

"Oh."

"Yeah," I continued, tugging at a flyaway strand of my hair. "They said Adam drowned and, from what they can see, there's no foul play." It turned out Victor had accidentally torn Adam's arm off when he went to grab what he'd thought was a stick. The severed limb was nothing more than a post-mortem injury. Same as the chunk missing from Adam's side. No proof of dangerous sea creatures. No proof of *sirens*.

"Who knew people used the words *foul play* outside of crime TV shows," she joked. "There's a girl missing too, right?"

"A girl and another guy." I cleared my throat, refusing to think about where Tamara might be. "The NIS are dragging the water in front of the resort, but they haven't found anything yet." As I said the words, I thought of my siren rescuer. Regardless of the supposed net, something—another siren?—had lured me into deep water that night on Lover's Point. Could the same thing have happened to Adam? But then why was his expression so peaceful? Mine certainly wouldn't have been.

Lynn let out a breath turned wind tunnel on the phone. "How's Mom?"

"Fine. Helping the agents handle a disgruntled audience."

"That's Mom for you." She chuckled, though it sounded forced. "Oh, hold on a sec, Annie." Noise came from the background like someone knocking. "Hey! You brought breakfast? Awesome! Did you remember—?"

A deep voice cut Lynn off. "Two sausage and egg burritos, got it."

"Who's that?" I asked.

"Oh, you remember Captain Wallace?" She didn't wait for me to respond. "He's been keeping an eye on me." I could hear the smile in her voice.

Captain Wallace. I clenched my jaw. He was the reason my sister was like this, that all of her dreams had been shattered, that she'd been snatched from me.

A muffled conversation ensued. Lynn must've placed her hand over the speaker. My leg muscles cramped, tired of being trapped in a crouched position. I staggered to my feet and glared at the bag of Skittles.

As Lynn continued talking to stupid Captain Wallace, I deliberated hanging up. Just as I was about to push "end call," Lynn's voice came back on.

"Sorry about that. Jim says hello."

"*Jim?*"

She cleared her throat. "Uh, Captain Wallace."

I crinkled my nose. No way would I give a "hi" back of my own. "What else did you want to know about the drowning?" I asked, done with this conversation.

Static buzzed for a moment. "Mom won't lose the resort, right? With all that's going on?"

"No."

"And you're sure you're okay?"

"Yes."

"Is there anything you need?"

"No." Not from you or your stupid *Jim*.

"Do you still have a crush on Nick Jonas from his Jonas Brothers days?"

"Okay, I'm hanging up." I lowered the phone.

"Wait, I'm sorry."

I froze. "What did you say?" My words came out annoyingly breathy and—worse—needy. To cover up my weakness I hip bumped the vending machine. The bag of Skittles shifted. The hook clutched the barest corner of the bag.

Lynn took a breath. I could picture her, eyes squeezed shut, nose crinkled. Even when we were kids, she hated apologizing. She pulled that face every time. "I'm sorry for avoiding you, Annie. Things have been really..." Her voice cracked. My emotionless, stoic Lynn.

"I've had a lot of adjustments," Lynn continued, her voice under control. "A lot of setbacks. I didn't want to call you until I was me again. The Lynn who ruffled your hair at the airport and made fun of your Nick Jonas fanfiction. The Lynn from two years ago." She took a deep breath.

I fought the burning tears in my eyes. My nose started to run, but I refused to sniff. I didn't want Lynn to know I was on the verge of crying.

"But when I saw the news earlier today, I knew I needed to call you. To make sure you were okay."

"Yoo-hoo, Annie!"

I jerked my head out of the vending machine cubby. Iona stood at the entrance to the cafeteria, hands on hips. She waved me over.

"Agent Floros wants to interview you." When that didn't make me vacate the alcove, she added, "Your mom is waiting for you since you're a minor. I'd wrap it up." She gestured to my phone. Warning given, Iona slipped back into the cafeteria.

"Lynn," I said, "I've got to go."

"Annie, you can't just hang up after that." She sounded annoyed.

The hypocrite! "Well, at least *I* answered the phone!" I ended the call and kicked the vending machine. The Skittles tottered and fell into the pickup slot.

I snatched the bag of candy with a huff of annoyance and jogged back into the cafeteria. Some employees still sat at the tables, chatting, but most people headed toward the exit. Mom stood outside a door that led to the cafeteria manager's office. Her arms were crossed, lips pinched at the edges. Yikes. Either the end of the meeting hadn't gone well, or she was fed up waiting for me.

As I passed Victor's table, I tossed the bag of Skittles at him. He caught them with a quick "Thanks!" Then I hurried over to Mom. She gestured for me to enter the office first.

Agents Floros and Papadakis waited inside, Papadakis sitting behind the desk and Floros leaning against a filing cabinet.

"Have a seat," Floros instructed with a wave of his hand.

I lowered myself onto one of the two folding chairs. Agent Papadakis gave me a warm smile, showcasing an endearing gap between her two front teeth.

"Hello, Annie," she said. "How are you doing? Your mom told us you were the one who found Mr. Finley." Her voice was surprisingly husky, as if she smoked.

I swallowed and glanced sideways at Mom who nodded at me. "Uh, I'm okay. Thanks for asking."

Agent Floros steepled his fingers and pressed them against his lips. "Annie, did you know Mr. Finley personally?"

So the questions began. I answered as honestly as I could. Yes, I knew Mr. Finley. Yes, I'd met his wife, and she seemed surprised by his disappearance. No, I didn't think Tamara was involved with Mr. Finley.

Throughout the interview, I gripped the sides of the metal chair. A debate warred inside my mind: tell the agents about the ruins or not? Yes, Benny's job hung in the balance, but so did lives, if Adam's death was any indication.

"Well," Agent Floros said with a sigh, as if this had been a waste of his time. He rubbed at his chin. I could imagine him mentally counting how many interviews he had left. "That concludes our—"

"Wait!" I lurched to my feet. The legs of the metal chair scraped against the tiled floor.

Everyone in the room jumped except Agent Papadakis. She'd scrutinized me throughout the interview, as if she suspected I was hiding something.

"Annie, sit down," Mom ordered. "What's all the excitement?"

I swallowed and tugged the chair back into position, lowering myself onto the seat. "There's something else." I glanced at Mom.

"And what is that?" Agent Papadakis asked.

"Ruins," I choked out the word. "There are ruins on the back of Viaii Nisi." Now that I'd begun the confession, I couldn't stop speaking. "Tons of human skeletons are there and at the end of a flight of steps are *siren* bones. I think… I think something might be in the water." *Not might,* I thought, remembering my siren rescuer. *There* is *something in the water.*

To my surprise, Agent Floros laughed. He adjusted his tie and cleared his throat. "I'm sorry, Annie. It's just… Your mother obviously didn't tell you."

I turned to Mom. Two spots colored her cheekbones, spreading to redden her nose. "Tell me what?"

"The previous owner," Mom explained, shooting a glance at both NIS agents, "planned to open a theme park here."

"A theme park?" I shook my head. "But what does that have to do with...?"

Agent Papadakis folded her hands on the desk, jacket buttons clicking on wood. "The ruins, the bones, the siren skeleton, they're part of the theme park." She watched me, gauging my reaction. "Your mom didn't want to move them out of respect for the deceased owner."

"The theme was *The Odyssey*," Agent Floros added. "A pretty unique idea, Greek gods and all that. Made quite a buzz back home. Until the poor woman drowned."

Their words didn't make sense. "That can't be," I whispered.

"It's the truth." Mom laid a hand on my knee. She seemed to have forgotten her earlier anger over me knowing about the cliffs, let alone the ruins.

I stared down at my hands, heart thudding. The ruins were just some theme park attraction? It couldn't be. The dread I felt amidst the cowering skeletons was real. And the siren who rescued me definitely wasn't a theme park attraction.

I just needed to prove it.

Lorelei's Song, Verse Six
"Fear also the gods' anger, lest they, astonished by
evil actions, turn against you."
~The Odyssey, Book Two

"Why do you suppose Queen Thessalonike ordered another gathering?" Acantha asked Lorelei, rolling onto her back and sending up a cloud of sand. "Oh, I've forgotten." She smirked. "You've taken a vow of silence. How lovely for the rest of us."

Lorelei bit her tongue to keep emotion from her face. Instead, she ran her fingers over the ridged shell of one of Acantha's oysters. Nestled inside this small creature would be a pearl. Acantha's oysters always produced pearls.

The image of the white luminescent sphere made Lorelei's stomach heave, which seemed impossible. She hadn't eaten anything for days, ever since that lung-breather touched her.

"Lorelei." Acantha's clicks came out sharp. She sat up, and her silver-white waves of hair rolled out in messy tendrils behind her back. "Stop tormenting my pets." She snatched the oyster from Lorelei's grip.

Lorelei felt a spark of annoyance, but it flickered out as quickly as it flared. She didn't have the energy for Acantha's goading today.

The siren's lips twisted in a pout. "Still silent, Lorelei? Don't you wish to comment on Queen Thessalonike's words?"

"It's not worth pondering." Niamh sighed. She lay a few shark-lengths away, back propped on a rock. Her tail hung over her face, and she plucked barnacles from the fins. "She will drone on as she always does."

"No she won't." Echo's gaze flicked to Lorelei and then back to her lap. A small fish darted between her palms. "The lung-breathers have prepared traps, and she wishes to warn us."

"Of course Echo would know in advance." Niamh peeked out at Echo from behind her raised fin. "That sounds rather droll. We don't know they're meant for us."

"Yes." Acantha swam to Echo, draping an arm around the siren's slender shoulders. "It could be for fish." Her tongue tickled the darting creature that had transformed Echo's hands into a playground.

Echo cupped her hands around the fish and nestled it against her stomach. "Acantha, don't frighten it. It's just a baby."

Bubbles escaped Acantha's mouth in a fit of giggles. "You're too soft, Echo." She tugged on a strand of Echo's hair.

"Leave her alone," Lorelei murmured, startling the sirens. It had been days since she last spoke. The roughness of her own voice sounded foreign to her ears.

Acantha's mouth split in a grin. She darted back to Lorelei. "At last, she speaks! Are you ready to hunt with me then, sister? That was the purpose of your silence, correct? To attune yourself to the sea?" She slid around Lorelei and grabbed the siren from behind, pinning her arms to her sides.

Panic burst in Lorelei's veins. She struck out, and her claws raked across Acantha's arm. Acantha hissed and released Lorelei, reeling back to cup a webbed hand over her wound.

"You are Maniae's own!" Acantha's lips pulled back to reveal rows of sharp teeth.

Niamh had lowered her tail at Lorelei's struggle and now sat up. "Don't be such a mollusk, Acantha. Lorelei barely scratched you."

Lorelei shook her head, freeing her mind from terror's haze. When Acantha had grabbed her, Lorelei was suddenly in the lung-breather's constricting arms, his hot breath and whispered threat suffocating her.

Shame, more at her own fear than the injury to Acantha, seeped into Lorelei's bones like a dark poison.

"Forgive me," she whispered and rushed away, cutting through the water. Her only thought was to distance herself from the others.

Lorelei's frantic strokes drove her deeper. The decreased temperature cooled the heat building under her scales.

"Lorelei!" Echo's chirp zinged through the water.

A growl of annoyance escaped Lorelei's clenched jaw. In moments, Echo paralleled Lorelei. She grabbed Lorelei's arm and forced her to halt.

"Acantha deserved that," she said simply, dropping her grip on Lorelei once they stopped. "You shouldn't run."

Lorelei swallowed. She kept her gaze fixed on the floating conch shells in Echo's dark hair. "I do not care what Acantha thinks."

"Something else then. What happened?" Her tail brushed against Lorelei's. "You can tell me. I kept your other secret, didn't I?"

"This is much worse." The fear curled deep in her belly shamed Lorelei. She'd overpowered the royal one, yes, but she still felt haunted by what might have been.

"Lorelei? Are you all right?"

"This doesn't concern you," she said, forcing venom into her voice.

"Don't be foolish!" Echo seized Lorelei's wrist. "I am trying to help you."

Echo's anger sizzled into Lorelei. A phantom desire to swim away and never return curled the muscles of Lorelei's tails. Except that was a pointless endeavor. Echo would catch Lorelei as she always did.

For the second time in less than a moon cycle, Lorelei confessed secrets she longed to keep hidden. "The lung-breather. I went to see him when I was to meet you."

Echo's flat nose crinkled. "So I assumed."

Lorelei's gaze fell to her own webbed hands, cupped in a tight ball to hide their trembling. "When I met him," she struggled to keep her emotions trapped behind a wall of indifference, "he attacked me. He said if he couldn't have me, he would kill me."

"I will destroy him!" The rage in Echo's voice jerked Lorelei's head up. "He will not escape after such behavior." Echo slid toward Lorelei, hesitant, as if she might flee. "Don't fear, sister." Her forehead brushed Lorelei's, an unspoken promise. "You will be safe. I won't allow anything to happen to you. Which is why..." She pulled back, determination flashing in her eyes. "Forgive me."

"Forgive?" Lorelei shook her head. Forgive what?"

The ocean seemed to pause, as if every creature, even the waves, listened. Echo's lips twitched in a regretful smile. "I must tell our queen. It's the only way." She spun around and darted away.

"No!" Lorelei cried, snatching for one of Echo's fins. Her fingers brushed the thin membrane... only to close around water. "Echo, stop!"

Queen Thessalonike might know what to do, but she would kill Lorelei for her disobedience. Echo didn't know the darker side to their queen. She'd never felt the sting of Thessalonike's whip across her back like Lorelei had after her first transgression. Lorelei had accidentally broken a section of the queen's coral while wrestling with Acantha. She'd been young then, practically a child. But that one mistake had resulted in eight lashes across her back. The others, years later, well... Lorelei had learned to avoid getting caught disobeying the siren queen.

"Echo!" Lorelei shouted again and shot after her sister. Not only did Lorelei fear Queen Thessalonike's reaction toward herself, but toward Echo as well. Echo had kept all of Lorelei's secrets about the lung-breather. How deep did the queen's favoritism toward the young siren extend? Lorelei did not want to find out.

A hulking shadow, a whale's length in diameter, blotted out the surface. Lorelei froze, comprehension ticking the back of her mind. That shape—she recognized it. Her memory called up the royal one's stories of the floating vessels, suspended only by Poseidon's grace on the sea.

The object was a ship. Lorelei frowned. If the lung-breathers were out this far, then their traps—

A scream reverberated through the water.

"Echo!" Lorelei screeched. She raced forward, muscles burning. A large net of crude rope materialized against the natural blue of the ocean. Lorelei dove for the lung-breather's trap.

Echo struggled in the midst of the rope. Red floated around her in a crimson cloud, directing Lorelei's attention to the barbs woven into the twine.

"Echo!" Lorelei shouted. "I'm here." She wrapped her hands around the rope, ignoring the stings of pain.

Echo ceased thrashing. Panic burned bright in her blue eyes. "Lorelei," she sobbed. "Lorelei, help me!"

"Don't worry. I'll get you out." Lorelei tugged on the ropes, her muscles bulging with the strain. Her blood mixed with Echo's in the water, yet the trap held firm. "Oh, Poseidon, help us," Lorelei begged. She brought her teeth down, ripping and tugging. Copper exploded in her mouth as the barbs dug into her gums and tongue. A twisted section of rope snapped, allowing a small square of freedom.

Echo stuck her hand out, sapphire scales flashing in the water. "Lorelei," she sobbed again.

Lorelei didn't answer; she tore at the next line of rope with her teeth. She would save her sister, she would get her out.

The trap shuddered, and the cords connected to the surface strained. They creaked as the net rose.

"No!" Lorelei shrieked. She tore at the rope, screaming in anger and fear.

"Lorelei, stop!" Echo's voice breached Lorelei's terror. Her hand strained for Lorelei's, her arm reaching out through the small hole in the net.

THESE WICKED WATERS · 145

Lorelei weaved her fingertips through Echo's. "I won't let you go," she vowed even as the net rose higher. It pierced the surface. Echo gasped a breath of air.

"Don't let go," Lorelei wheezed, muscles along her arm screaming in agony.

"I'm scared."

"I won't let them hurt you." Lorelei caught sight of lung-breathers' faces in the lantern-light. They leaned over the boat's side, eyes hungry and savage. She wanted to rip their throats out, one by one. They would not have her Echo. *They would not!*

The net smacked against the side of a hulking ship. Lorelei cried out as her shoulder slammed into the hull. Hot agony made sparks erupt in her vision. Her fingers slipped from Echo's. Echo's final scream was suddenly silenced as Lorelei tumbled into the cold embrace of the ocean.

DAY NINE, 12:08 A.M.

Cicadas and crickets chirped around me in a nighttime concert. I paused to listen, shifting the straps of my backpack.

Sneaking out of the villa before the doors locked had been easy—borrowing snorkeling supplies from Aquatic Adventures even easier. A quick test showed that the villa's locked doors would open using my employee resort ID, so getting back in would be simple. Unless Mom checked the logs, she wouldn't know about this little excursion. My plan was practically perfect.

The one downside was timing.

I couldn't exactly come out to the pier during the day or even late evening, not when shoppers swarmed all over it. I'd had to wait until the stores closed at ten-thirty and the workers returned to the villa. Now midnight's darkness twisted the least threatening object into a lurking predator. This far from the villa, this late at night, the only light came from the sliver of moon above and the quaking beam of my flashlight.

Scary was an understatement, but I refused to turn back now that I stood on the Welcome Center pier. Below the jutting slats of wood, the ocean roiled and foamed. I swallowed hard.

"For Tamara and Adam," I rasped, tightening my hands into fists. "And Vladimir, too."

The pier creaked with each hesitant step. *Run*, the wood seemed to beg. *It's not safe.*

Talk about eerie.

I crept to the end of the pier and swung the beam in a slow arc. A seagull keened overhead, and I jumped. The flashlight clattered to the boards.

"Chill out," I snapped, retrieving the flashlight and sucking in a breath of salty air. Despite my exterior bravado, knowing what I meant to do made my toes curl with dread.

I flung the backpack onto the pier and tugged out my borrowed supplies: two ropes cut to different lengths, an underwater flashlight, and goggles. I cinched one rope tight around my waist, excess coiled at my hip and looped the other around my neck like a scarf. With goggles strapped on and the flashlight in one hand, I started down the ladder. My sneakers clanged on the metal rungs, and I cursed my fear for making me stupid. I should've taken my shoes off. Too late now.

After tying the other end of the first rope to the ladder, creating a tether, I took a slow breath and transferred the second rope to my hand. The flashlight reflected a hazy spotlight on the water's surface. I stared at it, jaw clenched.

"One, two, three… four… five…" I swallowed hard. "Oh, just do it." I breathed deep and jumped.

Water enveloped me in a cool embrace. My muscles contracted in momentary panic before my fingers, still gripping the rope, closed around the lowest rung of the ladder. I swept the flashlight in a slow arc, illuminating the ocean below the pier. Sand floated to and fro with each wave, catching the moonlight and sparkling.

Where the pier met the land, a wall of rock rose from the seafloor. My flashlight caught a deeper black near the first support pole—a narrow crevice. In its shadowy depths a glint of orange caught my eye. I squinted, fingers tightening on the ladder, lungs burning.

Oxygen trumped curiosity. I shoved to the ocean's surface with a gasp. Warm air tickled my skin and wet strands of hair stuck to my face. I pressed my forehead against a cool rung. I would need to leave the ladder to investigate the crevice. That thought made my throat tighten.

"You can do this," I breathed. "You'll be—" A splash cut me off, as if someone had smacked the surface of the water just behind me. Cool droplets splattered across the back of my neck and onto my cheek. My spine went rigid, breath catching. I turned by reflex, swinging my flashlight out to cut through the night.

The beam fixed on a scaled face inches away from mine.

I screamed, shooting up the ladder. The flashlight splashed into the water. My sneaker slipped, and I slid down, knee slamming into the lowest rung. Pain exploded across the spot. I cried out.

The siren's form was all shadow in the darkness. She slid closer, and I tensed for an attack. Instead, she snatched the flashlight and pointed it at me.

I winced, turning from the light. Darkness returned, and when I glanced back the siren had moved to float at the ladder's base. She held the flashlight toward me, beam pointed down, eyes narrowed as if she expected my skin to split and reveal a monster.

I cleared my throat, prying a hand off the ladder to accept the flashlight back. "Thank you."

As soon as the flashlight was in my possession, the siren shot back, turning up froth. Yards of inky ocean separated us. Her golden eyes studied me, just as my blue ones studied her. Both of us were curious, I realized. My flashlight swept across the fiery scales scattered over a flat nose and long ears that were more like fins than skin-covered cartilage.

"Hello," I croaked, voice hoarse. I cleared my throat. "I was hoping to run into you." I trailed off, unsure where I was going with the introduction. Did the siren even speak English? "Uh, what's your name?" I finished lamely.

The siren tilted her head, knotted hair cascading over a shoulder. Somehow I got the feeling my behavior amused her.

Well, what else could I say? "Come here, siren, I want to capture you and take you home?" Yeah, that would go over well.

Not.

Except, while I watched her, I realized there was no way tying a rope around her would work. I'd been naïve to think so in the first place. The corded muscles along her arms and the speed in which she moved... Not to mention her teeth. Capture would be impossible. My grip on the loop of rope I still held loosened in defeat.

The siren studied me before drifting closer. Almost as if she had decided to trust me. Or because she wanted to eat me.

The siren's mouth opened, and a throaty grunt creaked out.

I shoved my goggles up into my hair to see better. The flashlight illuminated razor-sharp teeth... and a swollen pink stub that was once a tongue. I gasped, sagging against the ladder.

At the sound of my surprise, the creature clamped her jaw shut and snarled.

"Sorry," I whispered, shifting on the ladder. My knee cried out in protest. "But... what happened to you?"

When she didn't respond, I held the flashlight toward my mouth. I parted my lips and stuck out my tongue. "What happened to yours?"

The creature's eyelids closed, thinner and more transparent than human lids. They reopened a moment later. She shook her head.

"What?" I asked. "What are you trying to say?"

The siren didn't reply. She slipped into the water without a sound.

"Wait!" I scrambled to lean away from the ladder, closer to where she disappeared. My flashlight swept the spot. "Please!" I called. "I shouldn't have asked about your tongue. I'm sorry!"

Minutes passed, and she still didn't resurface.

I waited for her until my legs went numb. But she never came back.

DAY ELEVEN, 12:15 P.M.

A splotch of purple and black engulfed the skin of my right knee. I ran my fingers across the bruise, conscience heavy.

Two days.

Two days had passed since I saw the siren, and I hadn't said anything. To anyone. I'd visited the pier each morning before the shops opened to try to lure her back with food, but she never showed. If I couldn't get her to return… I had no idea what I was going to do for proof.

Sunlight warmed my skin from a cloudless sky. Around me, a spattering of beachgoers lounged on the sand or splashed in the waves. Many guests had left after Adam's body was discovered and the missing employees became common knowledge. The numbers were so bad that Mom relieved me of maid duty yesterday—the actual employees didn't have enough work as it was. She hoped reopening the beach today would help but wasn't optimistic.

Now my only scheduled job was to hand out towels in the afternoons. When I'd first come to the villa, I would've been happy to ditch cleaning toilets. But now I would've chosen to clean the dirtiest toilet in the world if it meant Adam, Tamara, and Vladimir came back.

And that was saying something.

"Hey, Annie!" Victor's voice made me glance up. He strode over in a red pair of swim shorts, lifeguard floatie slung over his shoulders. White sunscreen was smeared across his chest as if he'd applied it in a rush.

I forced a smile. "Hey."

He stopped in front of me, arms crossed. "You okay?"

For a thrilling moment, I wondered how it would feel to be honest. To tell Victor about the siren bones, about my encounter two nights ago.

As quickly as the urge surfaced, it died. "I'm fine," I said.

He looked ready to disagree, but a girl on the lifeguard stand shouted his name.

"Be right there!" he called. Then to me, he said, "Well, if I can help, let me know."

"Thanks."

"That's one nasty bruise!" he called over his shoulder as he jogged away, kicking up sand.

I grimaced, ducking a look around for Mom. So far I'd managed to hide the injury from her, but if she noticed, I had a story all cooked up: an unfortunate stumble against the edge of a bathtub while cleaning.

My gaze drifted to the ocean, watching the sunlight dance on its surface. What other dangers lurked beneath these waves? Were sirens responsible for the missing people? Did they lure guests and employees into the water at night?

Gnawing truths toyed with my mind, truths I'd tried to avoid the last few days. I always assumed I'd find Tamara. I never once considered that when I found her...

She might be dead.

In the distance, a shadow darted underneath the buoy line. I squinted, holding up a hand against the sun. The swimmer picked up speed, staying close to the turquoise surface.

No. It wasn't a swimmer. It moved too fast for a human. I followed the figure's trajectory to where a little girl played waist-deep in the foam, water wings sagging on her skinny arms.

"Victor!" I screamed, launching to my feet. My bad knee gave out, and I hit the sand. "The little girl!" I cried.

Victor's gaze caught on the shadow. He leapt from his life-guard chair with such force the thing teetered, a bright red float slapping against his back. He sprinted into the surf just as the little girl disappeared under the water.

Whistles along the beach blew. I pushed up with an arm, wiping sand from my tearing eyes.

"Everyone out of the water!" the other lifeguards to the left and right shouted. Swimmers who'd been staring at Victor scrambled for shore.

Leaving the shallows, two lines of froth struck toward open ocean. A small form popped to the surface. Bright red hair, done up in pigtails, shone in the sun. The little girl's mouth opened wide in a shriek as she was dragged through the waves. Her cry sputtered. Her head slipped under.

I hobbled for the shoreline, joining a group of onlookers. My hands formed tight fists, fingernails breaking skin. A siren had taken that little girl; I knew the truth of it in my bones.

But was it *my* siren?

Victor cleaved through the water toward the girl. Yards separated them. My heart thundered as if I were the one per-forming the rescue.

A woman's sobs pulled my gaze away. She stood ankle-deep in the ocean, sunburned hands wringing together, her fiery hair pulled back in a messy bun. The crowd gave her a wide berth, casting nervous and sympathetic looks her way.

I shouldered past people and limped to her side. I took one of her hands in mine. She didn't turn, but her fingers squeezed tight around mine.

Victor intersected the little girl at the buoy line. Something tugged him under the waves. The frothing water stilled. Victor's red rescue float bobbed on the surface.

The woman's fingernails dug into my hand. Tears burned my eyes.

Come on, Victor. Come on!

Another lifeguard—Max, I realized—streaked into the ocean, floatie strapped to his back. A female lifeguard forced the crowd back and spoke frantic commands into a walkie-talkie.

Victor's head broke through the turquoise water as one arm hooked around the red float. Resting against his chest was a coughing girl, her pigtails drooping.

The woman—the mom—collapsed, tugging me with her. Tears trickled down her cheeks to patter against the sand.

Max met Victor halfway from shore and took the little girl. Victor's lips moved as he spoke to Max, but I couldn't hear from so far away. Max nodded and swam toward us, the little girl holding tight to the rescue float. He lifted her into his arms as they reached shallow water, signing to the female lifeguard with his free hand.

"Medical assistance," the female lifeguard said into the walkie-talkie. "We need medical assistance in sector two."

A few people tried to surge forward to see the little girl, but the female lifeguard pushed them back again with a barking order. "Stay back! Let us do our job."

The mom staggered to her feet, splashing into the ocean to meet Max.

"Mommy!" the girl sobbed, holding out pudgy hands for her mom, who held her tight.

My stomach dropped as I caught sight of the kid's leg.

"Out of the way!" The medics knocked me aside. I staggered as if in a dream, hand clutching at my left arm. Four gashes carved into the little girl's pale skin, just like the marks the siren left on me—but deeper.

"Annie." Victor's breathless voice jerked me out of my stupor.

I whirled around. He stood a foot away, water making trails down his skin, eyes bloodshot.

"Victor!" I hurled myself into his arms. He staggered back before he caught me and softened. "You're okay," I whispered into the muscles of his chest. "You did it. You saved her."

His head lowered so his lips brushed against my ear. Chills raced across my skin.

"Annie," he murmured. "Why did you ask me about sirens that day?"

I jerked back to meet his wide brown eyes. "Do you mean...?"

He nodded.

My heart decided before my brain could consider otherwise. "Do you have tomorrow off?"

He opened this mouth to reply but just nodded, as if stringing words together was too difficult just now.

I lowered my gaze, studying Victor's smooth collarbones. "There's something I need to show you."

He shifted. I looked up at him only to see his stare focused over my head.

I turned, watching as the little girl was carried on a stretcher toward the villa, gauze pressed to her leg. Her mom followed, holding tight to her daughter's hand. Agents Floros and Papadakis hurried onto the sand, speaking in Greek.

Agent Floros's voice carried. "That stupid Florence woman. She should've listened to me and kept the beach closed!"

"I think you mean listened to *me*," Papadakis said.

"Excuse me," Floros called, in accented English now, waving his arms to get everyone's attention. "Do we have any witnesses?"

I turned away from the NIS agents to see smooth, tan skin and a set of sharp collar bones. I stepped back, my t-shirt sporting wet spots along the front from our embrace.

"Tomorrow, then?" Victor's voice drew my gaze up. His lips formed a thin line, skin ashen.

I swallowed. "Yes. Tomorrow."

Lorelei's Song, Verse Seven
"That is the gods' work, spinning threads of death through
the lives of mortal men, and all
to make a song for those to come."
~The Odyssey, Book 8

For the first two nights, the lung-breather's castle had been silent. Lorelei clung to the cliff-side, half submerged, listening for Echo. Her injured shoulder throbbed with the strain, but she couldn't pull herself away. The need to slither up the stone staircase, to the lung-breathers' fortress, radiated through her. But six of the vile creatures guarded the dock where she could ascend.

So she waited.

On the third night, the guards spoke of Echo, calling her a "temptress" and "sorceress," and of the torture the royal one planned for her.

Lorelei ambushed the guards. She'd reached the staircase's center, shrieking for Echo, before the lung-breathers attacked her with sharp blades. She'd barely escaped capture.

Now, the fourth moonrise, Lorelei curled tight underwater. The horrors the guards spoke of, the pain Echo would suffer, leeched into her mind. Guilt gnawed at her with serrated fangs. Lorelei should confess Echo's abduction to Queen Thessalonike. But she was afraid—so, so afraid. It paralyzed her, devoured her from the inside out.

When the moon rose high in the starless night, the screams began. They reverberated through the water, a shattering melody.

Lorelei's stomach heaved. She sobbed a tearless cry, burying her head against her scaled knees.

"Echo," she moaned. "Oh, Echo." Lorelei could not bear this. Whatever agony Queen Thessalonike bestowed as punishment, even death...

Lorelei didn't care. Echo meant everything.

Everything.

Lorelei's muscles flexed, and she shot through the water, leaving Echo's shrill pleas for mercy behind.

16

DAY TWELVE, 10:28 A.M.

Ferns tickled my ankles as I tramped through the undergrowth. Despite the sun breaking through the foliage above, a somber cloud hovered over us. Victor and I had been quiet all morning, lost in thought.

I glanced over my shoulder. A yellow inflatable kayak rocked back and forth over his head with each step. His large hands gripped either side of it, muscles taut. Sweat beaded at his temples and darkened his t-shirt. This one had a brown cartoon otter below the words *I want to be loved bayou.*

"Are you doing okay?" I asked.

Victor blinked and appeared disoriented for a moment. Then his eyes focused, and he nodded. "Yeah, fine. Just thinking."

"It's just a little farther," I promised and turned around, recalling the small inlet I'd found when I first saw the cliffs. Victor appeared to be in shape, but I doubted he'd ever rock climbed. The inlet was mostly overgrown with cattails, but it was the perfect place to launch a two-person kayak, courtesy of Aquatic Adventures.

Through the curved palm trees ahead, blue water sparkled. I broke into a jog, eager to release some nervous energy. Victor grunted as he kept pace.

I waded through cattails as high as my waist before plodding onto sand. Ocean stretched out, kissing the hazy horizon. Frothy waves lapped against a large boulder a few yards out before sliding ashore. I took a deep breath of the salty air and turned to watch Victor's progress. Hysterical laughter burst out of my mouth.

The kayak had jammed between two palm trees, and Victor was tugging helplessly at it. He looked at me over his shoulder and rolled his eyes with a smile. "Mind giving me a hand?"

"Sure." I hurried over, trying to stifle my giggling, and reached for the trapped boat. The tips of my fingers brushed the soft plastic. I grumbled, hopping onto my tiptoes.

"On three," Victor ordered. He wiped the side of his face against his sleeve.

"*Three!*" I cried.

We tugged. The kayak squeaked against the trees' bark before slipping free. Victor and I stumbled back. I looked at him, grinning in triumph. Cast in the sunlight, his eyes resembled two copper pennies, matching the necklace he wore. Gooey warmth spread through my stomach.

Victor cleared his throat and looked away, bending to inspect the kayak for holes.

To hide the frantic thudding of my heart, I busied myself undoing the bandana securing my hair and wiping my face with it. The red material came away damp.

By the time I redid my bandana headband, Victor had tugged the boat over the sand toward the water.

"Everything shipshape?" I asked, following him. After a beat when Victor didn't respond, I added, "*Ship*shape. Get it? Our kayak?"

He shook his head and tossed me a paddle. "Very punny."

"Just lightening the mood over here." I caught the paddle in the crooks of my elbows. The stuck kayak had expelled the skulking shadow over us. I wasn't too eager for it to descend again. "My joke is no worse than your dumb shirts."

He wagged his finger at me, paddle secured underneath an armpit. "My shirts are cute." He jerked a thumb at the grinning otter emblazoned on his chest. "See? Otters are cute. Which makes me cute."

I looked him up and down. Well, I couldn't argue with that. "Let's just get in the boat."

I eyed the kayak, imaginary bees swarming in my stomach. I hadn't been out on the water since before my drowning accident. Hopefully I still remembered all the mechanics.

Victor steadied the kayak while I climbed into the front, the plastic shifting under my feet and almost tripping me. I managed to settle on the front seat without falling and laid a paddle over my lap. Beyond this inlet the siren bones would be glistening in the morning sun, just waiting for us. A chill raced along my spine at the thought of sharing them with Victor. What if he agreed with Mom and the NIS? That the bones were some amusement park attraction?

"Whoops, almost forgot," Victor said, seconds before something smacked me in the back of the head.

"Hey!" I spun around. A bright orange life jacket lay in a heap on the floor of the kayak. "Ah. Thanks." As a kid, I'd hated wearing life jackets whenever Lynn and Dad took me kayaking. Now? I put it on, making sure to loosen the straps first.

After Victor secured his lifejacket, he looked up at me. "Okay, I'm coming in." The kayak shifted toward the water then sunk down in the back. Victor let out an *oomph*. "Ready to push off?"

"Yup."

The kayak jerked forward a few inches until it rested solely on the water.

"Once we get out of this inlet, we need to head that way." I pointed to the gray cliffs. "Just avoid the big, obvious boulder right there."

"Got it."

I moved to sink my paddle in the water. It smacked against Victor's with a thud. "Watch it," I grumbled, turning to look at him. Then I realized I'd forgotten to ask a very important question. "Sorry, but have you kayaked before?"

Victor swung the paddle so it lay horizontally across his lap. "Actually, no."

"I see." I tugged at the life jacket. Sweat dripped down my chest and sides. "Since you're in the back, you put the strength behind the strokes. Both of our paddles have to move at the same time. Just watch mine and move yours the same way."

"Easy enough." Victor gripped the center of the paddle.

"You'll want your hands a little farther apart." When he shifted his hands to the proper distance I nodded and faced front again. At first I moved my paddle slowly so Victor could catch on. It took us at least ten minutes to get out of the inlet, not counting the time we spent detaching ourselves from a head-on collision with the boulder. At least the detour gave us practice. By the time we reached open ocean, our motions were succinct, almost perfect. Victor was a quick study.

Though the sun beat down on us in fiery force, I relished the way we glided over the water's surface and the rhythmic dripping noise the paddles made with each stroke. Dancing kelp waved goodbye as we floated over it and schools of fish scattered in our wake.

"Hey, Annie!" Victor tapped my back with his paddle to get my attention. "See those fish?" He pointed.

Underneath our kayak flitted a school of cobalt blue fish, scales rippling in the sunlight, their movements a timed dance. Each fish followed the perfect, inborn rhythm.

"They're blue chromis," he explained, sounding like a TV nature series narrator. All he needed was a British accent. "Their scientific name is *Chromis cyanea*. They eat zooplankton and hang out near the surface." He dipped his fingertips into the water. The school of fish burst apart and scattered. "And like most sea creatures, they scare easy."

I watched him for a moment, knowing a girly smile had slipped across my mouth.

He caught my stare and pursed his lips. "What?"

"You're glowing. When people talk about things they love…" I shrugged. "I can tell that marine biology makes you really happy."

The corner of his mouth quirked up, and he leaned forward, elbows on knees. "Is that the only thing you find interesting about me, Annie Mayfield?"

My heart lost its steady rhythm. "Don't flatter yourself," I huffed, spinning around.

Gray rock thrust from the ocean. Surf foamed against it as waves broke along the surface, immovable, permanent. The steps cut into the cliff-side became more defined the closer we paddled.

"Make for that rock there." I gestured to the flat platform where the siren bones waited. At the far end of the rock, the smooth tips of sun-bleached ribs curled toward the sky.

"I'll get out first and hold this thing steady," Victor said once we reached the end of the platform. He shifted, ready to hop out.

"Hold on." I gripped the warm rock to steady us and looked at him. "I need to warn you about something."

Victor waited for me to summon my courage.

I took a deep breath. "This might sound crazy, but… There are siren bones on this rock." Surprise flickered in his eyes as his gaze swept the area ahead, but he didn't speak. I continued, "And there is a mass grave in the ruins atop that cliff." I gestured to the area over our heads.

This time his mouth fell open. He started to ask a question, but I cut him off. "My mom and the NIS believe the bones and the ruins are theme park attractions the last owner of Viaii Nisi left behind. But I know you saw something in the water yesterday. I need you to tell me if you think… if you think they're real."

"What happened to him or her?"

My brow furrowed. "What?"

He inclined his head toward the island. "The last owner. Where are they now?"

I hesitated. "Dead."

"I see." Victor's fingers flexed on the paddle. He let out a breath. "Okay, well, let's get out of this kayak and check things out." He hopped onto the platform without waiting for my response. The kayak squeaked as he tugged it onto the rock while my body shook with the motion. I barely felt it. My gaze fixed on those arched bones. They reminded me of fingers curling up toward the sky, eternally grasping for something just out of reach. A shiver scuttled down my spine.

"Annie."

I blinked. Victor knelt beside me, one hand on the kayak, the other held out to me, expression somber. I clasped my hand in his and staggered out of the kayak.

"Ready?" he asked, fingers trailing against my palm as he dropped my hand.

I nodded a lie. "This way."

I slowed as we approached the bones.

Victor's muscles tensed. His eyes widened in disbelief. "What the hell?"

"Here, look." I grabbed Victor's hand and tugged him closer to the skeleton's hips. I held my breath and watched his face.

His thick brows knit together as he examined the skeleton, starting at the skull and working his way down. The tension started to melt away from his limbs, morbid curiosity and confusion replacing it.

"This..." His gaze hovered on the elongated spinal cord and thin fish-like bones protruding from it. "From here to here," he gestured to the human half of the skeleton, "it resembles the bone structure of a person, but farther down... Annie, I can't even..." His hands fisted in his hair. "They resemble that of an enormous fish. The extended spinal column..." Victor's gaze met mine. "This changes everything. I need to tell you about yesterday."

The words gushed out of me before I could catch them. "You saw a siren in the water, right? I already guessed that."

"Yes, but there's more. Just to be clear, this is something I didn't tell the NIS. I thought I was seeing things."

"Seeing what?"

"When I rescued that girl, there was this *thing* latched on to her leg. It tugged me down and tried to bite me. For a moment, I didn't think I'd..." He trailed off, gaze faraway, reliving yesterday's horrors. Then he shook himself and looked at me again. "I punched it in the face, pushing it upward, but it panicked. I think it was afraid of the sun."

My eyes widened. *Afraid of the sun.* When I rescued the siren by the pier, it had lashed out after the sun peeked through the clouds. Was that why it hadn't reappeared each morning I visited?

Victor's voice drew me out of my thoughts. "The fish thing left the kid alone and then swam off through a hole in the net. I told your mom about the hole, but..." Victor let out a breath. "Not about the fish thing. That creature had two tails but, like this skeleton, was humanoid at the top."

My heart gave a hard double thud. The siren I met on the pier had two tails. "What color was its scales?"

He frowned. "Why does that matter?" When I didn't answer, he sighed. "I don't remember. Everything happened so fast. Listen. After I told your mom about the net, divers checked it out. They found multiple holes. Huge ones. No normal sea animal could've done that so soon, but... Now it makes sense." His dark gaze burned into mine. Goose bumps danced across my skin despite the heat. "These bones are real, Annie. And the ruins you mentioned have to be too. Your mom, the NIS... One of them is hiding something." Victor paused, brows drawn together. "That guest who drowned—and that maid and Vlad. Do you think the sirens...?"

"Yes. At least, maybe." I let out a breath, relieved Victor and I had drawn the same conclusions.

"This is unbelievable." He examined the bones anew. "We have to do something."

"What do you have in mind?"

"We should tell the guests. They have to get off the island. They need to know about the sirens."

"Are you crazy?" I cried. "It'll cause chaos. It's not a good idea."

"We should tell your mom at least. If these things are attacking us—"

"She won't listen," I whispered, not meeting his eyes. "I already tried, remember?"

He kept grasping at possibilities, the same ones I had run through a thousand times. "Okay, if not your mom, the NIS."

"Again, I already tried. We need more proof," I argued. "They know about these bones and don't care. Yes, you saw a siren in the water, but they'll twist that on you."

"No, they—"

"Yes, they would. They think logically. Sirens aren't logic."

He fumbled, still grasping for a reason. "That girl's leg. That's some proof, at least."

"Victor..." I shook my head. "Think, okay? We're talking about *sirens*. Mythological beings from *The Odyssey*. Who in their right mind, other than someone who has *seen* a siren, is going to believe us?"

"Have you seen one?" he asked, studying me.

"Yes." I swallowed, toying with the laces of my sneakers, avoiding the shocked expression on his face.

"Why haven't you said anything?"

"I tried! But I need real proof. A siren body kind of proof. Promise me you won't say anything," I pressed. "To anyone. The beach is closed permanently now. Everyone is safe as long as they don't go in the water."

He groaned. "Why did you even show me these bones if I have to keep them a secret?"

Well, that wasn't the response I hoped for. "It was the shock on your face after you rescued the girl. I didn't want you to think you were crazy and... And I need an ally in this." I wiped the back of my hand over my damp forehead. "Let me do a little more research, get something real to bring to the NIS." *Give me time to talk to the pier siren,* I added silently. I'd give it one more try. Tonight, I would visit her again.

Please let her be there, I thought. If she didn't show, I had no idea what to do next.

"Do you want me to help you?"

I looked up at Victor. When we'd first met, I never suspected I'd be turning to him for help of any kind. Especially after the towel incident. But he'd taught me to swim. Found Adam's body with me. His expression was genuine and concerned. Concerned for me.

I gave him a tentative smile. "If I can't figure it out by tonight, then yes."

He ran a hand through his hair, looking back to the bones. "Sirens are real. Man. This is insane."

I glanced down at the siren bones, thankful to have Victor on my side. "Tell me about it."

DAY TWELVE, 3:50 P.M.

"**G**o fish," I muttered, eyeing the cards in my left hand while my right palmed my chin. I'd been roped into manning the guest services desk after passing by when one of the guys needed a cigarette break. Didn't people realize just because I was Florence Mayfield's daughter, I didn't know the ins-and-outs of every position?

Tommy, the towel-thief-turned-friend, leaned forward, revealing his cards. "What did you say?" he shouted over the chaos of the lobby.

Beyond the guest services desk where Tommy and I hunkered, people loitered in the lobby. Suitcases littered the marble floor while adults chattered uneasily. The bus had already made two trips to the ferry's dock. It seemed the villa had lost half its remaining guests in one afternoon. The attack on the little girl provided a good incentive to check out early.

"Go fish!" I yelled.

"Darn." Tommy reached for the card pile.

Chatter quieted as the next bus arrived. Benny stood at the front doors, directing groups of people outside. Despite the chaos and less-than-friendly attitude of the guests, he looked cool and collected. His ability to people please exceeded that of the snazziest politician. He caught my gaze and winked. I smiled back.

A tap on my shoulder made me turn. Agent Floros towered over me, mouth twisted in annoyance. Then his lips parted in surprise as recognition dawned.

"Agent Floros? What do you want?"

"Annie Mayfield? What are you doing at the front desk?"

"Filling in for a few minutes."

Floros's gaze flicked to the deck of cards. I sprawled atop the contraband game, swiping them into a drawer despite Tommy's protests.

"And is this your assistant?" Floros gestured to Tommy who studied the agent with a suspicious gaze.

"Why aren't you wearing sunglasses?" Tommy asked. "All FBI agents wear sunglasses."

Floros smoothed his black tie. "That's because I'm not an FBI agent." He turned to me. "I was wondering if you've seen Agent Papadakis today."

I shook my head. "Sorry, no. I've only been here a few minutes." It felt like a century had passed since I showed Victor the siren bones. But it had only been that morning. I glanced at my watch. A few more hours and I could sneak away and try to meet the siren again.

Floros crossed his arms, watching the crowd board the bus outside. "I tried her cell, but it went to voicemail, and she's not answering her room door." He shook his head, frustrated. "That woman. I bet she's sick or something. I told her not to leave her windows open overnight. The signs said not to do it and sea breezes aren't—"

My toes curled with dread. "She slept with her windows open?"

Floros frowned. "What does that have to do with anything?"

I fumbled for the skeleton room card. A nagging voice warned I was jumping to conclusions, but the frantic beat of my heart argued otherwise.

"Let's check her room." I lurched to my feet, card in hand. "Tommy, go find your parents."

He started to complain, but I ignored him and hurried to an elevator. Floros followed me, shoes clacking on marble.

"What floor is Agent Papadakis's room?" I asked, jamming my thumb into the elevator call button.

"Two, room 216. Your mother could only fit us in employee rooms."

"Right." I chewed my lip, shifting from one foot to the other.

Floros watched me with furrowed brows, muttering to himself in Greek. I automatically translated the phrase and glared at him.

"I'm not crazy," I said, resisting the urge to push the button again. "I'm just worried. You're right. Agent Papadakis could be sick. We need to make sure she's okay."

Floros' lips parted in surprise. "You speak..."

The elevator dinged as the doors slid open. "I do," I answered in Greek and led the way inside. "Hurry up."

Once outside Agent Papadakis's room I reached to swipe the skeleton card. Floros caught my damp hand in his dry one.

"We should knock first." He released me. "She might be..." He fumbled for the English word. "Indisposed." Pink warmed the golden skin at the back of his neck.

"You two have a history, huh?"

He ignored me. "Agent Papadakis?" He knocked once, twice, three times. "Are you there?"

Both of us waited in silence for a few beats. A busboy with a cart full of dirty dishes rattled past.

"Can I open the door now?" I asked.

Floros nodded, jaw set.

I swiped the key. The door creaked open, and we craned our heads through the crack. The small hallway ended in a studio-styled room, nicer than mine. From here I saw a couch, TV and the corner of a messy bed.

Floros sauntered inside, calling out, "Papadakis, you here?" When silence answered him, he repeated the phrase in Greek.

He roved toward the kitchenette, hidden in an alcove. "Hear anything?" he asked me over his shoulder.

I paused to listen for a shower running or the flush of a toilet. These kind of rooms would have a private bathroom. Lucky. "Nothing."

"Where is she?" Floros grumbled. "We have a web call with the director."

My feet led me to the disheveled bed. The two windows beside it were flung open. A warm breeze crested through, riffling the pages of an open book. I picked up the novel, fingers moving over the sticker at the bottom corner of the cover: *One More Page Books.* Over the edge of the book, my eyes caught on a tangle of sheets cascading from the bed, as if they'd been shoved off in a hurry. They piled on the hardwood floor leading toward…

"No."

The book fell from my numb fingertips. It hit the pile of blankets with a muffled *thunk.* I staggered to an open window, its screen torn, big enough for a body to fit through. My fingers curled around the sill, gaze raking the ground below. Agent Papadakis's room was only two stories up, but a jump from this height… I winced at the concrete underneath her window before my gaze landed on the ocean crashing nearby.

"Find anything?"

Floros's voice made me jump. I spun around. "Agent Papadakis is in trouble."

He scooped the book from the floor, rolling his eyes when he looked at the steamy cover. "What do you mean? Other than she's acting like a slob. Which is unusual." He indicated the bundle of sheets at our feet. "Enjoying an unsanctioned day off. That sneaky little—" He started to turn away, but I caught his sleeve.

"I don't think she's at the villa."

Floros hesitated. "What are you talking about?"

I squared my shoulders. My conversation with Victor this morning rang in my ears. *Please don't tell anyone about the sirens*, I'd begged. But things were different now. If Agent Papadakis could be snatched from her bed... No one was safe.

"There are sirens on Viaii Nisi," I began. "I think one of them lured Agent Papadakis out the window." I gestured to the broken screen.

The corner of Floros's mouth twitched as if he fought back a smile. He fisted a cough. "Did you say sirens? As in *The Odyssey*? A fictional work by Homer? I'm surprised kids are still reading that garbage."

"Yes." I gritted my teeth. "That's exactly what I said."

Floros burst into laughter. He struggled to collect himself when he caught the fury on my face. "I'm sorry, Annie, but you should stick to card games." He patted the top of my head, igniting a rage that clamped my jaw shut. "I'll have your mother check security feeds for my partner, just in case. Thank you for your help and the interesting story. I'll see myself out." He untangled himself from the sheets, set the romance novel on the nightstand, and strode for the door.

"Just lis—" I started, but Floros was already gone. "Great." I fell back against the blanket-less mattress. Foreboding twisted my stomach.

Using the tongue-less siren as proof wouldn't be enough to keep the remaining guests and employees at the villa safe. Even if she was the one luring guests into the water. I needed reinforcements.

I sat up, hair a messy bush around my head, and dug into a pocket for my cell phone. I flipped through the contacts, thumb trembling over Lynn's ID. Lynn never doubted my theories, not even when eight-year-old me was convinced Bloody Mary lurked behind the bathroom mirror. Lynn tested the story with me, baseball bat in hand.

But things between us had changed. What would she think?

Before I backed out, I tapped her name. The line rang once before I heard a crisp, "Annie?"

"Lynn." I let out a shaky breath. "Something's happened. I need you."

"What's wrong?"

The sweat from my palm made the phone slick. I tightened my grip. "Please believe me. Promise you'll believe."

Lynn's voice was firm when she answered, "I will always believe you."

My body relaxed enough for me to breathe deep. "There are sirens on Viaii Nisi. I think—no, I *know*—they're responsible for the deaths."

"Deaths? I thought just one—"

"Three other people have disappeared."

Lynn swore a particularly colorful combination she must've learned in the Army. "The resort's only been open twelve days and *four* people have gone missing?"

"You need to get here as soon as possible. Bring guns and earplugs. We're going to need them."

Lynn was silent for a painful minute before she said with finality, "Give me thirty-two hours."

DAY TWELVE, 10:39 P.M.

I peered out my bedroom door, head swiveling left to right. The mouthwatering scent of nachos curled down the hall from the cafeteria. Snippets of late-night snack chatter reached my ears, but the corridor was empty.

I eased my door shut and hurried to the emergency staircase that no one liked to use. Which suited me just fine. The less people who knew I was leaving the villa, the less likely word was to get back to Mom.

I took the two flights down and stepped out into a long hall, a pair of French doors at the end leading to the pool and jogging trail. I shot a glance over my shoulder before I tugged the doors open. No one in sight, except for a mom dragging her protesting kid toward the lobby.

"It's adult swim time," the mom said. "You can't be out there anymore."

"But that's not fair!" the kid whined.

Outside, the steady beat of some 80's song pulsed through the air. Lights flickered underneath the pool's surface—red, blue, green. People danced in the water while others floated in groups, talking, holding drinks.

I hurried around the pool, dodging lounge chairs and people with adult beverages, until I reached the wrought-iron fence that encircled the area. I swung the gate open and hopped down a flight of steps. Gravel crunched under my sneakers as I broke into a jog along the trail and followed the path as it veered to the right.

I could've taken the trolley to the Welcome Center before it shut down at eleven, but then I would've had to wait in front of the villa for it to show up. Way too much risk involved. Agent Floros spent the day ghosting around the resort in search of Papadakis. With my luck, he would've chosen this moment to lurk outside the trolley pickup spot.

The trail curved left, but I continued straight. Instead of gravel, hard-packed sand sifted under my sneakers. I hurried toward the narrow road the bus used. This half of the island seemed deserted; even the lights at Aquatic Adventures were off. Just me and the sliver of moon above. I pulled my flashlight from my backpack and clicked it on.

As I zigzagged through the Welcome Center's shops, the knife stowed in my backpack seemed to double in weight. The thought of using it made my skin crawl, but if the siren had grabbed that little girl and snatched the other people…

I might not have a choice.

My pace slowed as I crossed the pier's thick wood beams. A thin film of humidity-induced sweat covered my forehead and the back of my neck, but I didn't wipe it away. I slunk to the ladder that led to the ocean, surprised to see a small speedboat, space enough for driver and passenger, bobbing below. Someone in Aquatic Adventures must have forgotten to put it away. How convenient. I turned around and began climbing down the ladder.

The boat rocked under my feet as I stepped inside. I allowed myself a moment to adjust to the movement before sliding into the front seat. Nervous energy prickled behind my calves.

I took a breath and pointed the flashlight's beam at the water's surface.

"Siren?" I called, tossing a handful of shrimp into the water. I didn't even know the creature's name. How rude was that? I waited a heartbeat before calling again. The flashlight illuminated dark water, but no golden-eyed creature of myth.

"A few more minutes," I reasoned, refusing to wonder what I'd do if she didn't show again, and lowered myself into the boat, back pressed against a plastic padded seat. I hunkered down to wait.

I didn't have to wait long.

A loud splash made me jerk upright. Droplets of salt water landed on my face and rolled down my cheeks. I fumbled to my knees and peered over the boat's edge.

The siren floated in the water nearby, her yellow eyes unblinking as my flashlight's beam landed on her.

We stared at each other. I cleared my throat. "Um, about a few nights ago... I'm sorry about what I said." At that, her face scrunched up in displeasure that made my heart skip a beat. "To make it up to you, I brought something." I transferred the flashlight into my mouth and swung my pack off my back, rummaging inside for the bag of shrimp. The tips of my fingers brushed a hard iron handle.

The knife.

I swallowed and moved around it, fingers snagging on the food bag.

While I'd been preoccupied, the siren moved closer. Her webbed fingers curled over the side of the boat, and she watched me, head cocked.

I brandished the bag of shrimp. "These are really yummy. I couldn't bring cocktail sauce, but I wasn't sure you'd like it. It's kind of spicy." I held the bag out to her.

She blinked once, thin lid closing over her bright eyes, and then accepted the bag. She sniffed the objects inside, and her eyes widened. She flung back her head, dumping the contents into her mouth. I caught a flash of sharp teeth and the stub of a tongue.

The siren chewed open-mouthed, eyes closed in delight. A warm glow lit inside me, happy that she was happy.

The siren gagged as she swallowed, making a loud huffing sound that startled me. She handed back the empty bag.

"Ah, you're not a litterer," I said with a forced laugh, taking the trash. I lowered a hand back inside my pack. My fingers curled around the hilt of the kitchen knife. The blade itself was wrapped in a hand towel to keep me from cutting myself. Whatever the siren's reaction to my question, I wanted to be ready.

"There's something," my voice cracked, "I need to ask you."

Her eyes darted to my hand, still submerged in the bag.

"People are disappearing from the resort." I sounded like a recording on fast forward. *Slow down, Annie.* I forced myself to take a breath and speak coherently. "Four people. And a little girl was injured two days ago, almost dragged out to sea." My fingers tightened on the knife's handle. "Did you attack her? Did you take those people?"

The siren's grip on the boat tightened. The plastic creaked and cracks spread across its surface.

Despite my desire to skitter back up the ladder, I asked again, more forceful, thinking of Adam and Tamara. *"Did you do it?"*

Her hands released the boat, sliding back to the water, eyes wide and haunted. A garble of noises fell from her mouth followed by a choked gasp.

Rather than attack me for asking such a question, she seemed afraid. Almost angry. That couldn't be the reaction of a blood-thirsty creature.

Which only meant one thing.

I licked my lips. "There are more of your kind, aren't there?"

The siren's gaze darted to the ocean below before meeting mine, eyes narrowed. She pointed to herself, to me, and then gestured toward the island.

I blinked, trying to understand what she meant. "You want to take me somewhere?"

The siren waited in silent affirmation.

I shook my head. "But why? Why can't we talk here?" Suspicion lit in my mind, making my body tense.

She patted her throat, shaking her head, then swirled a finger on the ocean's surface.

"Oh." Her suggestion clicked. "You want to write in the sand since you can't..." I trailed off, not eager to insult her again by mentioning the tongue thing.

As I stared into the siren's golden eyes, understanding the hope in their depths, I squashed my doubts. I felt connected to her, somehow. Safe. As if we'd known each other for centuries.

I nodded. "Let's go."

The siren slid into the water, resurfacing by the front of the boat. Her fingers worked the rope securing it to the pier. Once she untangled the knot, her head disappeared again. The boat gave a hard tug. I tumbled backward, catching myself on one of the seat backs before I ended up falling off.

The boat picked up speed, the bow slicing through water. Cool night air whisked across my face and toyed with my hair. The lima bean tip of Viaii Nisi loomed into view. I focused on the strip of land as it approached, recognizing our destination as the small inlet Victor and I visited this morning. Unlike us, the siren deftly avoided the enormous boulder. Her head bobbed above the surface as she fought to tug the boat onto the sand.

I jumped over the side, flashlight in my mouth. The water lapped around my hips, but my feet found purchase on the seafloor. I shoved the boat hard, and it glided onto the sand with a groan.

I followed, my sneakers squelching with each step. I sat and tugged my shoes off. The siren slid across the sand next to me, her arms and tails moving seamlessly as if she were a snake. More than a little disturbing.

I looked away and spat the flashlight into my palm. The taste of plastic lingered in my mouth. I tried to swallow it away.

The siren hunched beside me, moonlight dancing across her form. I couldn't help but stare. She was the most beautiful creature I'd ever seen. Her orange scales glistened under the beam of my flashlight, darkening to a fiery hue as her human half turned fish. The dual tails were shaped like legs with smaller fins protruding from her thighs and enormous flippers in place of feet. When I dared a glimpse at her chest, I realized she didn't have female parts there at all, just toned plains of muscle.

I looked up to her face, and our eyes locked. She gestured toward me with her sharp-nailed fingers. It was time to ask my questions.

I stabbed the bottom of my flashlight into the sand. Its beam illuminated a small circle around us. The siren watched it, transfixed. Her fingers weaved through the light, lips pursed in curiosity. I might've explained it to her if I had any idea how a flashlight worked.

"You aren't responsible for the attacks," I began, watching her. "Are you alone? Or are there others?"

Her attention shifted from the light, back to me. The hardness in her eyes seemed to soften as she studied my face. She ran a finger across the sand. Shapes formed under her touch. Shapes I recognized.

I leaned closer and blinked. "That's Greek!" My cry of excitement made the siren snarl. I winced. "Sorry. It's just... I can read this. It means *others*, right?"

She nodded, lips spreading to reveal sharp teeth. I tried not to start at the sight of them.

"So these *others* took away the people and attacked that the little girl?"

Another nod.

My hands formed tight fists. "We found one of the people they took. He was dead. Are the others...?"

The siren stared at the darkness beyond our halo of light. She scrawled the Greek word for "unknown."

"Do you at least know where they are? Is it possible they drowned like… like Adam?" Tamara's face, bloated and pale haunted my thoughts. My voice became hoarse with sudden tears. "They took a girl. She was my friend and—"

The siren held up a hand, stopping me. Her fingertip swept the sand in a flurry of words I squinted to read.

When she finished, I spoke them aloud, struggling with the translation, "They are coming…" I shifted to read better, careful not to disturb the sand. "For… you. No. Sorry. They are coming for… They are coming for *us.*" I sucked in a breath, gaze darting to hers. A spark of panic ignited deep inside me.

"The sirens aren't going to stop luring people from the Villa, are they? This is just the beginning. They're going to attack." The words rang true in my gut, even as the siren nodded. Hadn't I guessed as much? Wasn't that why I called Lynn with a plea for guns?

"When?" I asked. "When will they come?"

The siren lowered her head. Knotted braids slid over her scaled shoulders.

"Please." I placed a hand on her arm. The scales were cool and solid under my skin. "I need to know I can trust you. This will help."

She started, looking up at me with wide eyes. Her lips moved in a silent word I couldn't understand. The siren slid forward, closing the distance between us. Her forehead pressed against mine, warm skin meeting chilled scales.

I closed my eyes. A sense of peace emanated from the contact, easing my panic. The siren pulled away, and loneliness and longing surged, crushing me. "What's your name?" I whispered.

This time the letters she traced were English, stylized in a first grader's scrawl.

"Lorelei," I breathed. "Your name is Lorelei."

Light glistened in Lorelei's golden eyes. She nodded and gestured for me to say it again.

"Lorelei," I repeated, wondering at the last time anyone spoke her name aloud. "That's beautiful."

She pointed at me as if to say, "And yours?"

"I'm Annie." I splayed my fingers across my chest, t-shirt damp. "I'm Annie Mayfield. Thank you for your help, Lorelei."

A corner of Lorelei's lips quivered. Maybe a smile?

"You don't know when these *others* are going to attack," I repeated. "But do you know how many of them there are?" I knew Lynn would appreciate the information.

Lorelei hesitated before turning her face up toward the night sky. She reached up, webbed fingers extended toward the glistening stars.

"That many?" My eyes widened. "We need to get off this island, don't we?"

Her hand dropped to the sand. It moved in fast, fevered strokes. The words I read aloud made my skin crawl.

"No escape."

Lorelei's Song, Verse Eight
"For iron by itself can draw man to use it."
~The Odyssey, Book 19

Queen Thessalonike snarled, and fury lit her milky blue eyes. The sirens who had pressed close when Lorelei rushed inside the queen's coral slithered back. Even Thessalonike's guards, positioned behind her, tensed with nervous energy.

But Lorelei held her ground, chin raised.

"Aegaeon's wrath upon you!" Thessalonike spat. "So this is where Echo has been these four moonrises. Do you wish me dead, you fool? To lure the lung-breathers to your queen?" She darted from her throne, moving faster than she had in centuries, and brought her face close to Lorelei's, lips curled back. "Be warned, Lorelei. You were created by me and for me. If I die, you and your sisters die."

"It would be worth the sacrifice," Lorelei growled, centuries of suppressed hate breaking free.

"I'll kill you, you worthless creature!" Thessalonike's hand shot out and cracked across Lorelei's face.

She crashed into the seafloor, sending puffs of sand dancing. Lights sparkled in front of her eyes. She blinked, forcing the glowing maelstrom away.

"We will attack the lung-breathers this moonrise," Queen Thessalonike shouted to the gathered sirens. "They will pay for this. Spread the word to your sisters throughout the sea!"

The sirens unleashed a guttural growl, writhing in their wide circle.

"No," Lorelei whispered. She pushed herself away from the sand. "They still have Echo. An attack would provoke them to—"

"Silence, Prodótis," Thessalonike spat.

The sirens lurking in the coral murmured to one another, repeating the word over and over. Prodótis. *Betrayer.*

Lorelei fought against the heat of shame building behind her eyes. They were right. Because of Lorelei's foolishness, Echo was...

She opened her mouth to speak again, to plead with Queen Thessalonike to change her mind, but Acantha streaked into the sirens' coral.

"My queen!" Acantha's chirps screeched through the water. She slid between Lorelei and Thessalonike. "The lung-breathers have our sister, Echo, on the surface."

Panic barreled through Lorelei. No! Dawn had struck hours ago! Memory of the lung-breather's revolting plan twisted through her mind.

"Where?" Lorelei snapped at Acantha. "Where is my Echo?"

"By their cliff," Acantha said, watching Thessalonike as though the queen asked the question. Confusion reflected in Acantha's furrowed brow. The siren had been absent for Lorelei's confession, responsible for that day's patrol. "My queen, they are dragging her down steps where they keep their floaters."

Their boating dock.

Lorelei exploded from the coral in a burst of bubbles, spiraling through the water.

"Stop her!" Queen Thessalonike roared. The guards surged up to obey their queen, but Lorelei flitted from their grasp and into open ocean.

It took Lorelei mere heartbeats to swim to the lung-breather's cliff, above which their hideous castle lurked. The boats that usually docked at the long flat rock were gone.

Even underwater, Lorelei heard the screams.

The surface rippled and ebbed, but Lorelei watched as two lung-breathers secured Echo's wrists inside thick manacles chained to the rock.

"Monstrous seductress," spat one of the men.

"The sunlight will purge her possession from the prince," the other said, straightening and following the first man toward the steps. More lung-breathers stood on each stair, strange bent branches in their hands. They watched Echo writhe, impassive. How could they be so callous? Did they not understand Echo's shrieks for mercy?

"This is your fate, my daughter, my Theía Kóri." Thessalonike's chirps drifted to Lorelei on the water. She whirled, bubbles twirling around her. Queen Thessalonike floated a whale-length below, her guard forming a protective half circle around her.

Lorelei rushed to her queen. The guards' circle clamped shut, blocking her path. Lorelei reached toward Queen Thessalonike over the shoulder of one. "Please," her voice broke. "Punish me. Do as you will. But if Echo stays exposed... she will perish."

Queen Thessalonike closed her filmy eyes and lowered her head.

"So you do *nothing*?"

Lorelei's words were met with a scowl. The queen raised her head in a regal sweep, cold fire burning in her eyes. "This is Echo's punishment for her loyalty to you. Instead of loyalty to *her queen*."

"Your spiteful jealousy will condemn her to unspeakable torment!" Hot anger pulsed through Lorelei's limbs. "Curse you, you hateful creature!"

Lorelei shot upward, bursting to the surface in a spray of water, and hurled herself onto the rock where Echo lay bound. Agony rippled along Lorelei's nerves, the sun sizzling against her back like the strike of a nine tailed whip.

"Echo!" Lorelei screamed. She scrabbled at the manacles binding Echo's wrists. Her sharp talons clanged off the metal. Already, Echo's sapphire scales were blackening at the edges, puckering and drying. She seemed oblivious to Lorelei's presence, lost in a haze of anguish.

"I'm here! I'm here!" Lorelei positioned her body over Echo's, trying to block the sun's rays. Heat slithered under her scales. It felt as if a fire burned on her exposed body, burrowing its way deep into her bones.

Echo's thrashing eased, but her body still spasmed. Shallow breaths whooshed in and out of Echo's lungs. A ragged sob crawled from her throat.

Long shapes whizzed toward Lorelei. They made pinging sounds on the rock and bounced off. She jerked her head up and snarled low in her throat. The lung-breathers held their strange sticks, the string attached to either end pulled back. Something sparkled then arced toward her.

She roared, curving up to bare her teeth. A sharp metal slammed into her lower abdomen with a heavy thunk. She glanced down to see a long shaft of wood protruding from her scales.

The world turned shadowed at the edges. Lorelei fought through the fog toward Echo.

She had to save Echo. She had to...

Her body jerked as two more shafts pierced her chest. The force knocked her off balance. She careened into darkness, tumbling off the rock and into the water.

DAY FOURTEEN, 2:52 A.M.

"**M**om!" I threw open the double office doors so hard they slammed against the walls. A wrinkled Chinese man watched me from a huge TV screen, mouth agape. I froze in the doorway as two heads swiveled in my direction. Mom glared at me while Benny rubbed sleep from his eyes.

"Um..." I fought to catch my breath. After the siren towed me back to the pier, I'd raced to the villa only to find Mom not in her room. How was I to know she'd be on a skype call at three a.m.? "Excuse me," I said to the Chinese man, giving him a nervous wave. He waved back, still stunned. "Mom," I looked to her, "I need to talk to you. It's important."

A muscle in Mom's jaw spasmed. Yikes. She turned back to the TV screen and the camera lens fixed in the top center. "I'm sorry, Mr. Zhao. I'll have Benson email you the specifics."

The Chinese man nodded. "Very well. Thank you for your assistance." He inclined his head in a slight bow.

Mom returned the gesture. Seconds later, the call ended with an instrumental beep. I swallowed hard as Mom got to her feet. She whirled to face me, arms crossed. Uncontrollable laughter, half hysteria, half amusement, burbled up my throat. Mom stood in a blouse, suit jacket, and plaid pajama pants.

"This better be important," Mom said, voice a scary calm. "That was Mr. Zhao, the man we're contracting with to get a subsidiary in China. One wrong move and the deal could fall through."

Benny got to his feet—wearing normal pants, I noticed—and placed a hand on Mom's shoulder. "But Mr. Zhao is a very nice man with a daughter of his own. The way it looked to me, he found the whole thing amusing."

"Maybe." Some of the tension drained from Mom's face. She yawned and the accompanying tears misted her eyes. "The time difference is draining." Benny couldn't help but yawn too, and soon I was yawning.

Yawn-fest ended, Mom's gaze pinned me. "Annie? All that drama and now you're silent?" Her brows rose in a *this better be good* way.

I cleared my throat, smoothing my still damp shirt. Sand tinkled to the floor. "This is going to sound crazy. You might want to sit down."

Benny dutifully sat. Mom crossed her arms.

"Or not." I curled my toes in my sneakers, sand gritting under my socks. The whole ride back to the pier I'd tried to concoct a way to tell Mom that would keep her from pulling an Agent Floros. Needless to say, inspiration hadn't struck. Simple truth would have to do.

I straightened my spine, imbuing as much confidence in my stance as I could. "There are sirens on Viaii Nisi." Before I hadn't wanted to say anything, but now I had proof if they didn't believe me. If Lorelei kept her promise, anyway—and I trusted she would.

Blank silence met my words. My eyes darted from Mom to Benny and back again, trying to gauge their reactions.

Mom was the first to move. She sighed, rubbing at her forehead. "Annie, didn't we already go over this in Agent Floros's interrogation?"

"Yes, but—"

Benny cut in, shaking his head. "This is all my fault. Annie, when I told you those ruins were cursed, I was just joking. Your mom had them checked out. They're fake."

An emotion flickered across Mom's face. Guilt? Worry? It vanished too quickly for me to tell.

"Yes," Mom affirmed. She turned to Benny, a brow arching. "And we've already discussed why you shouldn't enable my daughter's dangerous activities, Benson."

Benny winced.

I ignored the barb, forging ahead. "It's not about those bones." *Lie.* "A few days ago a siren saved me by the pier. That's where I got that scratch." I pointed at my arm and the faint pink lines still visible in the obvious shape of claw marks. "I met with her tonight. Her name is Lorelei. She told me that people are disappearing because sirens are luring them into the ocean. But they're not going to stop there. If we don't leave, they're going to *attack* us."

As I spoke, Mom and Benny's faces lost the sleepy fuzziness. Benny watched me, intent. Mom listened but with a suspicious pucker to her lips. Quiet followed my confession. My heart thundered in the silence, and I took a breath to help ease its panic.

Mom shook her head. "It's a very nice story—"

"It's not a story," I snapped. My body pulsed with a frenzied energy. They had to believe me. If they didn't, despite Lynn's help, horrible things would happen. A bunch of tourists and resort employees didn't stand a chance against sirens as numerous as the stars. "I can show you." Before I left Lorelei, she showed me how to summon her.

"How?" Benny's tone was serious. I drew strength from his belief, no matter how thin.

I thought back to my time with Lorelei, of her promise to visit me after dark if I needed her. "She said she would come back if I called her, but we have to wait until tonight. That's when we agreed to see each other again."

"This is ridiculous." Mom threw her hands in the air. "Annie, you can't expect us to—"

"Florence," Benny said. "Let's trust her. With Agent Papadakis missing, we need to look at every angle. No matter how unbelievable."

Mom didn't answer at first. She watched me with a steady gaze, no doubt wondering if this was a "cry for attention." Finally, she sighed. "Okay. We'll go. Meet us by the central lifeguard stand at 9 p.m."

Relief made my knees week. I grabbed the doorframe for support. "Thank you."

"Annie Marie Mayfield," Mom took a step forward with each part of my name, "if this is some game you're playing, you'll be on the first ferry back to the US. And you'll be spending the rest of the summer at corporate with your father."

I licked my lips, tasting salt. "Trust me, Mom. This is anything but a game."

The day moved at a turtle's pace with no jobs to do. But, finally, 9 p.m. rolled around. Victor hurried across the beach at my side, hands jammed in the pockets of a hoodie. When I texted him earlier about my meeting with Lorelei, he'd been furious...

For five seconds.

Curiosity quickly replaced his anger. After asking half a million anatomical-related questions that were too difficult to answer over text, he insisted on accompanying me to the beach.

"Are you doing all right?" Victor asked beside me, his flip-flops kicking up sand as he walked. Moonlight and the villa's lights cast half his face in shadow. "Nervous?"

"I'm terrified. And you asking me if I'm nervous isn't helping." I jabbed him in the side with my elbow.

Three figures at the shoreline caught my flashlight beam. I frowned. What was Agent Floros doing here?

"Hurry up," I said to Victor. "Everyone's waiting."

We jogged to join the group, each member with a flashlight of their own. Tension sparked in the air, only part of it due to my nerves. Mom and Agent Floros kept an unfriendly distance between them, purposefully avoiding each other's gaze.

"What's going on?" I asked the group in general.

No one spoke until Benny relented. "I invited Agent Floros to join us." He sighed as Mom glared at him.

"Which he shouldn't have done," Mom huffed.

Floros snorted. "My partner is missing, Mrs. Mayfield. Benson claimed your daughter had a lead." He crossed his arms. "You're just upset because I called headquarters, and they're sending more operatives tomorrow. You're afraid the resort is going to be closed."

"Don't put words in my mouth, Agent Floros," Mom snapped.

Benny and I winced at the same time. Her sleepless night was definitely catching up with her.

Victor turned to Floros. "So you believe us about the sirens?"

Us. I fought the urge to squeeze Victor's hand in pure relief. At least I had someone completely on my side.

"I'm reserving judgment. Do you?"

Victor nodded. "Absolutely. I've seen one."

The adults around us shot him a disbelieving look. He just raised his brows as if daring them to contradict him.

Floros coughed, inclining his head at the surf before us. "Is something supposed to happen here?"

"Right." I passed the flashlight to Victor. His warm fingertips brushed my cold ones.

He leaned close to whisper, "Relax."

"Easy for you to say," I grumbled, kicking off my flip-flops, handing him my cellphone, and tiptoeing into the water.

"What're you doing?" Benny called, striding forward. "Annie, you shouldn't, you can't swim—"

"She's fine," I heard Victor say. "Just don't ask her to do
the freestyle. It's a mess."

I frowned at the commentary. Victor's teasing humor did
little to loosen the knot of apprehension that twisted my insides.
My jaw was clenched so tight, my teeth creaked.

I stopped when the waves reached mid-calf, bouncing on
the balls of my feet. This was not going to be pleasant. I sucked
in a breath and dropped under. The water was warmer than I expected, brushing across my skin. I opened my mouth and
chirped the way Lorelei taught me hours earlier. The notes
rolled through me, sweet and melodic, much different than they
had when I'd practiced them on land. They resonated through
the water with clear tones. I lost myself in the sound.

A hand on my shoulder brought me back. I jerked my head
upright, spluttering. I shoved damp curls from my face and
wiped at my eyes. Mom stood beside me, staring, face pale in
the dim light.

"What were you doing?" she cried, grabbing my shoulders
and giving me a firm shake.

"Mom, it's okay." I shrugged off her hands. "It's how the
siren told me to call her." I glanced down at the splatters of sea-
water on Mom's designer skirt. "Let's get back to shore."

We splashed through the surf together, Mom not leaving my
side. When we reached the sand, Victor tossed me the towel I'd
asked him to bring.

"Thanks." I wrapped myself in its warmth.

"How long do we wait?" Floros was the first one to ask.

"A few minutes," I offered, unsure. Lorelei swam so fast…
It couldn't take too long to get here from the pier.

Half an hour ticked by. I hunkered on the sand, keeping
time on my cell phone. Victor had been forced to go inside fifteen minutes ago, covering a late shift at the outdoor pool. Agent

Floros paced along the shoreline while Mom and Benny huddled together, both typing messages on their phones.

"This is ridiculous." Floros stopped before me, eyes narrowed. "I hope you know that you've wasted a federal officer's time, young lady. That's a criminal offense."

I opened my mouth to protest, but Benny beat me to it.

"Agent Floros," Benny said, striding over. "I understand you're concerned about your partner." He clapped a hand on the agent's shoulder in an attempt at camaraderie. "Why don't you all head inside?" He looked at me and my mom, then back to the agent. "I'll wait a little longer. I've got work I can do." He waggled the Blackberry he held in one hand.

Floros hesitated. "I don't—"

"Benson, are you sure you want to...?" Mom cleared her throat. The unspoken words *waste your time* hung in the air. "Stay out here? According to Annie, a siren can get you at any moment."

A lump formed in my throat that I swallowed back. I staggered to my feet, slipping on sand. "She'll come! I know she will."

But why would she? Nothing bound her to me. Maybe she'd seen all these people gathered on shore and had been afraid. Or maybe she just didn't trust me. I should've asked her to come when I was with her last night, instead of waiting for Mom to ask for proof.

"Hey, hey," Benny soothed me. "I believe you. Agent Floros, why don't you head in? We'd hate to waste any more of your time. And Florence? You go inside too. You need to sleep. I'd really like to stay."

"I appreciate that." Floros shot me an annoyed glare before he tugged at his blazer. "I suppose I'll leave you to it, Benson." Judging by his expression, he doubted Benny would actually find anything by waiting out here. Or by trusting me.

Mom looked ready to disagree but sighed. "I do have some paperwork in the office." She glanced at me. "I will be calling your father in the morning, young lady."

"Mom," I started. "Just lis—"

"No. I've had enough." She smoothed her damp skirt, suddenly unable to meet my eyes. "We'll discuss this tomorrow."

I swallowed hard and looked down at my feet.

After a few awkward goodbyes, both of which I didn't return, Mom and Floros headed for the villa, Mom speed walking ahead of the agent.

I glared at the dark ocean, eyes burning. This was my one shot to make them believe, and I'd failed. What would Lynn think when she showed up tomorrow? How furious would both she *and* Mom be at me? I cringed. Soon it wouldn't even matter, not if Mom had her way. In a few days I would be with Dad at corporate, relegated to licking envelopes and refilling staplers.

"Hey, kiddo." Benny slung an arm around my shoulders. "Go inside. You need to warm up." As if on cue, my body shivered. I tugged the towel tighter around me. "I'll stay out here for another hour. If your siren shows up, I'll call. Promise."

"Do you really believe me?" I asked, voice small.

"Sirens are a hard concept to buy." He squeezed me tight. "But it's you we're talking about. I believe *in* you. So I have to believe *you*. Make sense?"

"Not really."

He laughed. "Regardless, get inside. My twenty new emails will keep me company."

"So you're not actually playing Pokémon out here?" I teased, my mood lifting at Benny's faith.

Benny's arm fell away in mock hurt. "Me? Never!" He adjusted his tie and said in a low tone, "Besides, I don't want to get sand in my DS."

"I love you, Benny." I hugged him tight, burying my head in his chest.

"Don't get mushy on me, kiddo." But he hugged me even tighter before pulling away.

"I'm going to shower and then I'll be right back. Take these, just in case." I handed him a pair of earplugs I'd gotten from the gift shop. At Benny's confused look I added, "Because they're sirens."

"Ah. Got it."

I took a few steps toward the villa before turning back. Benny bent over his phone in the sand. The bright screen reflected off his face, highlighting his intense concentration as he read an email.

"Thank you, Benny," I murmured. "I don't know what I'd do without you."

20

DAY FOURTEEN, 7:02 A.M.

Persistent buzzing invaded my dreams. I groaned and fumbled for the source. Last night I'd taken a shower, intending just to sit on my bed and text Lynn before joining Benny on the beach, but I must've drifted to sleep. I groaned, my groping fingers sliding under my pillow, finding my vibrating cell phone. I cracked my eyelids open.

Lynn. I bolted upright, suddenly very awake.

"Hello?" I answered.

"Sorry," Lynn's voice sounded far away, as if she spoke through a tunnel. "I'm sure I woke you up. Look—" Static interrupted her.

I clamped a hand over my other ear so I could hear better. "You're breaking up. What did you say?"

"We're flying through some really nasty weather." Her voice crackled. "Make sure the helipad is prepped with lights."

"Wait, I thought you would take the ferry."

"Look outside."

My gaze drifted to my room window. Darkness engulfed the sky like a hungry beast. Lamp posts illuminated trees bending in the gusts of wind. Rain spattered against the glass, racing down the pane. It was the first time it had rained since I had arrived. "Oh. I see."

"I called in a favor. See you soon. Over and out." The line went dead.

I flung my sheets off and jumped out of bed. I made it half-way down the hall before I realized I was barefoot and still in my pajamas. Oh well, I'd looked worse.

The elevator carried me to floor twelve. I rushed down the empty hallway. When I got to Mom's room, I allowed myself a steadying breath before I brought my fist down on the door.

Through the wood shuffling sounds reached me. Then the door swung open to reveal Mom's wide-awake, made-up face.

"Annie?" Mom's mascaraed eyes widened. "What are you doing up here?" Her gaze slid from the top of my head to my feet. "In your pajamas…?"

I stepped past her into the room. "There's something I need to tell you."

"Oh?" Mom sighed and joined me in the living area. She toyed with the cream drapes hanging from a rod over the window but didn't fling them open. "Don't tell me there are centaurs on the island now, too. I never got a text from Benny confirming your theory. I'm very disappointed, Annie. Your father—"

I ignored the pang of disappointment over Lorelei. "Lynn's coming."

Mom's eyes narrowed. "What do you mean, *Lynn's coming?*"

"I called her and told her about the sirens. *She* believes me."

"But she can't come here." She flung open the drapes. A slate gray sky loomed, more foreboding at this height. Through the blowing wind and driving rain, I could barely see the ocean.

"This weather is keeping the ferry docked," Mom murmured as she watched the storm. "Even the NIS agents Floros called can't get here."

I gulped. "Is it really that bad?"

Mom sighed. "It's just a small storm, thankfully, or we'd have to evacuate. But it's enough to ground any boats or aircraft."

I called in a favor, Lynn had said. She was out flying in that. Because of me.

Mom started to close the drapes but hesitated as a thought occurred to her. "Please don't tell me Lynn is headed here now." When I didn't answer, she clapped a manicured hand to her mouth. "Exactly where is my daughter?"

I winced. "In a helicopter."

"In a…" Mom fell into a conveniently placed leather chair. "In this weather? She could be killed! What were you—what was *she*—thinking!"

Killed. I scrambled to reassure Mom. And reassure myself. "Lynn just called me. She's fine. But we need to make sure the helipad is ready with the lights on and everything."

Mom let out a shaky breath. "There's nothing I can do," she murmured so softly I almost didn't hear. She repeated the words like a mantra, as if she'd spoken them many times in the past. Finally, she cleared her throat and straightened. "The three of us are going to have a talk when your sister gets here. Meanwhile, I'll have Benson check—" She broke off, brow furrowed. "Actually, have you seen Benson?"

I shook my head. I'd been dead asleep until about three minutes ago. "No, why?"

Mom's worried gaze made the hairs on the back of my neck stand up. "He's usually up here by now. We eat breakfast and discuss the day's schedule together. I tried calling his cell and knocking on his door this morning, but there was no answer. He's never…"

Mom's words faded into the background. Something splintered and cracked in my chest. I tore from Mom's room and down the hall, sprinting past the too-slow elevator. I flung open the door to the emergency staircase so hard it banged against the wall behind it.

Mom called for me to stop, but her words faded away as I darted down staircase after staircase.

I threw open the door to the lobby, squeaking across the floor in my bare feet as I turned. The marble entryway was empty save for a woman behind the reception desk and Mrs. Samson, who sat in a lounge chair with a book spread across her lap.

"Rybka?" She looked up, but I was already rushing for the doors.

At my first shove, the door didn't move. I thrust at the handle bar with all my strength. The door creaked open, howling wind tearing through. I sprung through the gap, and the door slammed behind me.

Wind slashed at my hair and clothes as I ran to the ocean. Each step felt sluggish compared to the frantic pounding of my heart. The pelting rain stung my skin like thousands of glass shards, and a cramp carved deep into my side, but I didn't stop.

I sprinted past trembling umbrellas, barely maintaining their cemented anchors in the sand. The lounge chairs had already been taken inside, or blown away, I didn't know.

I couldn't see the water until I was halfway down the beach. A human-sized mass, darker than the slate-gray surf, bobbed at the tide's edge. The world staggered to a halt. The howling wind and piercing rain drifted away. The only sound was the *thump thump* of my heart and the whistling of my ragged breathing.

"Benny!" I screamed. My words broke the spell. Pain and noise rushed to fill the void.

I ran to him, then knelt in the pool of crimson that surged around his still form. Benny's body lay half in the water. Deep grooves scored his abdomen, and chunks of flesh had been ripped from his arms. Blood still pumped from the vicious wounds. The ear plugs I'd given him lay discarded in the sand beside his blackberry. Tremors shook me. Sour bile coated my tongue. I gagged.

What could I even do to help him?

A whimpering sob crawled out of my throat. He said he'd wait an hour and then come back inside. I'd given him ear plugs.

He should've been safe. Oh, God. And I'd fallen asleep last night while he...

"Help!" I screamed into the storm. "Someone, help me!"

"Annie?" Benny's ragged whisper brought my gaze down. His face was deathly pale, almost waxy.

"Benny. Oh, Benny," I moaned. I brushed rain from his forehead and cheeks. He was ice cold. "You're going to be okay."

But his eyes weren't focused on me. They stared up at the sky as if something beautiful hovered there instead of ominous clouds. His eyelids twitched with every raindrop that pelted his face.

"The voices," he wheezed, head lolling side to side, searching for something. "So... beautiful. I wanted to hear better. Sirens..." His lips curled into a haunting smile, and his body went limp.

I screamed, voice cracking with the effort. I staggered to my feet, fighting the storm back to the villa. My cries of "Help! Help! Help!" were stolen by the wind, but I didn't stop shouting.

The door to the villa stuck again, and I scrabbled at the handle with my nails, ripping it open.

"Help!" I wheezed as I stumbled into the lobby.

Mrs. Samson jumped to her feet, the book on her lap hitting the marbled floor. My gaze anchored on the fanned pages.

"Rybka, what's wrong?" Mrs. Samson's hands found my shoulders. I realized I'd fallen to my knees. My bloody handprints marred the marble floor.

"Benny," I rasped. "On the beach." My mind swirled in a wash of colors.

"She's in shock," I heard Mrs. Samson gasp. She disappeared. I wanted to cry out for her to get to Benny, but a ringing picked up in my ears.

Suddenly I was on the floor, staring at pairs of running feet. Shouts reached me and then Mrs. Samson was back, her cold hand on my forehead. So, so cold.

"It's okay, Rybka. It's going to be okay," she murmured. Then she started to pray.

Lorelei's Song, Verse Nine
"Be strong saith my heart...
I have seen worse sights than this."
~*The Odyssey, Book 11*

"Lorelei!" Echo's laughter drifted through the sea. "Lorelei, stop it!" Echo darted behind a chunk of coral, her tail smaller and face fuller, younger. Lorelei dove after her, spiraling through the water, a piece of kelp in hand.

"I'm going to get you!" Lorelei cried between giggles. "Swim faster, sister!"

This is a memory, Lorelei realized, even as she knew it was a dream. Except sirens weren't supposed to dream.

That knowledge tore her from the scene, from the two sirens gliding through the coral, shrieking with laughter.

The first thing Lorelei felt was a burrowing pain. She forced her eyes open and blinked to focus her vision. Two siren guards floated on either side of her, securing her arms. The others watched in a silent half circle as Queen Thessalonike approached, silver hair billowing in the current.

Lorelei tried to break free from the guards, but pain lanced through her core and back where the sun burned her. Looking down, she saw three deep divots on her abdomen where scales had been. Raw, fleshy skin showed underneath.

Queen Thessalonike stopped a tail's length from Lorelei. The queen's gaze bore into her, hateful... and sad. "From this day forth," Thessalonike's chirps rebounded through the water, "I banish Lorelei, the Prodótis, for crimes against me and her sisters, resulting in the capture and death of Echo."

Death of Echo. The words made Lorelei gag. She shook her head, unbelieving. It couldn't be; Echo couldn't be gone. Around her, the sirens whispered the word over and over again until it became a haunting melody. *Prodótis. Prodótis. Prodótis.*

Lorelei found Acantha in the line of guards behind Queen Thessalonike. She watched Lorelei with an impassive gaze, as if they hadn't matured together, raced dolphins in the deep, hunted octopus and shark. She looked at Lorelei as if she were a stranger.

Queen Thessalonike inclined her head at the guards flanking Lorelei. They shifted, one yanking Lorelei's hands behind her, the other grasping Lorelei's face. Lorelei snarled.

"For associating with the lung-breathers," Thessalonike raised a hand, flexing the taloned fingers in preparation, "I am taking your voice."

Lorelei bucked against the guards. Their grip tightened, muscles like iron, unmovable, unbreakable.

"No!" Lorelei keened. "No! Please, no!"

The guard forced Lorelei's lips apart. Her fingers grated against Lorelei's scales as she struggled.

Queen Thessalonike moved forward, claws outstretched. Lorelei's eyes rolled in panic, searching for help in the crowd. Her gaze found Niamh. The siren held Lorelei's stare for a moment only to lower her head.

"I beg you," Lorelei choked out. "Show mercy."

"This is mercy." The queen's hand shot forward, talons closing around the meaty flesh of Lorelei's tongue. A wet sucking wrench was followed by blinding pain. Lorelei's vision flashed white. She screamed, gagging on blood.

Queen Thessalonike slid back, forked tongue clenched in her fist. Red seeped into the ocean from Lorelei's gaping mouth.

"It is done," the queen said.

The gathered sirens swirled in Lorelei's vision. She went limp in the guards' grip.

"Release her," Thessalonike ordered. The guards obeyed, and Lorelei sunk onto the sand, eyes open but unseeing.

"Behold," Queen Thessalonike addressed the gathered sirens, tongue held aloft, "the fate of those who disobey. My laws are for your protection and for that reason…" She gestured to

Lorelei's limp body, blood flooding around her head like a crimson cloud. "If any of you are caught near this Prodótis, you will suffer the same fate. And, Prodótis," Thessalonike addressed Lorelei.

Lorelei tried to lift her head, but it wouldn't move from the seafloor. The queen's threat rang in her ears long after the sirens departed.

"If I see you again, I will *obliterate* you."

21

DAY FOURTEEN, 8:58 A.M.

Dried blood coated my skin. I picked at the flakes on my hands and under my fingernails. A faraway part of me thought, *This is Benny's blood.*

I should've felt repulsed—washed and scrubbed my hands until they stung—but that would take effort. And I was too cold to even move.

An hour earlier I woke in a small medical room. A guest services employee, charged with keeping an eye on me, described what happened after I passed out. He said they carried Benny's body to Doctor Denton. I had rushed to the Jamaican's office, shoving open the door, but Mom caught it.

"Wait outside," she murmured through the small crack. Then she shut the door. When I tried the handle, I found it locked.

Numb, I collapsed on a bench outside Doctor Denton's office. And I hadn't moved since.

I stared down at my hands, flexing my fingers. Last night I'd held Benny close in a hug. Last night Benny had been whole. Safe. Untouched.

"I need a chopper!" Mom's shout pierced the thick wood door. My head jerked up. "It's an emergency!"

A helicopter... Hadn't she told me earlier today—was it today?—that getting one to Viaii Nisi was impossible? My blood pulsed faster with panic. Mom couldn't get a helicopter. Benny was going to die.

I caught myself. No. *Benny won't die.* He wouldn't leave me.

Benny would be fine. Doctor Denton would save him. A few stitches and my childhood crush would be up and smiling, calling me kiddo.

As I tried to convince myself that Benny would live, a vision of his torn body rose before me. Those gashes, chunks of missing skin. And so much blood.

The room spun. I started to slip again, back into that darkness.

The smacking of flip-flops made me turn, stealing me back. Victor hurried down the hallway, eyes on me. The sight of him sent a conflicted wave through me: half anger, half longing.

He stopped a few feet away, as if unsure of his safety if he came closer. "What are you doing?" he asked.

"Waiting." The word croaked from my lips.

"Is it all right if I wait with you?" He offered a tentative smile.

"How can you be totally fine?" I snapped, pushing myself into a seated position. "Didn't you hear what happened to Benny? What those monsters did to him?" I glared at Victor, even as I knew my boiling rage wasn't his fault. "If only I hadn't let him stay out there. I gave him ear plugs. He said he'd only wait an hour. He should've been safe. Instead of checking on him, I accidentally fell asleep. If only…" My words dissolved into heavy sobs, and I hid my face in my arms, rocking back and forth.

The bench creaked as Victor eased down beside me, and his warm arms pulled me toward him. I buried my face into his chest, the fabric of his t-shirt catching my snot and tears.

"It's okay," he murmured, rubbing my back. "It's okay."

But it wasn't okay, and it would never be okay. I cried and whimpered against him until my sobs turned to sniffles. I kept my head on his shoulder, nose dripping, the bulging eyes of a green frog stared up at me.

"What does your shirt say?" I asked around a hiccup.

"I'm hopping you'll like me," Victor replied, words rumbling deep in his chest. His chin nestled on the top of my head. "If it helps, I know how you're feeling. This waiting. The unknown. The worry."

I looked up and Victor's chin slammed into my eye.

"Ouch!" I pulled back and started to clap my hand over the injury, but Victor caught it. His touch sent tingles of sensation through my skin.

"Annie," he gasped.

I followed his line of sight to the dried blood. "It's not mine," I whispered.

"Come on." He got to his feet and tried to tug me to mine.

"I'm not leaving." I started to pull my hand free. Victor tightened his grip.

"We'll be back in a second. There's a bathroom right there." He jerked a thumb behind him. A women's restroom waited three doors down from Doctor Denton's office.

"Only if we're quick." I allowed Victor to help me to my feet.

"We will be." He shoved open the bathroom door and shouted, "Anybody in here?"

When no response came, he plunged ahead, stopping at the first of three sinks. My reflection in the mirror showcased wild hair, almost translucent skin, and wide eyes. The pajamas I wore were stained dark red in splotches, matching my hands in macabre fashion.

Victor released my fingers and twisted the hot water nozzle. While the water warmed, he hurried over to the paper towel dispenser and waited for the electric machine to let him snag a few sheets.

"You're in the girl's bathroom," I said in a daze as I watched him wave his hand in front of the sensor for the fifth time.

"So I am." He swept his gaze around the elaborate stalls with white trim and the bright sconces lining one wall. "You should see the men's bathroom. We have a taco stand in there."

A smile twitched at the corners of my mouth. "A taco stand?"

"Yep." He came back to me with a handful of paper towels and placed them behind the faucet on the sink. "The ones on floor six even have water slides, but shhh." He held a finger to his lips. "Keep that on the DL, kay?"

Victor tested the water with a finger. He winced and turned the cold nozzle. After a few seconds, he felt it again. "Perfect. Now, don't get used to this."

"Used to what?"

He held his palm under the soap dispenser on the sink. After waiting for a good amount to pool in his hand, he looked up at me and whispered, "This."

Victor grasped one of my hands in his and ran it under the water. The heat sunk deep into my muscles and bones, eating away the chill of fear. He slid his fingers over my palm, lathering the soap into suds. Flowery perfume filled the air as he massaged my left hand and then the right. Crimson water swirled down the drain in a miniature whirlpool.

I stayed silent as he turned off the water and patted my palms dry with the paper towels. When he finished and had tossed the used towels in the trash, I murmured, "How do you know?"

He turned to look back at me. "Know what?"

I ran the fingers of one hand over the palm of my other. They felt so smooth and fresh after Victor's touch. "The fear of waiting."

Victor sighed. "That's a conversation better suited to a hallway, not a bathroom." He shoved the door open and gestured for me to go ahead of him.

The door to Doctor Denton's office was still closed. I couldn't even hear Mom's voice through the door. My mind's eye painted Benny laid out on that hospital bed, the paper sheet crinkled under him stained red. Doctor Denton would be leaning over, applying bandages, and Mom would be chatting to Benny about some Mayfield Corp business.

At least, I hoped that was the scene beyond the door.

Victor collapsed onto the bench. I took the space next to him, my now-clean hands clenched in my lap.

"My dad gave me this," he said, flicking the penny he wore around his neck. The copper caught the lights above. "The day he died."

I turned to him. *"What?"*

Pain shimmered in the depths of Victor's dark eyes. "My dad used to be this big corporate guy. We moved for his job. But then he got laid off. To keep us fed, he worked two jobs. One during the day as a manager at some fast food chain and another at night as a security guard.

"Before Dad left for his night job, he always gave me a penny he got that day. He'd say, 'Save these, Vic. They'll be worth something someday.'" Victor smoothed the front of his shirt. "The night he gave me this," he flicked the penny once more, "a drunk driver hit him on the sidewalk."

A hollow sorrow leached the fresh heat from my skin. "Victor…"

Victor stared up at the ceiling, releasing a slow breath. "It doesn't hurt as much anymore." He shrugged in a way that made me doubt the words. "My family and I get along fine, but not well enough for college. I tried the military, but I've got a heart condition so couldn't get in. Now I'm just earning my way and scraping together all the money and scholarships I can.

"When I tell you this, Annie, understand that I know what I'm talking about." Victor reached over and squeezed my clasped hands. "Whatever happens to Benny in there, you *will* be okay. Maybe not today or tomorrow, but one day you'll wake up thankful for the memories. Those can never be taken away."

The door to Doctor Denton's office creaked open. Mom slipped out and shut it behind her. Make-up smeared dark rings under her eyes and ran in streaks down her pale cheeks. A mess of blond hair tumbled out from her clip, tangling around her shoulders.

"Benson is dead," she whispered, struggling to meet my eyes. "He's... he's gone."

For a moment, I couldn't breathe, couldn't think. "I don't believe you." I pushed to my feet, stumbling for the door to Doctor Denton's office. Mom blocked my path. She grabbed my shoulders. Her red nails dug painfully into my arms. "Get off me," I cried, trying to break free. "I need to see him. Benny! Benny, I'm here!" I peered around her, catching sight of the tip of Benny's designer dress shoes propped on the hospital bed. Then Doctor Denton's back blocked the rest of him from view.

"Enough, Annie!" Mom cried, giving me a hard shake. "There was nothing Doctor Denton could do. This isn't a hospital! Annie, please—" Mom's voice broke. "He's *gone*."

The truth burned before my eyes, harsh and too bright. "It's my fault." I staggered back, body limp. "Benny is dead because of me." I raised trembling hands to my face. They were clean now, but I could still see the blood. So much blood.

I ran.

Guests meandered around the lobby as I rushed by, most of them glaring out the windows at the storm, oblivious to my anguish. I staggered into a corner, half obscured by a potted indoor plant, and crouched low, knees to chest.

Around the large pot, I watched Victor skid into the room. His gaze swept the guests but didn't find me. He rubbed a hand down his face and turned to the guest services desk.

My mind replayed my final moments with Benny. The storm. The sea. The blood. Benny's final word echoed through my mind like the residual clang of a bell. *Sirens.*

The sirens.

Fury fisted in my chest. They would pay.

I shoved to my feet and sprinted across the lobby, using my momentum to force open the front doors. Wind whipped through the gap, stirring up my hair.

"Annie! Wait!"

I glanced back to see Victor hurrying toward me, knocking guests out of the way.

The door caught on my shoulder as I fled into the storm, but the sting felt faraway and unimportant. I sprinted, desperate to hurt the monsters as much as they hurt me. Rain pelted my hair and clothes, stinging my skin.

I tore down the beach and into the water, splashing up to my knees. The waves rolled around me, not high enough to knock me over, but rough by Viaii Nisi standards.

"You monsters!" I yelled into the storm. Rain and salt splashed into my mouth. My hands clenched into fists as I screamed, the sound merging with the wind. "Face me, cowards! You won't get awa—"

Something cold and hard clamped around my ankles and tugged. I sucked in a gasp as my back slammed into the waves. Victor's strangled cry of "Annie!" reached my ears before water rushed over my head.

22

DAY FOURTEEN, 9:40 A.M.

Water choked my scream. I hurtled through the ocean, back scraping against rough sand and broken shells. I jerked and wriggled. Still, my captor didn't slow.

A tinny ringing picked up in my ears as my frantic heart thundered harder and faster. *Thump, thump, thump.* The noise sounded like a bass drum. I convulsed as my body wrestled for oxygen. I tried to kick. To fight. To free myself. To *not* drown...

The grip on my ankles released. I floated in darkness for a moment until my sluggish brain registered the change.

I kicked upward, praying it was in the right direction.

I broke the surface, gagging and sputtering. Something hard as steel locked under my arms, rough scales raking my skin. I blinked to clear the scorching salt from my eyes. To my right and left bobbed the flat faces and finned ears of two unfamiliar sirens, their scaled hands holding my arms. Powerful beats of their tails kept all three of our heads above water too deep for me to touch the bottom. At least they weren't letting me drown. Yet. I let out a waterlogged cough.

I'd been dragged into a dank cave. The stench of rotten meat and fish hung heavy in the stagnant air. Green slug-like bugs glowed on the walls, casting the gathered sirens in an eerie light. As my eyes grew accustomed to the dimness, I realized sirens surrounded me on all sides. Some perched on rocks, others floated in the water, all with stony stares fixed on me. A shiver of fear skittered down my spine. There had to be at least fifty of them crowded in the space.

A few feet away, on a throne of hewn stone and surrounded by a half circle of sirens—guards, maybe?—reclined a siren with milky eyes. Gray scales glistened over her body, darkening at her hips to a midnight black. Her pale, almost white hair, knotted and tangled, sat piled on her head. The bones of some fish were set into the mess like a tiara. She leaned forward, long talons clicking on the stone. Her lips spread wide in a toothy smile.

I swallowed hard.

"I am Thessalonike," the siren said, snapping her jaws, voice devoid of any accent, as if she'd spoken American English all her life. "Queen of these waters. The creatures gathered around you are my daughters, my subjects, my guards." A forked tongue darted out in a hiss. "*You* are in my domain, lung-breather."

Challenging these creatures had been a huge mistake. A *deadly* mistake. My heart raced as my gaze darted around the cave for a way to escape. On a ledge near the row of guards, a pale shape caught my eye. I squinted, recognizing it as a foot, three toes missing, torn off in ragged chunks. Connected to the foot was a slender leg that looked almost black from a layer of dried blood. The rest of the body was swathed in shadow except for the cascade of tangled dark hair and the bright red of a scrap of fabric.

I sucked in a gasp, eyes burning. No. No. No.

"Tamara," I wheezed, my throat constricting. As my eyes adjusted, I realized there was another body entwined with hers. It was noticeably male, wearing one of the Mayfield Villa uniforms. That body had to be Vladimir. I wanted to puke. I wanted to sob. Had Tamara and Vladimir died before they were brought here? Or... or had the sirens kept them alive, using them as snacks whenever they got a craving for human flesh?

I glared at Thessalonike, may hands curling into fists. "You are disgusting," I spat. "Where is Agent Papadakis? Where is the other woman you took?"

Queen Thessalonike gestured to one of the guards in front of her throne. A gold band winked against the green scales on the guard's arm as she swam to a jutting rock on the opposite side of the cave from where I was held. She snagged a body clothed in a flimsy white nightgown, now stained with grime and blood, off the ledge and dragged it through the dark water to Thessalonike.

"Agent Papadakis," I whispered, horrified.

The queen grasped a handful of Agent Papadakis's blond hair and pulled her up so the tips of her toes created ripples on the water. Her right leg hung at an odd angle, the knee looking almost backward. I cringed at the gashes in her pajamas, revealing ragged flesh that still seeped blood. Her whimper echoed through the cave.

She was alive.

"Let her go," I begged, jerking forward against the sirens holding me. "Agent Papadakis, it's me! It's Annie."

Papadakis's eyelids fluttered. She mumbled something I couldn't understand.

If I could just save one person, it would be worth it. "Everything's going to—"

Thessalonike's free hand curled around Papadakis's throat. With one quick twist of her wrist, she snapped the agent's neck. The crack rang through the cave. I gagged, bile rising in my throat. Thessalonike tossed Papadakis aside and her limp body splashed into the water. The waves and ripples slapped against my neck and shoulders. Another siren guard snatched the body and tossed it to the ledge with Tamara and Vladimir's corpses. It landed with a sickening thump.

I trembled. Cold seeped through me. Not the coldness of fear or sorrow. The coldness of a deep, incomprehensible horror.

"You killed them all," I whispered. "Adam, Tamara, Vladimir, Papadakis... And Benny—" My voice broke.

"I see you found our final warning." Thessalonike tilted her head as she watched me fight back tears.

"You will pay for this," I growled. "Not all of the sirens are loyal to you. Lorelei!" I shouted, scanning the sirens around me. She had to be here. She had to help me. "Lorelei, where are you?"

Queen Thessalonike leapt from her throne and into the water. In the space of a blink, she was in front of me, teeth bared. "You dare mention that name!" she screeched. Her talons pierced the soft flesh of my neck as she snatched my chin. Warm blood trickled down the skin of my throat and dripped into the water. Thessalonike's flat nose pressed against mine, stale breath whistling between her teeth. "She is a traitor, banished centuries ago. Mention her again and you will join the other corpses."

I gasped in realization. "You're the one who cut out her tongue."

"Yes." Thessalonike released my chin and slid backward toward her throne. Her guards parted for her, and she slithered back up onto the rock. Her gaze stayed locked with mine as her forked tongue flicked over her talons, gleaming with fresh blood. *My* blood.

I swallowed back nausea.

"You lung-breathers set your minds to owning my possessions." She chuckled low in her throat. "Well, you saw what became of those in their house of stone."

My eyes widened. All those skeletons. All those lives cut short. "That was *you*?"

"Your kind stole my precious daughter and left her in the sun to die." Thessalonike's eyes drifted closed as if reliving the memory. "Our attack was vengeance. And every lung-breather life we've taken since is retribution. This island belongs to me and me alone."

I shook my head. "But we're not the same people who tortured your daughter. How can you punish us for a sin we didn't commit!"

A blurred shape streaked through the water beside me, bursting to the surface at Thessalonike's side. Water droplets splashed across my face, and I coughed.

The siren bowed, silvery hair cascading over her shoulders. A gold band encircled her upper arm, and I noticed matching bands on the other siren guards that flanked and encircled Thessalonike's throne.

"Speak, Acantha," Thessalonike said with a bored wave of her hand, her gaze fixed on me.

Acantha's slitted eyes looked to me then back to Thessalonike. The siren's lip curled up in disgust as she spoke, too quickly for my two years of Greek to understand. But my mind caught one phrase: *o prodótis eínai edó.* The betrayer is here.

"Is that so?" Thessalonike spoke in English, head cocked as she watched me, milky eyes unblinking. "What is so special about you that she would dare face me, I wonder." She moved back toward me.

Goose bumps skittered down my arms. I tried to move away, but the guards tightened their grip on my arms.

Thessalonike snagged my chin again. This time I gasped at the sting of her sharp nails as they dug deeper. She moved my head side to side.

"Echo," Thessalonike murmured, her harsh grip softening. She stroked my cheek with the smooth scales of her other hand. "You have Echo's bearing..." Warmth softened her eyes, eyes that had been so cold moments before.

Suddenly her face hardened, and lips parted in a snarl. The waft of decay made my stomach roll. "You and your kind will vacate the island before midnight, or we will slaughter all of you."

Images of Mayfield Villa littered with massacred bodies rose before me. The young, the old. The siren queen would slay anyone in her path.

"Wait, please!" I cried. "No one can leave the island. The storm is too—"

Thessalonike inclined her head, releasing my chin and swimming back a few feet. "I believe you lung-breathers call this kind of storm a *hurricane*. Or, at least, it will be. With Aegaemon's help."

Horror clawed my insides, though my conclusion made no logical sense. "You caused this storm?"

A scream reverberated through the cave, as though it came from far away. Followed by another and another. The word "Prodótis" slid into the air on whispers that echoed.

The guards' grip on my arms loosened. They turned toward the front of the cave, eyes narrowed. Even Thessalonike's attention shifted.

I kicked out, throwing my desperation into the blow. My heel slammed into Thessalonike's stomach. She careened backward and smashed into the lip of her stone throne with a cry. The siren guards rushed to form ranks in front of her.

The sirens on either side of me bared their teeth in a violent hiss. I tensed, ready to fight.

An underwater shadow collided with the siren securing my left arm. The one on my right released me with a snarl and dove to join the bubbling fight beneath the surface.

I splashed under the water, trying desperately to stay afloat like Victor had taught me. Cries in Greek and high-pitched clicking echoed through the cave. My limbs seized in fear and I sunk under the surface. Scales brushed my shoulders and cinched tight around my waist. I jerked back.

I tried to force my eyes open, but salt water bit into them. Something cool pressed against my forehead.

Lorelei!

The arm around me tightened, and we shot through the water. The cries and splashes around us faded. Fire roared in my lungs, and my body started to tremble, hungry for air. I squeezed Lorelei's wrist as tight as I could.

She shot upward. My face broke the surface, and I burst into a fit of coughing, arms and legs treading water as Lorelei's grip fell away.

Rain pounded against my skin in icy torrents, colder than the ocean. A loud roaring grew in front of me, and I felt myself sucked forward. I forced my burning eyes open to see the outline of Lorelei's face and an enormous wave barreling toward us.

"Lorelei!" I screamed and pointed. She turned and hissed. The wave swooped us up along its curve.

Lorelei lunged for me. Her scaly body slammed into mine, arms and tails wrapping tight around me as the wave crashed. We were buffeted through the water, our heads knocking against each other. I sucked in a breath to cry out, remembering too late. Ocean rushed into my mouth.

I fought Lorelei's grip, struggling to break free, to breathe. She spiraled back to the surface. We broke through. This time, she didn't let go.

I sputtered and retched, wiping salt from my eyes as another wave crashed, slamming us under. Lorelei squeezed me close and darted forward. Already, I could feel the telltale need in my lungs. Panic seized me. I grabbed Lorelei's constraining arm.

I need air! I wanted to scream at her. She didn't relent, and she didn't resurface.

I dragged my fingernails over her scales. Lights danced behind my closed lids and a whirring reverberated in my ears. I writhed and fought to escape, but Lorelei held me firm, trapped.

As my vision tunneled, fear leached the fight from me. I sucked in a mouthful of ocean.

Prodótis was right.

Lorelei had betrayed me.

Lorelei's Song, Verse Ten
"There will be killing till the score is paid."
~The Odyssey, Book 22

Rasping breaths shuddered from Lorelei's mouth. Useless, pointless breaths. Sirens breathed once every five hours, not the steady rhythm of lung-breathers.

But Lorelei wasn't a siren any longer. She was nothing.

Her talons dug grooves into the rock platform as she hoisted herself up. The pain in her abdomen and back were mere shadows compared to the hot sorrow in her chest. Trickles of red blood seeped from the corners of her mouth, turning to clouds in the water below.

She unleashed a grunting howl as she hurled herself up and onto the surface of the rock. Part of her had hoped that Thessalonike lied. A lie to cause more pain than a lost tongue. A lost voice. But now Lorelei saw the truth.

The remains of Echo's charred and blackened body lay chained to the rock. Her once sapphire scales had splintered and curled on themselves, turning a deep crimson, the color of dried blood. All that remained of Echo's sweet face was gaping eye sockets and wisps of dark hair.

A scream flung Lorelei's bruised lips apart. She hurled her head back and released her pain to the cloudy sky. She cursed the lung-breathers, Thessalonike, and... herself.

She lowered herself atop Echo's corpse. The tears that Lorelei longed to shed wouldn't come despite the burn in her eyes. Sirens could not cry. Thessalonike alone possessed that blessing, a gift used to create daughters from the sea foam. Lorelei's grief would stay trapped until it devoured her whole.

She longed to sob Echo's name, to apologize, to explain, but even that had been stolen.

A crack of thunder split the cloudy sky, followed by a streak of lightning. As if a veil had been torn, rain burst from

above and fell in a great torrent. Soon, Lorelei felt the ocean rising, the cool caress against her fins, then her waist. Thessalonike
had prayed to Aegaemon.

And he was sending his storm.

Lorelei didn't leave Echo's side, not when the rain turned to
blistering hail, not when the ocean crashed over her head,
pounding at the cliff side as if it too hungered for the deaths of
the lung-breathers. The tide rose and rose until it crested against
the men's castle of stone. Until the sirens could attack and take
their revenge.

Lorelei didn't care. She let the water soothe the sunburn
along her scales. She lay beside Echo, her head cocooned in the
hard plains of her sister's chest. Hate seeped out of her until a
blank slate of emptiness remained.

Screams of hunger and fury echoed through the water above
as the sirens attacked. Her sisters would take blood for blood, a
life for a life.

No. No longer her sisters.

Lorelei squeezed her eyes shut and curled closer to Echo.
She submersed herself into the memory her dream had conjured:
Lorelei chasing Echo with a piece of kelp, weaving in and out of
the coral. She had never caught her sister, of course, but the fun
was in the laughter and the chase.

Something slammed into the waves above. Bursts of crimson drifted down to her from the shattered remains of a lung-
breather. He or she had sought escape from the sirens' rampage
and had found it in death.

Lorelei envied the lung-breather's easy demise. While
Thessalonike's heart still beat, Lorelei was cursed to live forever, yet not live at all. Unless she sacrificed herself to the sun or
to the lung-breathers' weapons.

But she was already a *prodótis* in the eyes of her kind. She
would not make herself a coward as well. No. She would wait
and grow stronger, faster. Faster even than Echo.

Then she would kill Thessalonike.

23

DAY FOURTEEN, 10:53 A.M.

My eyes tore open. I sucked in a ragged gasp as rain splattered against my lips and down my throat. Victor straddled my waist, leaning over me, blocking out the darkening gray sky. His clasped hands hovered inches from my chest.

"What're you doing?" I asked, voice hoarse.

"Annie!" he cried, shaking his head. Droplets flew from his face. "I was giving you CPR, but it doesn't seem like you need it." He squinted down at me, raindrops rolling off his lips and down his chin.

A shadow hovered at the corner of my eye. I shifted to find Lorelei kneeling at my side, the tips of her long fins still submerged in the foam.

"You saved me," I croaked, reaching toward her with pruney fingers.

Lorelei's gaze flicked to Victor. Her muscles tensed in distrust and suddenly I realized he was still straddling my hips. Heat pulsed at my cheeks, and I shoved myself upright. He rolled off in time to avoid smashing foreheads.

"Are you okay?" he shouted over the wind, holding up a hand to shield his eyes from the driving rain.

I nodded, swiping my damp hair out of my face. We didn't have time to stand here talking. I turned to Lorelei. "I need you to come with me inside the villa. Can you do that?"

Her talons tore deep grooves in the sand as she shook her head violently, still watching Victor. Four long tears marred the front of his shirt, plastered against his chest from the wind. When he caught me staring he plucked at the fabric. "I startled her, that's all. I'm fine."

"Lorelei." I shifted to my knees, inches away from her face. The wind buffeted me from every side, and I curled my fingers into the sand, trying to stay upright. "Please. Thessalonike is going to attack everyone on this island." I heard Victor's sharp intake of breath behind me. "But no one will believe me unless you come. I need proof. I need *you*."

Lorelei's webbed fingers relaxed their grip on the sand. Her eyes met mine, glowing despite the storm around us. She nodded once.

I resisted the urge to throw my arms around her. She seemed balanced on a precipice as it was, especially with Victor nearby. "Thank you." I hesitated, remembering my final moments trapped under the ocean's surface, when I swore Lorelei was a traitor. I had been so, so wrong. I called over my shoulder for Victor. He approached, eyes wary as they took in Lorelei.

"Are you going to explain what's going on?" he asked as he sunk down beside me. A wave crashed and the foam rushed past our knees.

"Once we get her inside," I promised. "Lorelei, you're going to need to let Victor carry you." I would've tried, but one look at the siren's bulk made it clear that my only option was Victor.

At this, Lorelei hissed and Victor balked. His hands went to the tattered remains of his shirt.

"It will only be inside the villa," I pleaded. "If you can't trust each other, trust me."

He grunted. "As long as she doesn't attack me again." He scrutinized Lorelei. "Okay?"

Lorelei's nose crinkled in disgust, and a fathomless darkness flashed in her eyes—fear? She nodded once.

After some awkward maneuvering, not helped by the strengthening storm, Victor scooped Lorelei in his arms. Her body went rigid, teeth clicking together in distaste.

"This way!" I called, leading the way toward the lights of the villa, almost obscured in the darkness.

"Annie," Victor began as we battled the wind, heads lowered. "What happened to you? One minute you were on the beach and the next this siren hauls you ashore and attacks me when I try to help."

"The other sirens grabbed me," I yelled over the wind. "The evil ones. Lorelei is on our side. Their queen is going to attack the resort. We have to talk to my mom."

"When we get inside, I'm going to expect a longer explanation."

I swallowed hard. Everyone would.

"Attention. Guests please report to the theater," a recorded female voice echoed through the empty lobby. "Attention. Guests…" The message played on a loop.

"Where is everyone?" Victor asked, voice strained. The muscles in his neck bulged as he fought to keep Lorelei upright.

I shook my head. "I don't know, but we'll find out. Let's wait in my mom's office." Goose bumps puckered my skin as the chill of the air conditioning washed over me. I crossed my arms as I started to shiver.

I jammed the elevator call button and waited, shooting a sympathetic glance Victor's way. Lorelei stared at the room in wonder. Every so often her gaze would drift back to the statue of Poseidon.

The elevator dinged and the doors slid open.   Victor staggered into the empty space, and I hurried to select the twelfth floor. In the small enclosure, the fishy scent of Lorelei's scales increased. Victor's reflection grimaced. Lorelei seemed entranced by the mirrors, cocking her head, eyes widening when her reflection followed.

The elevator doors whisked open to a silent hallway. I peeked out to the left and right. Empty on both sides. It felt like a bouldering mat had collapsed on my chest. Though this floor had never been busy, the emptiness still made my hair stand on end.

I strode toward Mom's office at the end of the hall. For a moment, my heart pounded as my gaze fell on the bench outside. Benny should be there, elbows on knees, DS gripped in his palms. He would look up, see me, and smile. "Hey, kiddo!"

But the bench was empty. And Benny was dead.

My grief surged forward, tightening my throat. I longed to curl up on my bed and sob, but that would have to wait. First we needed to see Mom. She would be able to fix all this. Make it better.

I hoped.

I stopped outside Mom's office and knocked. Victor's labored breathing tickled the back of my neck. When no response came, I flung open the doors.

Mom's office, like the lobby, was empty. As I entered, the lights flicked on, illuminating her desk, couches, and wall-to-wall bookshelves.

"Over here." I guided Victor to the closest couch. He lowered Lorelei with a grunt.

"Are you okay?" I asked Lorelei.

"I'm—" Victor started, massaging his shoulders with a hand, only to glare when he saw who I spoke to. "Oh, thanks a lot."

Lorelei nodded, webbed fingers probing the soft material of the couch.

I looked around, chewing my lip. In a way, it'd been lucky the lobby was so empty. My muddled brain hadn't considered the panic Lorelei would cause bystanders. But where was Mom? If she didn't show up, I'd have to go hunting for her. The last thing I wanted was to leave Victor and Lorelei alone.

"Your mom will be back," Victor said.

I turned to see him eyeing the paperwork scattered across Mom's desk.

"She's left her phone and has missed at least fifteen calls already." He crossed his arms, over-worked muscles bulging. The motion tugged at the slit in his t-shirt, showing off the tip of his abs. I looked away quickly and fiddled with my ruined pajama top.

"Meanwhile," Victor continued. "Maybe you can give me the long version of what happened." He inclined his head toward the siren.

I brushed salt encrusted hair out of my face with a trembling hand. "I'll tell you everything. But it might take a while."

"We've got time."

In the span of fifteen minutes, I told Victor a shortened version of the events in Thessalonike's cave. He paled as I described the fate of Tamara and the others. Just remembering Papadakis's death made my stomach roll. I had been there. But I hadn't been able to do anything to save her.

"I can't help but feel it's my fault," I finished, feeling awful. At some point in the story, I had gravitated toward Victor, hopping onto Mom's desk while he leaned against the bookshelf behind it. "If I'd told someone sooner, *made* them believe me…" I trailed off, staring at my dirty knees.

"So you're a blood-thirsty siren then?" Victor asked, voice hard. His flip-flops squeaked on the hardwood floor as he moved to stand in front of me. I didn't meet his eyes. "You're the one who kidnapped Vladimir, Tamara… all of them? *You* killed them, right?"

I sighed. "Of course not, but if I'd tried harder." My hands formed fists. "If I'd done something, Benny—"

"Benny would still be dead."

My head sprang up at Victor's harsh tone. "How can you say that?"

His hands grabbed the desk on either side of my knees. I tensed at his closeness, my heart picking up speed.

"Because it's true." His voice was rough as he looked into my eyes. I became keenly aware of our siren observer. "No matter what you did, no one would've believed you. Who knows if I would have, if I hadn't seen a siren attack that little girl?" He let out a breath. "You've done the best you can, and there's still more you—*we*—need to do."

I leaned forward, wrapping my arms around him, burying my head into his damp t-shirt. "Thank you," I murmured, inhaling his salty scent.

The doors slammed open. Lorelei snarled, talons digging into the couch's upholstery. Victor and I jumped apart. He stumbled, a flip-flop sliding off his foot.

"Annie!" Mom shouted as she stormed inside, Agent Floros and Iona close behind. "What do you think…?" She trailed off as her enraged gaze found Lorelei. "Oh, my… Oh, my…." she cried out, stumbling back into Floros and Iona.

I hopped off the desk and rushed to Lorelei's side, mostly to keep her from attacking anyone. "It's okay," I told the siren. To Mom I said, "Mom, this is Lorelei. She's the siren I mentioned earlier."

"Did someone say siren?" Floros elbowed his way to the front. He blanched when he saw Lorelei crouched behind me, lips pulled back. Colorful Greek expletives exploded from his lips. He clapped a hand to his forehead. Behind him, Iona's orange freckles stood out on her white face. She pressed against a wall as if Lorelei might attack.

"It will be all right," I murmured to Lorelei in Greek. The familiar language seemed to soothe her. She released her attack-ready hunch, but her muscles were still tense. I glanced at the couch and the padding sticking out of the gouges she made. Luckily, Mom was too freaked out to notice.

"Uh, Annie," Victor said from across the room. "Maybe you should have everyone sit down." He watched Iona with concern. She did look as if she might faint.

"Right. Could you, uh," I gestured toward the startled trio near the door, "take care of that?" I worried that if I stepped away from Lorelei, even for a moment, the fear in her eyes would trigger instinct to take over. I rubbed my scarred arm unconsciously.

Once Victor got everyone seated near the bay windows, the furthest seating from Lorelei, I relaxed. Floros still watched the siren, murmuring under his breath. Some color had returned to Iona's cheeks.

"What is going on?" Mom asked me, squeezed between the two on the couch. She looked torn between annoyance and shock. "What is that thing?"

Rings of smudged mascara and eyeliner still hung under Mom's eyes. Her trademark pink lipstick had been smeared away, most of it ending up on her teeth as if she'd gnawed her lip.

I fumbled for the words. How to begin?

"F-Florence," Iona stammered. She stared blindly ahead, probably thinking she was dreaming this whole scenario. "We need to get back to the theater. The hurricane—"

"*Hurricane?*" Victor cut in, looking at me, likely remembering Thessalonike's threat. "When did the storm become a hurricane?"

Mom massaged her temples, obviously struggling not to stare at Lorelei like the two people beside her. "It popped up on the radar out of nowhere thirty minutes ago. It's only a category two, but with our island so small I'm supposed to evacuate the guests. Except we'd never make it in a ferry. And there aren't enough helicopters. We had to opt for emergency protocol and take shelter in the theater. That's why I didn't go after you, Annie. When you ran."

An icy fist squeezed my heart. So Thessalonike hadn't been bluffing. A hurricane really was headed our way.

I found my words. "Mom, Iona, Agent Floros, I need to explain something to you, and I don't have a lot of time." I quickly shared a condensed version of the story I told Victor. When I got to the corpses in the sirens' cave, I took a deep breath. "All of the missing people were taken by the sirens," I said, unable to meet Floros's eyes. "And they're all dead."

Floros' brows drew together. "Are you saying... You're saying that the sirens killed Papadakis?"

I nodded, unable to come up with any words that would calm the turmoil in his eyes.

"Damn you!" Floros jumped to his feet, rushing for Lorelei, veins bulging in his face and neck. "You killed her!"

"Stop!" I shouted, blocking his path. His chest slammed into me, and I stumbled, righted myself, and then held firm. Lorelei growled behind me. "She didn't do it. She *saved* me. Not all sirens are the same."

A muscle in his jaw ticked. "I don't give a..." He squeezed his eyes shut, raising a hand to hide them as a single tear ran down his cheek. "Damn it."

My throat tightened. "I'm sorry, Agent Floros," I whispered. Then I raised my voice. "Sirens are real, and they're going to attack the villa in a matter of hours."

Iona held a trembling hand over her mouth as if she might be sick. "What are we going to do? I can't even... This doesn't seem real."

Mom watched Lorelei, her expression somber. I knew she wanted to tell me I was wrong, but with the proof a few feet away from her, she couldn't. "What do you suggest?" she finally asked.

I opened my mouth to reply, to admit I had no idea what to do, when a steady beeping rang through the office. Lorelei unleashed a deep-throated snarl, eyes rolling for the source. Her talons tore another set of deep grooves in the couch.

Victor frowned, looking around. "What's going on?"

"The proximity detector," Mom said, brow furrowed. Then her eyes widened. "Lynn."

24

DAY FOURTEEN, 12:59 P.M.

Mom, Victor, and I raced to the roof. Floros and Iona split off, hurrying to oversee the guests in the theater. I left Lorelei in Mom's office, locking the door to keep her in—dangerous as she was—and humans out.

We paused at the door to the rooftop and helipad. Victor squeezed the metal handle, turning back to us. "It's gonna be windy. You two ready?" A loud whirring sound vibrated on the other side of the metal door: the unmistakable spinning blades of a helicopter.

"We're ready, come on!" I turned the knob and shoved hard on the door. At first it wouldn't budge, but then Victor added his weight. The door flew open with a lurch, and Victor and I tumbled into the storm. Mom stepped out behind us, gasping at the strength of the wind.

I squinted into the lights of the helicopter, already landed on the roof. Its whizzing blades slowed as the chopper's engine died.

A loud click followed, and the headlights snapped off. The only light came from a lamp fixed above the staircase door and inset lights on the circular landing pad.

A silhouette hopped down from the helicopter, and my heart did a little hop of its own. Then I realized the shadow was too bulky and tall to be my sister. Lynn hadn't been cursed with short genes, but she wasn't *that* tall. The figure turned and held their arms up for a second person.

Lynn.

She'd just touched down on the roof when I barreled into her, arms flung open wide. I crashed against her. She stumbled and would've fallen if she hadn't caught herself on the still open hatch of the helicopter. Something cool and foreign brushed my calf.

I pulled back as if burned, my eyes falling to the metal rod sticking from Lynn's capris and disappearing into a gray sneaker. Light glinted off the piece.

"Annie!" Lynn cried through laughter and tears. She righted herself and grabbed me again in a tight hug. I gasped in surprise, my stare forced away from her prosthetic leg.

I sniffled into her neck. "You came," I managed to choke out.

"Of course I did."

"Lynn!" Mom shouted as she approached. "I'm so glad you made it safely."

"Mom!" Lynn eased away from me and met Mom halfway.

"Hey there, Annie!" The distinctively male voice cut through the wind and rain. I peered up at the shadowed face of Captain Wallace.

Ugh. Not *him*.

"Why are you here?" I snapped. An elbow jabbed my side, hard enough to get my attention. I glared at Victor.

"Be nice," he mouthed.

I clenched my jaw. Victor had no idea what this man did to my sister.

Lynn came back to lean against Captain Wallace's broad chest, ducking against the wind. "This would be a conversation better suited for the indoors," she advised in a shout.

At the subtle command, Mom, Victor, and I tromped for the stairwell, where we waited in relative shelter while Lynn and Captain Wallace worked together to secure the helicopter to the helipad with heavy ropes. They returned minutes later, Captain

Wallace with a massive duffel bag hanging off one shoulder. "The guns!" he shouted to me when he caught my curious look.

Once we were all out of the pelting rain and wind, I brought up my question to Lynn again.

"Why is Captain Wallace here?"

"Annie," Mom warned beside me. "Manners." But the hypocritical way she eyed at Lynn and Captain Wallace proved she was just as curious.

Lynn pushed tendrils of wet hair out of her eyes, the longest part of her pixie cut. "Jim—Captain Wallace," she corrected when she caught my glare. "Flies helicopters for a corporati—"

"RayMeadow Corp," Captain Wallace cut in with his deep voice.

Even better. He worked at RayMeadow. A direct competitor of Mayfield Corporation.

I gave Lynn a seething look.

She kicked the tip of my shoe with her prosthetic leg. I clenched my jaw against the desire to jump back. This was my sister. I loved every part of her. I just wished the prosthetic didn't make me feel so uncomfortable.

"Captain Wallace," Lynn continued, "was able to cash in some favors and get us the helicopter. One strong enough to fly through storms... and hurricanes, it seems." She let out a breath and shook her head. "I didn't think we'd make it. Things are bad out at sea."

Captain Wallace smiled at mom and tipped an invisible hat. "Nice to see you again, Florence. I'm Jim, if you've forgotten." He held his hand out to Victor. "Nice to meet you. Lynn, Annie's sister, and I served together in the Army."

Victor shook Captain Wallace's hand. "Victor Hale. Annie and I work together." The penny around Victor's neck caught in the dim light and flashed copper.

Captain Wallace's eyes widened. His gray eyes matched Lynn's gray sneakers. What were they, color coordinating?

"Mind if I take a look at your necklace?" he asked, leaning forward. He fished a pair of glasses out of his jacket.

"Uh, sure." Victor stepped closer, shooting me a curious glance.

Even with glasses on, Captain Wallace was attractive. The thick black frames gave him an artsy smart look. No wonder Lynn was interested in the guy. Back in high school, she always flirted with the weird art and drama boys.

Captain Wallace let out a whistle. "I know this isn't the time for it." He moved back and flicked off his glasses. "But I'm a coin collector, and you've got a wheat penny hanging around your neck. With that year, that coin's worth $2,000. Even with the hole drilled in it. I'd love to talk to you about it after..." He trailed off and turned to me. "Lynn says you need us because sirens were going to attack?" His brows knitted together, and he looked to Mom for clarification. "*Sirens?*"

"It's true," Mom affirmed.

Lynn rolled her eyes at Captain Wallace. "I ask you for a helicopter and enough guns to take down a small militia, and now you're doubting."

"Actually, you asked to *borrow* my guns." Captain Wallace smiled. "When I heard your family's resort was in trouble, I threw in a helicopter and my companionship for free. But I do expect a special *bonus* for using my L85A2. She and I have quite the rapport, but nothing compared to me and you." He dropped a quick kiss on Lynn's temple.

Flames flickered at Lynn's cheeks. "Jim!"

Oh, gag.

"Lorelei?" I called, easing Mom's office doors open. I peeked inside, relieved to find the siren still on the couch. She looked up from the book she held, muscles taut. I'd given her a *National Geographic* hardcover full of pictures.

"I'm alone," I promised, stepping into the room and shutting the doors behind me. "Everyone is deciding what to do about the attack, but I wanted to make sure you're okay." I knelt beside her. Her fiery scales looked dry around the edges. I frowned. "Are you okay?"

Lorelei nodded, running a hand over her tails before pointing outside and shrugging.

"You can stay out of the water for a long time, can't you?"

She nodded again.

I rested my cheek on the lip of the couch near her hip. "There's something I want to ask you. You don't have to answer."

Lorelei waited for me to speak, eyes warm.

"When Thessalonike held me captive, she told me that you were a betrayer. Did... did it have anything to do with the bones on the far side of the island?"

She lowered her head. Braids slid over her shoulders, tickling my face. I waited for her to respond or at least shake her head. When she didn't, I cleared my throat.

"Never mind. You don't have to say the details."

Finally she looked at me, fingers brushing my temple, her lips moving. "Echo," she mouthed.

A shot of familiarity made my nerves burn. As if Lorelei had called me the name before, a long time ago. I shook my head to clear it. I was probably just tired. "Lorelei, I want you to get far away from here."

Her stare hardened.

"You can't be here. You'll be safe in the ocean." Even while I said it, everything inside me yearned for her to stay. Lynn's arrival and the sight of Captain Wallace's guns made it all too real. Creatures of myth were coming to kill us. Creatures much stronger and more powerful than we could ever be. "The other sirens don't like you, and the humans here don't trust you. I don't want you to get hurt."

Lorelei watched me for a beat. Her mouth twitched and a phantom smile flickered there. Then she nodded.

"You'll go?" My voice cracked.

She grabbed my hand and traced Greek letters onto my palm. "Go," I said aloud in English. Then, "Close."

"You'll go, but not far," I murmured in understanding. She nodded. I hurled myself against her chest. She started in surprise, body tightening. "Thank you, Lorelei," I said. Tears burned in my eyes. "I'm so scared."

Her arms went around me, hesitant at first, and then confident. She choked, trying to speak. It took me a moment to understand, but when I did, the growing terror in my chest eased.

"Ah Po-tet," Lorelei grunted. "Ah. Po-tet. Oo."

I protect you.

Once Lorelei was back in the ocean and I had changed into fresh clothes and forced food down my throat, I returned to floor three and the theater. Inside sat a bunch of kids and a scattering of daycare employees keeping them entertained. I picked Tommy out in the crowd and gave him a halfhearted wave before settling into a seat in the back. Mom must've summoned all the adults into a meeting. I wondered what she would say.

Ladies and gentlemen, an army of sirens are about to attack our resort.

Yeah, that would go over well. Hopefully the oncoming hurricane was enough of an explanation for why no one could leave the theater.

I closed my eyes against the kids' chatter. A myriad of emotions battled for dominance: grief, terror, anger, hope. Too much had happened in the last twelve hours for me to process anything. A hard numbness was sweeping through me. And I welcomed it.

A cold hand on my shoulder made me look up. Mrs. Samson smiled at me, her eyes alight with excitement.

I sat up straighter. "Oh, hi."

"Hello, Rybka." She took a seat next to me. "It seems we have trouble on our hands." As she spoke, the Russian accent slipped. Then she cleared her throat and it was back. "Your mother explained about the hurricane." She glanced around at the kids and leaned forward to whisper, "And told a group about the sirens."

My eyes widened. "She did?"

Mrs. Samson nodded. "A few will fight with Captain Wallace's guns. I'm one of them."

This time my mouth dropped open. "You can't be serious."

She chuckled. "I didn't give them much choice, once I admitted knowing about the sirens."

"Wait... you *knew*?"

Mrs. Samson shrugged. "There are things about me, Rybka, things that you have yet to discover. Besides, I'm an old woman." She patted her hair. "It will be nice to have some action, even if I'm going to be on the fourth floor scouting."

Some of my surprise diminished, interest replacing it. "What did they decide to do?" I asked.

"You will have to ask Captain Wallace." Her animated face grew serious. "Rybka, this will be very dangerous. You need to be aware and watchful."

My brow furrowed. "Why do you say that?" I asked. "My mom is making me stay in the theater. I won't be in any danger."

"You never know what might happen." Mrs. Samson grunted as she rose. "Blessings on you, child." She patted my cheek, then strolled down the aisle.

I looked down at my watch. Eight hours until midnight. I prayed it would be enough time.

25

DAY FOURTEEN, 10:48 P.M.

"**M**om?" I called, sidestepping employees as they jogged down the hall. Storm shutters blocked the tall glass windows, casting the corridor in ominous shadows.

Nandan hurried toward me, arms loaded with board games.

"Hey!" I shouted slowing as we bisected paths. "Have you seen my mom?"

"She's in the lobby with Agent Floros," He gave me a curt nod and hurried away. Seemed someone still had a grudge over the whole towel incident.

A burst of wind rattled the storm shutters, and the entire villa creaked as if in pain. The chandeliers above flickered. I swallowed hard, opting to take the stairs down to the lobby.

I splashed into an inch of water when I reached the first floor. Storm surge must've engulfed the beach, and waves now crashed against the front of the villa. Water levels were rising fast.

I found Mom in a pair of rainboots near the Poseidon statue in the center of the empty entranceway. She stood in a circle with Agent Floros, Captain Wallace, and a broad-shouldered man I didn't know. Furniture had been piled against the doors of the villa, chairs and tables haphazardly balanced.

As I approached, I caught the tail end of their conversation.

"The lobby and the first floor are clear," Agent Floros said. "Second floor is almost complete."

"We can set up after everyone is in the theater," the stranger added, a sharp New York accent coloring his words.

Mom opened her mouth to speak when she saw me standing nearby. "Annie, what are you doing down here?" Everyone turned to look at me.

"I wanted to know what was going on," I explained, forcing myself to meet the group's gaze. "I waited for hours, but you never came back to the theater. It's getting close to midnight now. Mrs. Samson told me she's part of some defense team? You realize she's an old lady, right?" I gave Captain Wallace a glare, assuming he chose the teams.

"She approached us," the stranger from New York said, drawing my attention. "Somehow she knew about the sirens. She'll be with me on the fourth floor. It's the safest spot. We're the sharp shooters."

"This is Carl." Captain Wallace gestured to the man. "He served in Desert Storm. I figured we needed a military man for this, so I filled him in."

"Lucky I was on a trip with old army buddies." Carl chuckled. "They're all pitching in. I almost didn't believe you when you asked for people with fighting experience, Wallace. And I'm still not sure this isn't just some joke."

"We'll find out sooner or later." Captain Wallace smiled, clapping the man on the shoulder.

"What is everyone else doing?" I asked. "Maybe I can help." Sitting in the theater for hours, watching guests mill about, annoyed that their vacations were being ruined, was enough to try anyone's patience. Worse, being still let my thoughts wander. I needed to act. To be useful.

Agent Floros scrubbed a palm over his face. "I'm second floor. My team is the first line of defense in case the sirens get in. I still don't know how fish plan to swim up to the front doors. What're they going to do, knock?"

Captain Wallace chuckled. "Who knows, but if we get that lucky, I'll be happy to keep them locked out." He looked to me.

"I'm the third floor with your sister. We're the last line of defense. The fourth-floor shooters will be our reserve if things go bad."

"Great. Where can I help?" I asked, looking from Floros to Greg to Captain Wallace.

"You're staying in the theater. With me." Mom raised her brows as if daring me to contradict her. I obliged.

"I've been involved in this from the beginning. You need me."

Mom sighed. "Annie, don't push me on this. You're a child. You're not helping."

"But, Mom." My voice cracked. "I need to do this. They killed Benny, Tamara, and so many other people. I need to do *something*."

"You have done something—you told us what was going on and called Lynn. Captain Wallace can take it from here." She turned to the men. "Let's head up to the theater and spread out from there. You have your teams assembled and briefed?"

"Yes, ma'am," Carl said while the others nodded.

"Annie," Mom turned to me, "come on." She inclined her head toward the corridor where the stairs were.

I gritted my teeth, wanting to protest.

Captain Wallace interjected, "Florence, I'd like to talk to Annie for a minute, if that's okay."

Mom frowned. "All right. But as soon as you two are finished," she fixed me with her obey-me-or-else stare, "Annie, I want you in the theater. Got it?"

"Fine," I huffed.

Mom left the lobby, Carl and Floros following close behind. The tense way Floros moved, back rigid, chin high, awoke my guilt. I should've done something to save Papadakis. I should've thought of something. I should've—

"Annie?" Captain Wallace's voice dragged me from my regret.

I blinked. "Sorry, what?"

He let out a breath, leaning against Poseidon's thick calf muscle. "I think it's brave that you want to help. You and Victor both. He was down here trying to convince me just a little while before you were."

I watched him, unsure where this was going. "Thank you?"

He fished into the duffel bag at his waist, retrieving a black handgun. I reached out to take it automatically, having gone to a range with Dad on and off as a kid. The weapon was surprisingly heavy—and cold—in my hands.

"What's this for?" I asked.

"For just in case." He pushed off of Poseidon. "I gave one to Victor too. Other than Florence and Iona, you're the only ones who will know about the sirens in that theater. If… if they get past us, you're all that's left to protect everyone."

Sweat slicked my palms. I squeezed the gun tighter, hiding my fear by checking the safety and the chamber.

"Lynn said you knew how to use it," Captain Wallace offered, breaking the awkward silence between us.

"Our dad taught us."

"You blame me for what happened to her, huh?"

I froze. "How did you know?"

Captain Wallace stared at his big hands. Criss-crossing marks littered his knuckles like a game of tic-tac-toe. "If you can believe it," he murmured, "I blame myself too. If I hadn't gotten injured…" His fingers moved to brush over the jagged scar running down his temple as if a phantom injury remained. "If Lynn hadn't been assigned as my nurse, she never would've been in that field hospital when it was bombed. Our section sustained the worst damage." His foot tapped a quick rhythm on the floor. The sound echoed in the empty space.

Captain Wallace watched me, gray eyes darkened to a thundercloud. "You're right. It's my fault."

I swallowed hard, not sure what to say. Hadn't I felt the same way about Benny? Tamara? Vladimir? Papadakis? Victor claimed I wasn't to blame. If he was right—and I painfully

wanted him to be—that meant Captain Wallace was just as innocent in Lynn's accident.

The crackling of the walkie-talkie at Captain Wallace's
waist interrupted. Lynn's voice came through the static.

"Jim? Over."

Captain Wallace shot me an apologetic half smile before he
held the walkie-talkie to his mouth and answered. "What's going on?"

"Everyone is in position. We're just waiting for you."

"Be right there. Over and out." Captain Wallace returned
the walkie-talkie to his belt.

I ran my thumb over the ridged handle of the gun. "Thank
you."

Captain Wallace hesitated, as if he wanted to ask what I
meant. Thank you for the gun? Or thank you for the honesty? He
shook his head and nodded toward the stairs. "We better get
moving."

Thirty minutes later, I leaned beside Lynn against a wall on
the third floor. The three other members of her team hunched
over their weapons nearby. Captain Wallace chatted with Mom,
indicating the storm shutters over the windows.

"I need at least four of these opened," he explained. "On
this floor as well as the second and fourth."

Mom nodded and showed him where the switches were lo-
cated. A loud groaning sounded as the storm shutters swung
back. The wall at my back vibrated with the motion.

"Thank you, Florence." Captain Wallace adjusted the strap
of the enormous gun he held. "You better get into the theater
and see to your guests." He paused. "I'll send Annie in shortly."

Wind gusted across the exposed window panes, making
them rattle. Little pings sounded against the glass. I squinted,
trying to figure out what they were.

"Hail," one of the men nearby explained. The villa groaned
in agreement.

The lights dimmed, flickering for a moment before they blacked out. My heart skipped a beat. Screams breached the closed theater doors. Lynn's hand squeezed around mine. I squeezed back.

Panicked whispers ran down the line of men to my left. The hum of a generator kicked in and red emergency lights came to life along the walls.

"Focus, men," Captain Wallace called as he set up two battery-operated lanterns. Their yellow light fought off the ominous red glow around us.

"Florence?" Captain Wallace asked into his walkie-talkie. His face was half shadow. "Will the floodlights outside the building work on the generator?"

"They should."

"Everett, get the lights," Captain Wallace ordered a man with a nose too large for his face. Everett scrambled to his feet and rushed down the hall.

Lynn shifted beside me, turning to look out the windows. Her gasp made my head pop up.

Waves rolled toward the villa. Dark ocean had already devoured the small beach and lapped at the lower windows. Bright floodlights illuminated pounding rain, turning it white in the darkness. Even the hail appeared unearthly as it pinged against the exterior walls.

Howling wind rippled across the front of the villa. The window near Captain Wallace shattered. He held an arm up to protect himself, swearing.

Air rushed into the hall, forming a funnel. My hair whipped around my head and jabbed into my eyes.

"You okay?" Lynn cried at Captain Wallace, holding a hand in front of her face to block the gale.

"Fine!" Captain Wallace answered. He shook off the glass shards. They clinked as they hit the floor.

Captain Wallace pointed at Lynn and mimed shattering the window behind her. Lynn nodded and had me step back before jamming the butt of her gun into the glass. Hairline cracks skittered across its surface. Lynn brought her gun back again. This time when she hit, the window burst into tiny pieces. Lynn jumped back as more wind rushed into the hall. The other men followed her example.

"Why is this a good idea?" I cried, gagging on the cyclone as Lynn dragged me back to the window. She kicked shards out of the way and crouched, instructing me to do the same.

"It's safer than letting it break on its own," Lynn said into my ear. "Besides, we need an open space to shoot from. We should get you into the theater."

"Just a little longer. Please." I checked my watch—11:55—then my gun, which I had secured in a holster that Captain Wallace gave me.

"Mom told me about Benny."

I looked up at Lynn where she kneeled under the window, gun propped on a shoulder.

"Yeah," I murmured, voice hoarse.

"Do you remember his mac n cheese?"

"What?"

She pursed her lips, the way she always did when trying not to cry. "The mac n cheese he made the nights he babysat us."

I scooted closer to Lynn, my shoulder brushing hers. From the corner of my eye I could see Captain Wallace peering out the window, eyes squinted against the wind.

"I never liked that stuff," I admitted.

Lynn smiled. "I know. He'd spend two hours making the noodles and cheese. I devoured it. Then he'd heat up the Kraft version for you." She shook her head. "He always made crazy desserts for my track team fundraisers... Benny was always there for us. I'll miss him, Annie."

I rested my head on her shoulder. "Me too."

"Mom didn't say," Lynn murmured. I could barely hear her over the wind. "How did the sirens kill him?"

Her question threw me. I fought against the image of Benny's tattered body. The blood. The gashes. His eerie smile. I opened my mouth but couldn't find the words. Captain Wallace saved me from responding.

"Enough chitchat you two." He lowered himself to the ground underneath the window. "It's 2400. Enemy is coming. Annie, I want you in the theater. Now." His tone didn't leave room for argument.

Lynn nodded. "Go on, Annie."

"Be safe," I whispered to her. I shoved to my feet, legs full of needles from sitting in one position for so long.

"Men," Captain Wallace was saying to the others, "earplugs in on my command. Keep your heads on a swivel. If you get in a tight spot… Well, we won't hear you scream. It's every man for himself."

The wind shoved against me as I walked. I ducked and fought my way toward the doors. My fingers closed around the handle when a familiar crooning drifted into the corridor, carried on the squall.

"The sirens are coming!" I shouted over the wind.

Captain Wallace swore and relayed the order for earplugs into his walkie-talkie.

Over his shoulder, a wave arched toward the villa. Floodlights glistened on bright scaled bodies. They rose on the cresting foam, arms outstretched, teeth bared.

I ran.

26

DAY FIFTEEN, 12:01 A.M.

The villa trembled as a wave slammed into the first floor. Loud thuds shook the wall where sirens hit the building, but as the water retreated, there were no scaled bodies in its depths. I froze. Where were they?

A scaly arm snaked through the window in front of Lynn, talons reaching out.

"Get inside!" Lynn yelled at me.

Captain Wallace started shooting, the other men followed his lead.

I shoved a door open, staggering into the theater. Arms wrapped around me and squeezed, pulling me farther into the room. The scent of sweet pea tickled my nose. I looked up into Mom's face. Behind me, Victor secured the doors.

The chaos in the hall, the screams and gunfire, didn't reach the sound-proof theater. Nervous chatter echoed throughout the space. Some of the maids milled about, passing out snacks to anxious guests. A few people looked my way, curious, but otherwise, no one seemed to know we were under attack.

"Are you okay?" Mom asked, guiding me to a row of chairs in the back. Her grip on my arm tightened. She didn't let go, even when we were seated. "You should've come in earlier. I wanted to go out and get you, but…" Her gaze drifted to Victor where he stood at the door, a somber sentry. "Is Lynn all right?"

I swallowed. "She'll be fine." *I hope.*

"It's my fault," Mom whispered. "All of this."

I shook my head, understanding the blame game all too well. "Don't be ridiculous. You didn't know sirens were real."

"But I knew those bones in the ruins were real."

I tensed. "What?"

"I had a friend examine them. Me and my micromanagement." She choked on a laugh. "They were authentic human bones. The skeleton on the rock wasn't. But I paid the examiner to report them as fake." She rubbed a hand over her face. "I felt so called to this island. It was an escape from so many things. I didn't want the bones to keep people from coming. None of the owners ever moved the bones. And I couldn't either. Something about them... Oh, Annie. I'm so sorry."

My hands formed fists. If she would've told the truth, maybe Benny, maybe Tamara... I stopped myself. Even if Mom had been honest, the sirens would still be out there. Killing.

"I love you, Annie," She whispered. "I don't tell you enough, but I do. I want you to know that I do."

"Mom..." I trailed off, not sure what to say. An *I love you too* hovered at the tip of my tongue but didn't battle its way past my teeth. Hurt and pride stood in the way.

"Things have been strained between us lately. Do you ever wonder why?" She reached up to smooth hair off my forehead.

Her touch transported me to my childhood. With every banged knee, stomach bug, or bad day at school, she would reach out, brush hair from my face and say—

"You're my girl, and you can do anything," Mom breathed. "I haven't said that since Lynn's accident. I didn't want you to do anything. I wanted you to be safe, always. When I realized I couldn't control you, I pulled away. I was scared. So scared of feeling that pain again." Her voice cracked. "It was weak and selfish. I promise I will do better."

"Oh, Mom." I reached across the armrest to hug her. "I love you," I murmured into her hair.

Something heavy slammed into the theater doors, making the metal tremble. I whirled around to see Victor leap back.

The theater was the hurricane emergency center in the villa, Mom had said earlier. The room was built to withstand strong winds and had pumps that would keep the water from rising too high—if any did get in. But that banging... That wasn't water.

Victor came over to me, gun in hand. "You doing okay?"

I eased open my clenched jaw, standing up to join him in the aisle. "My sister is on the other side of that door. What do you think?"

"Right. Sorry."

"Annie!" a familiar voice shouted.

I looked up at the balcony. Tommy leaned over the railing, waving frantically. He acted like a hurricane was the most exciting thing to happen to him. His mom grabbed Tommy around the waist and tugged him back.

Another series of loud bangs shook the door. Three indents buckled the metal. Panic shot through me. I bolted for the doors.

"Annie, stop!" Mom cried.

Victor's fingertips brushed my wrist but fell away as I picked up speed. "Annie!" he shouted. "Don't!"

I shoved at the doors, forcing my weight against them. They swung open, and I stumbled forward, falling to my knees.

Lynn lay in the froth a yard away, her gun held horizontal like a staff. The flat face of a siren bore down on her, mouth split wide in a toothy snarl around the barrel.

"Lynn!" I screamed, scrabbling for my gun as I pushed to my feet and ran forward. A wave crashed against the villa, sending more water gushing through the shattered windows and into the hall.

Blood streamed from a gash at Lynn's forehead, painting half her face crimson. She let out a cry of desperation and frustration. Gunfire echoed, lights flashing as bullets burst from chambers. Shadows darted around me, humans and sirens battling.

I slid to a stop, nearly tripping over the door to the stairwell. It had been torn off its hinges, the stairs covered with rushing water.

Lynn gritted her teeth, swinging a leg up at the siren's abdomen. The creature flew backward. In seconds Lynn had her weapon up. She fired. The gun kicked back in her grip. A hole tore open the siren's forehead with a gush of red. The creature let out a keen and tumbled into the flood with a splash.

Another siren slithered toward me, mouth open, teeth gleaming. I staggered back. She opened her mouth, lips curled to sing. I reached to cover my ears. Too late.

The sweet melody wrapped around my limbs, making them heavy and loose. I found myself smiling, filled with peace and longing. The world blurred.

Wake up! a voice wailed inside me. *Wake up!*

An inhuman screech split the air. Hazy shapes returned, focusing as I blinked. I realized with a start that the cry came from me, my mouth still split open in a scream.

The world slammed into focus. The siren before me snarled. She lunged.

"Annie!" Lynn's yell carried on the wind. She swung her gun around, ready to fire.

The siren's talons slammed into me. I fell backward into the stairwell, my stomach dropping. Pain and water exploded around me as I hit the landing. The siren's weight forced air out of my lungs and my head underwater. I struggled beneath her, breaking the surface. My eyes tore open, burning with salt, as she darted for my neck.

A series of gunshots echoed through the enclosed space. The siren's body convulsed before collapsing onto me. The weight forced my head back under. I flailed with panic, trying to shove the body away.

Suddenly the pressure eased. Warm hands wrapped around my shoulders and tugged me up. I sputtered, sucking in ragged gulps of air. Beside me, the siren's corpse lay on the next level of steps, water spreading her hair out in a purple halo.

"You are such an idiot," Victor snapped.

I swiped at my face, rubbing my eyes. Victor knelt before me, water dampening his swim shorts up to the thigh.

"Thanks for saving me," I wheezed.

Victor sighed. "You're welcome." He glanced up the stairs to the third floor as another round of gunfire sounded. "We need to find a place to hide. The theater's out. We can't expose the guests to the sirens' song. We almost lost a handful of them when you barreled out. I would have been ensnared too if it hadn't been for these." He showed me the earplugs in his palm.

I winced. Selfish, selfish, Annie. Lynn didn't even need my help. "Sorry."

"Maybe we can take shelter with Floros down here." With a grunt, Victor pushed to his feet. He held a hand out for me. I took it, grimacing as my wet shorts rubbed at my thighs.

We splashed down the staircase, skirting around the siren's corpse, one hand on the railing. I slipped once and would've fallen if Victor hadn't grabbed my arm.

"You okay?" he whispered.

I nodded.

"Stay quiet. If the sirens were up on our floor..." He trailed off, leaving me to assume the rest. "You seem to be able to snap out of their song. If you hear it, tell me to put the earplugs in."

He was right. Twice now I had escaped the sirens' grasp. Why could I resist when the people around me couldn't?

The second floor was cast in a red glow that deepened the shadows around us. Water splashed up to our ankles, filled with debris: upturned furniture, dishes, and ragged plants. The levels ebbed and flowed as wave after wave hit the resort too fast for the water to drain down to the first floor.

"Do you hear that?" Victor asked, teeth glinting in the half-light.

I cocked my head, listening. The faint echo of the battle above and the storm outside trickled down the stairwell, but the second floor was silent.

"I don't hear anything," I said slowly. Then dread squeezed my heart as I realized what that meant. "Something happened to Agent Floros."

Victor gritted his teeth. "Exactly." His gaze swept the corridor before us, employee rooms stretching out to end in the communal sitting area. A gush of water rolled toward us, the level rising to mid-calf. I grimaced at the cold.

"Over here." Victor grabbed my wrist and forced me to halt. He scooped an orange life vest from the water where it had tumbled out of a stand and jammed my arms into it.

"Victor!" I hissed. "Now isn't the time—"

"We don't know what's going to happen." He clipped the final buckle and tightened the straps. "And I'm not taking chances when it comes to you. Hold on to this." He curled my fingers around a flashlight. "Captain Wallace gave it to me earlier. It's waterproof."

I took the flashlight. It felt like a brick in my hand.

"Come on." His fingers entwined with mine as he started down the hall. "My room is at the end with a window over the pool. We can hide there and jump if we get cornered."

"Okay."

A few doors we passed were closed, but most of them hung open, darkness leaching into the hall, reaching for us with phantom claws. My heart gave a jolt as I saw my room ahead, and I tugged free of Victor.

"Annie, what're you doing?" he asked, watching as I waded through the water.

"Tamara's necklace is in there. I should've gotten it when I changed, but I was so preoccupied…" I slid inside my room, reaching my bedpost by touch alone. I secured the crane pendant around my neck after a few failed attempts and hurried back into the hall. A pang shot through me at leaving Adam's hat behind.

But this necklace meant something to Tamara's family, not just me.

Victor hunched under an emergency light, checking the bullets in his gun. He looked up when he heard me approach, tense shoulders relaxing.

A shape shot from the water at his back. Scaled arms slung around his neck and dragged him down. Droplets splattered the wall as he and the siren went under.

I screamed.

The gun was in my hand. A flash of scales caught my eye. I fired. Once, twice, three times.

Blood turned the water an inky black, and then a shape heaved upward out of it. Only after an agonizing second did I see Victor, shoving the siren body off his shoulders. I fell to my knees beside him, shaking from adrenaline and fear.

"Annie," he choked, water dripping down his face. His eyes found mine in the red light.

I forced a shaky smile. "Figured I'd return the favor."

Victor's fingers knotted in my hair, tugging my face toward him. His lips crashed against mine. I gasped. Salt sparked on my tongue. Water from his hair ran down my cheeks. I leaned into him, letting the chaos around us fade. He pulled away suddenly, our heavy breathing echoing in the silence.

"What was that for?" I rasped.

Victor staggered to his feet, pulling me with him. "I've wanted to do that since I caught you on the pier. With the odds the way they are, I didn't want to miss the chance in case..."

In case we didn't survive. "Oh."

Victor coughed. "C'mon. My room's down here."

We'd moved halfway down the hall when hissing and snarling reached our ears.

I turned to Victor. He held a finger to his lips, and I nodded. We crept further down, pressing ourselves against a wall and peering around it. In the employee lounge, five sirens hunched over lifeless shadows. Their scales flashed as they tore into flesh, teeth snapping. The nearest body stretched out, fingers half curled, head floating, eyes open, mouth parted in a silent scream.

Agent Floros.

I gagged. Victor swore.

A siren's head swiveled in our direction. Blood dribbled down her chin, splashing into the water. Our gazes locked, and I recognized the creature from Thessalonike's cave.

"Acantha," I whispered.

She snarled, catching the other sirens' attention. They growled low in their throats, looking up from their victims.

Victor swore again. He shoved in his earplugs and angled his body so he stood between me and the sirens, grip on the gun white-knuckled. I drew mine and moved to stand beside him.

Acantha roared and shot toward us, claws extended.

27

DAY FIFTEEN, 12:56 A.M.

A dark shape burst through the broken windows on our right. Fiery scales flashed as our rescuer slammed into Acantha, teeth bared.

"Lorelei!" I shouted.

The other sirens skittered around Lorelei and Acantha, launching themselves at us. Victor and I fired simultaneously. Two sirens dropped mid-air. Lorelei broke away from Acantha, shoving a third siren against a wall.

Victor's gun gave a dull click. "I'm out," he said, voice overly loud.

I barely heard him as I shot at the fourth siren until my clip was empty.

"We've got to get out of here!" He grabbed my arm, towing me toward the shattered windows.

I tried to pull free. He turned to look at me, and I mouthed, "Lorelei!"

Victor helped me onto the window ledge. "She can take care of herself!"

I hesitated, one foot on the window frame, Victor's shoulder brushing mine. The ocean roared below us. Wind buffeted my hair against my cheeks. Fear twisted my gut.

I glanced behind me. Acantha attacked with a roar, but Lorelei was stronger, faster. She raked her claws across Acantha's abdomen. Acantha shrieked. She darted toward Lorelei, only to stop when she saw us at the window.

"Jump!" I screamed.

Nothing but air surrounded me for a freeing moment. Then I smacked against the ocean. Icy water stole breath from my lungs. I floundered against Victor's constricting arms before the life jacket buoyed us to the surface.

Beating wind tore at my skin, and hail pelted me like bullets. I squinted around us, trying to orient myself.

A body splashed into the water nearby, and I cried out, Victor's grip tightening. Then I recognized Lorelei's glowing eyes.

"What should we do now?" I cried, spitting salt from my mouth.

She pointed toward the villa. I peered ahead, barely able to see a half-submerged towel hut let alone the building beyond.

"Come on!" Victor started kicking. Lorelei led the way, her scales shining in the floodlights above like a beacon of safety.

"Don't let go!" I shouted to Victor over the wind even though he probably couldn't hear me.

Yards away from the villa's shattered windows, a telltale sucking sensation pulled at us. A wave crested and curled forward with a growl.

"Victor!" I screamed.

Lorelei caught the front of my life jacket, hurling us into the towel hut. My head brushed the roof as Victor smashed me against the back wall, grabbing the lattice. His chest pressed into me, heartbeat thudding against my back. The frantic sounds of our breathing filled the open space.

Then the wave slammed into us.

Victor's body pressed hard against mine, keeping me anchored, though the wave fought to tear us apart. I squeezed my eyes shut and held my breath.

A muffled cry sounded by my ear. Victor thrashed behind me. His reassuring weight vanished, and suddenly nothing held me to the wall of the towel shack. The wave retreated, towing me with it. I tumbled in the surf, my cries turning to bubbles in the water. A flash of scales darted toward me—Lorelei's hand outstretched. Then the wave ripped me away. I spun in the darkness, lungs screaming.

The life jacket popped me to the surface. "Victor!" I yelled. The distance between me and the hazy lights of the villa stretched out, swallowed by roiling ocean. I could barely make out the details of the building.

"Annie!" Victor's voice reached me as a far-away echo. I clicked the flashlight on and pointed it in the direction of his voice.

"Victor!" I called again, praying for him to respond. Only the roaring wind and pelting rain and rushing ocean answered. Panic burbled inside me. "Lorelei!" I cried, my voice a cracking sob. "Someone, anyone!"

The wind and rain beat against my exposed skin as another wave scooped me up and smashed me down. I kicked frantically to turn in a circle, trying to find the villa. A faint light in the distance was all I could see of it. A few feet away, the water rippled in a line toward me, forming into a siren's silver body as it slithered through the water.

Thessalonike.

She reared up like a serpent to strike. I screamed and flipped backward, right onto a hard edge. Pain exploded in my back. I instinctively reached behind me and latched onto the obstacle with my free hand, desperate not to be washed away again. Firm rock greeted my fingertips. *The cliffs.*

Realization stole my breath. The storm had dragged me to the backside of the island.

When the next wave crashed, I dug my fingernails into the rock, fighting to stay anchored. A shape rose beside me, orange scales sparkling in the light. Lorelei's nose brushed against mine, her forehead cool against my flushed skin.

"Lorelei!" I sobbed and hurled myself at her.

She allowed the embrace for a few seconds before she wriggled free. Her hands explored my life jacket as if trying to figure out what it was. A groaning whoosh sounded from behind us, and we were sucked backward. My flashlight illuminated another dark wave. A whimper creaked from my throat.

Lorelei slung an arm around me and shoved through the water. She didn't move as fast on the surface as she did under, but we still beat the wave. Lorelei heaved me into the stairs by the ruins, and together we crawled up until the wave hit—mercifully crashing at our feet. Water sprayed over the cliff and splashed across my face. I buried my head into the safety of the stone.

Lorelei patted me all over, and I looked up, illuminating her face with my flashlight.

"What're you doing?" I asked in a hoarse whisper.

Lorelei didn't answer. She kept running her fingers over my arms and face as if checking for injuries.

"I'm okay," I coughed. "Are you?" I swept the flashlight over her body. The light caught on a curve of deep red holes piercing the scales at Lorelei's shoulder. Crimson still seeped out of the wound. I winced on Lorelei's behalf and reached toward her only to pull back at her annoyed look. "I saw Thessalonike."

Lorelei nodded.

I swallowed hard. "Victor, the boy you saw on shore when you saved me. Do you know what happened to him?"

She shook her head.

I took a trembling breath as another wave battled the cliff side. I jumped as water splattered over the ragged top and rained down. The memory of Victor's salty kiss caressed my mind, warming my lips. *Please be safe.*

Ocean rushed up the stone steps. On the tip of an oncoming foamed arch, gray scales glinted like a dull blade.

The siren queen.

Fury roiled inside me. I stood, snatching a rock off the steps, and threw. It arced past Thessalonike's head and crashed into the wave.

Lorelei leaped toward the siren queen, but Thessalonike knocked her aside with a snarl. Thessalonike slammed into me as the wave crashed. The back of my head bounced against stone. Fireflies danced and burst before my eyes.

"You tainted Echo's spirit," she keened. Her talons raked across the front of the life jacket, cutting open the outer material with ease. "I will not allow you to live!"

I grunted and swung my flashlight up, smashing it into the side of Thessalonike's head. The beam flickered for a moment then strengthened.

She howled, arching back. Her talons knotted in my life jacket. She lifted me, and for a moment I dangled above her, her luminous eyes glaring up at me in pure loathing and disgust. Then she hurled me to the side.

My left arm shot out to catch my fall, and as I collided with the cliff, a wrenching pain slashed through my forearm. I screamed and tumbled down the steps, rolling to a stop at the submerged rock platform.

Shadows hovered at the corners of my eyes. Despite the swinging of my flashlight, I couldn't dispel the darkness. My stomach rolled. But the agony in my arm was the worst—a sharp pain that seemed to grow and grow until it was all I could think about. I bit my lip to keep from screaming again.

Lorelei's screech made me look back. Using the queen's tactic, she had ridden a wave and leapt as it crested, straight toward Thessalonike, claws extended. She crashed into the siren queen, and they tumbled down the steps, slashing and hissing. I hunkered in the scanty shelter provided by the cliffside, cradling my injured arm, as the two sirens slammed into it, Lorelei's body beneath the siren queen. Thessalonike crushed Lorelei's neck against the rock, then reared back and swiped a clawed hand across Lorelei's abdomen.

I gritted my teeth and fumbled for a makeshift weapon to help Lorelei. Something smooth brushed against my fingertips in the water, and I tugged hard. The object gave way with a snap, sending me staggering to my knees.

Lorelei flung Thessalonike off with a shriek. The siren queen smacked into the roiling ocean.

"Lorelei!" I shouted and hurled the weapon toward her. As if sympathetic to our plight, the wind lifted the object higher and dropped it into her outstretched hand.

Thessalonike burst from the water with a howl. Lorelei shoved herself up to meet the queen, weapon first. A wet *thunk* sliced through the storm's rage. Thessalonike let out a ragged gasp and fell against the steps, sliding down a few feet, head banging on each stair. I swept my flashlight over the siren queen and cried out.

Buried in the middle of Thessalonike's chest curled the end of a long white bone.

"You've destroyed us all," Thessalonike wheezed. She clutched at her chest but seemed unable to find the protruding bone. "Prodótisss." The watery hiss twisted from Thessalonike's lips and her milky blue eyes lost their focus. Her body gave a violent tremor and exploded into foam.

The biting wind sucked backward in a whirl, tugging at my hair, and then was stilled. The pull and growls of the hungry ocean calmed with each passing second. A heavy silence descended as the rain and hail morphed to drizzle. Within moments, the slate grey clouds lightened and dispersed, revealing a twilight sky smeared with red.

I staggered back. The motion jarred my arm, and the world went black around the edges. A ringing in my ears got louder and softer and louder again.

"Lorelei." I stumbled toward where she lay on the platform. Blood seeped steadily from deep gashes clawed into her chest and stomach, dying the rock scarlet.

I fell to my knees beside her.

She raised a trembling hand to my cheek, rubbing away a tear. A sigh escaped her lips as she watched the brightening sky. Warm sunbeams crept into the crevice. Lorelei turned her face toward the light, smiling. Her scales seemed to ripple and shine before they burst apart, leaving nothing behind but froth.

The ringing in my ears intensified, and I fell forward, my injured arm catching on the edge of a stair. I tumbled into nothingness.

DAY TWENTY-ONE, 1:34 P.M.

My body curled against the cold. I shifted and rolled onto my side, tugging a thin blanket over a shoulder. Steady beeping sounded, but I blocked it out. Just a few more minutes and then I'd get up and put that maid uniform on.

A shrill alarm jerked me awake. I cried out as my eyes tore open, the skin tender. Instead of my tiny room at the villa, I lay in a hospital bed in the center of a large private room. Flowers, balloons, and stuffed animals crowded every available counter space. It looked like I bunked in a garden or toy store, not a...

Where was I exactly?

The door to my room swung open and a nurse hurried in. She had a long pixie cut that reminded me of Lynn. Her eyes matched the powder blue of her scrubs.

"Why, Miss Mayfield, you're awake!" she said with a smile that revealed perfect white teeth. "Hey there. Let me get this." She fiddled with the shrieking machine. After a few taps it lapsed into a delicious silence.

I shifted higher up on my pillows, realizing there was a bulky cast wrapped around my left arm. Hazy images wavered before me. Snapshots of the attack on the Villa, Lorelei battling Thessalonike, and then...

Lorelei's body had burst into foam.

I slumped against the thick mattress and stared at the ceiling, eyes too dry for tears.

"Let me just say," the nurse said, crossing her arms. "I'm glad you're awake. You move a lot in your sleep, and it messed with the heart monitor."

I rolled my head toward her and checked out her ID badge. "Eve, what hospital am I in?" My voice was hoarse, and I cleared my throat.

She leaned a hip against my bed. "I'll give you a hint. Your dad owns it and half the hotels in the area."

Well, that explained the flowers and toys.

"There's my girl!"

I looked up as a man stepped into my room, decked out in a high-end suit. His blue eyes crinkled when he smiled, and his nose leaned a little too far left.

"Dad," I choked, surprised.

"You look pale." He hurried to my side. "Are you up for a hug?" At my shaky nod, he scooped me up tight. His earthy cologne washed over me, a scent so familiar. I closed my eyes and breathed it in. The pain in my chest eased ever so slightly.

Dad pulled back and sat on my bed. His gaze turned to Eve. "Thanks for taking such good care of my daughter. Mind giving us some time alone?"

Nurse Eve crinkled her nose. "I need to check her vitals."

"It can wait," Dad said in his I-own-this-hospital voice.

"Five minutes." She squeaked out of the room.

"That would drive your mom crazy," Dad muttered to himself. "Squeaky shoes." He cleared his throat and gestured at my vibrant floral garden. "I overdid it a bit with the flowers, huh?"

I held up a hand, forefinger and thumb close together. "A little."

He ruffled my greasy hair. "You weren't supposed to agree."

A knock sounded on the open door of my room. I leaned around Dad to see Mom in the doorway. She wore an all-black dress that flared out at her knees.

"Can I come in?" she asked, directing the question more at Dad than me.

Dad slid off the bed. "Of course, Florence." He gave me a tense smile. "I'll wait outside. I know you two have some things to talk about." He tugged at his black suit coat. After hesitating a beat, he pressed a kiss on Mom's cheek as he passed.

Mom held her fingers up to the spot as if savoring the gesture. Once Dad left, she moved over to me, high-heels click-clacking on the floor.

"I'm sorry I wasn't around when you woke up." She shifted her big black briefcase to her other hand. "Lynn just went to the cafeteria to get some lunch."

Lynn. The last time I saw my big sister, she was fighting an army of sirens. "She's okay?" I asked.

Mom nodded.

I let out a breath. Lynn was safe. More memories surfaced, and my earlier relief evaporated. I sat up, catching the IV in my arm on the bed railing and pulling it taut. I unlooped it impatiently. "Have you seen Victor? Is he all right? I—"

Mom put a hand on my shoulder and squeezed. "They're all fine, Annie. He's with Lynn now. Captain Wallace too. I texted them and they're on their way back." Her hand moved to her bag, fluttering over it in a nervous gesture. "The reason why I wasn't here when you woke up…" She trailed off, straightening her spine with effort. "Benson's funeral was today."

"I missed Benny's…?" My throat started to close up. For a blissful moment, I'd forgotten that he was gone. The reminder made me want to sob. "I should've been there. Why didn't someone wake me up?"

"Oh, Annie." Mom toyed with the hospital bracelet on my wrist. "You've been in a medically induced coma for the past few days. There was some swelling in your brain. Benson would have understood." She paused. "Actually, he left something for you."

My ears perked at that. "He did?"

"Sort of. He told me he wanted you to have this when you left the villa." She clicked open her bag and reached inside, pulling out an object I knew well. "Maybe he was joking, but I decided to take him seriously. And I'm glad I did."

I took the worn Nintendo DS from Mom's hand. Pokémon Black and White was still inserted into the game slot. Hot tears burned the backs of my eyes.

"Turn it over," Mom instructed. Her lashes fluttered as if she blinked back tears of her own.

Brow furrowed, I did as instructed. Taped on the bottom of the DS was a single sentence:

Beat the Elite Four for me. Love, B.

A tear rolled down my cheek and pattered on the note, staining the white paper. Then I started to cry.

"Oh, my girl." Mom wrapped her arms around me and rocked me side to side. "It's okay. It's going to be okay."

No. Right now, it was not okay. I had lost Benny and Lorelei—two people who I felt understood me better than most.

But I wasn't alone in my loss. So many other people had died at the villa. Tamara, Adam, Papadakis, Floros… And that wasn't all.

"How many?" I rasped. "How many people died in the attack?"

Mom pulled back, swiping my tears with her thumb. "Twelve." The word came out matter-of-fact. Before I would've considered it harsh, but now I knew it was how Mom dealt with pain. "Agent Floros's entire team. One member of Captain Wallace's. The sirens' victims. Benny."

"Twelve," I echoed. "What happened to the sirens?" Lorelei and Thessalonike's body had burst into sea foam. Did that mean the others…?

"They disappeared. There's no evidence of them—anywhere." Mom frowned as if she still attempted to solve the mystery. "Authorities attributed all the deaths to the hurricane despite some outspoken contradictions from our witnesses." She faltered. "They never found the ones the sirens kidnapped, but by now they're assumed dead. I made sure to put in a good word for Tamara, so she hopefully doesn't get the blame. Everyone who helped defend the resort has kept their mouths shut about the truth. It makes sense, since the creatures literally disappeared before our eyes." She paused. "We did save the necklace you had on and, well, see for yourself." Mom pointed near the windows.

Afternoon sunlight trickled through the glass, showcasing city buildings against a sapphire sky. A necklace dangled from a coatrack, the silver crane soaring. Beside the necklace hung a familiar neon blue hat with *Viaii Nisi* sewn on the front.

A trembling smile worked its way to my lips. "Thank you." I looked at Mom, her mouth pinched with worry. "I'll be fine," I assured her.

She brushed a curl away from my face. "You're Annie Marie Mayfield. You've always been better than plain old fine."

I gave her a watery smile.

Movement at the corner of my eye made me look up. Lynn, Captain Wallace, and Victor crowded in the doorway. I grinned at the sight of them. A bandage was taped across the top of Victor's forehead and a bruise colored his eye, but he looked fine otherwise. And, as always, he wore a pair of swim trunks.

"I'll see myself out," Mom said. She nodded at the group and strode past them.

Lynn rushed over to give me a hug. Black stitches marred the skin above her eyebrow. "How are you feeling?" she asked when she pulled back.

"A little groggy." I rubbed sleepiness from my eyes, yearning for a mirror. If I looked as bad as I felt, I definitely didn't want Victor in the room. My mouth tasted bitter, teeth thick with film.

"You scared us," Captain Wallace chided. "Rescue teams had to scour the island for you and your boyfriend." He jerked a thumb at Victor.

Boyfriend?

Victor gave me a shrug as if to say, *What can you do?*

Lynn huffed, "Okay, Jim, that's enough. You're banned from the room. Annie, can I get you anything? It has to be light because of the medicine you were on."

"A toothbrush would be great," I whispered. "And maybe some chips?"

"They'll have to be plain chips," she warned.

"That's fine."

"Be right back." Lynn towed Jim out of the room, her dress dancing over her metal leg.

Victor watched the two leave before he moved to my side. Up close, I noticed something was missing, but my muddled brain couldn't determine what. I did remember the kiss, though. It seemed like it was seared into my mind.

Then it hit me. "Your penny necklace is gone."

"Oh." He ducked sheepishly. "I sold it to Captain Wallace." Then he met my eyes, and a smile shone on his face, almost too bright. "It's the last amount of cash I needed. I'm going to college in the fall. They were able to squeeze me in."

My mouth fell open. "Victor, really? That's fantastic!"

He nodded. "I almost can't believe it."

"Are you going to wear your punny shirts around campus? Attract all the girls?" I asked, jabbing his chest where a little seal perched above the words "You have my seal of approval."

He caught my hand in his, eyes serious. "I'm only interested in attracting one girl."

I laughed nervously. "Right."

He opened his mouth to speak, but someone cut him off.

"Excuse me," Eve said as she stepped into the room. "I need to check Annie's vitals. Mind stepping out?" The last part she directed at Victor.

"Oh, sure." Victor nodded. To me he whispered, "Was Captain Wallace right?"

My brows drew together. "About what?"

He shot Nurse Eve a side-eye. "About me being your boy-friend."

My face warmed. Couldn't he have saved this conversation for later, when I was showered and didn't have medically-induced-coma breath?

At Nurse Eve's *ahem*, Victor winced. "Sorry," he said to her before leaning in close, lips brushing my cheek on the way to my ear, breath hot. Chills spread across my skin, nerves still slow and sleepy. "I'm glad you're awake, Annie." He pulled back and shot me a wink before striding out of the room.

Eve watched him go before she hurried to shut the door. Then she glided to the foot of my bed. Her form glimmered, growing fuzzy, and then solidifying. Instead of the nurse, Mrs. Samson stood at the end of my bed, bright pink lips curled up-wards. I rubbed my eyes, but the sight before me didn't change.

"Hello, Annie," she said. "Or should I say Rybka?"

I struggled to speak, my mouth dangling open. "Y-you... How? What *are* you?"

"Sorry, Rybka," Mrs. Samson said, words now colored by a light Greek accent. "I won't pester you after this, but I decided you needed to know in case the future proves... stormy. I was once a goddess named Amphitrite."

"Amphitrite," I murmured, forehead wrinkling. "Goddess of the sea... Poseidon's wife?"

She smiled. "You always did so well in Greek mythology."

My mind reeled, refusing to believe it. But then again, hadn't I battled against sirens days ago? Why did a Greek god-dess showing up in my hospital room surprise me?

"Okay," I hedged. "What does that have to do with me?"

"You intrigued me," Mrs. Samson admitted, hands resting on the end of my bed. "I've watched you from afar for a long time—since you almost drowned as a child. I was one of the paramedics that day." She waved off my budding questions. "I harbored my suspicions, but when you arrived at Viaii Nisi, I knew. You, my dear, are a reincarnated siren."

I stared at her. She stared back. I held up a hand. "Okay, no. This is where I draw the line."

Mrs. Samson shrugged. "Suit yourself, but it explains your resistance to their song. Dear Echo died in such torment, it's no surprise her spirit didn't ascend. Why do you think I called you Rybka, which means little fish, when you don't swim?"

I massaged my throbbing temples. "Why are you telling me this?"

"Because I fear what the future holds after Thessalonike's death. New powers will rise. I wanted you to be aware of your heritage. And of me." She smiled.

"How... nice."

Mrs. Samson pushed away from my bed. "Don't give it too much thought. Rest. I'll keep an eye on you."

I yawned, trying to keep the sarcasm from my voice. "Oh, yes. I feel very safe."

She laughed, the sound echoing through the room like the tolling of a bell.

I blinked, and Mrs. Samson was gone. I fell back against my pillows, squeezing my eyes shut.

"These drugs are making me hallucinate," I grumbled.

$\mathcal{E}$PILOGUE

DAY SIXTY-NINE, 10:33 A.M.

The helicopter's blades whooshed overhead in a slow descent. I peered through a dirty window as sand rushed to meet us. The skids touched down, and Jim killed the engine.

I tugged off my headset with a hand and plopped it onto the seat next to me.

Lynn leaned around the co-pilot's chair, her engagement ring sparking in the tropical sun. "Are you sure you want to go out there alone?"

"I'll be fine." I turned to Jim. "Thanks for flying me out here."

"Anything for a future sister-in-law." He winked.

Lynn rolled her eyes, but I didn't miss the glance she stole at the diamond ring on her finger. "Be careful, Annie," she warned. "There's still a lot of debris. The cleanup crew Mom hired hasn't gotten out here yet."

"I will."

Lynn heaved the door open, and I hopped out, off balance due to the sling supporting my left arm. The broken remains of the villa stretched before me. The entire building stood strong, but the windows were shattered and the white front had been stained a dark gray. The boardwalk along the beach was destroyed, boards scattered across the sand. I skirted around broken chairs and umbrellas, heading toward the tree line. My imagination painted guests stretched out on towels, kids running

from the villa with floaties, employees serving bright drinks
with paper umbrellas.

Shade cooled the sweat on my skin as I entered the tropical
forest. I let myself remember everything, from the moment I
stepped off the ferry and lost my hat to every encounter after.

When I reached the cliff, I stripped off the sling, stretching
my now-naked arm. The breeze felt chilly against the pale skin.
I reached for the first hole in the rock. As I swung up to the next
opening, my left arm strained at the weight. It was too early in
my healing for rock climbing, and I didn't have any of my
equipment. But I needed to do this again. To sweat. To remember.

Time slowed as I moved up the cliff. My chalk-less palms
slipped on the rock once or twice, but I didn't stop until I
reached the top.

I bypassed the ruins, choosing to forget the horror the sirens
unleashed in the past. I had lived it.

I followed the rock-hewn staircase. Déjà vu skittered across
my skin. I felt like a ghost revisiting a burial site, forgotten by
the living. Then again, if Mrs. Samson was right...

I shook my head. No. I attributed her appearance to a drug-
induced dream. After her "visit," I'd awoken to the real Nurse
Eve checking my vitals.

My sneakers scuffed the platform, sun beating down on my
shoulders. In the far corner, two rusted manacles remained
drilled into the rock. But the bones chained there, the siren that
had suffered on this ledge, was gone.

I stared out at the ocean, stretching forever to the horizon.
I'd lost so many people in such a short time. Even now, months
later, I couldn't grasp the entirety of my grief. Each time I tried
to pick up Benny's DS, my hands would shake. And when I
tried to wear Tamara's necklace—her family refused to let me
give it back—it felt like a noose around my neck.

Whenever I thought of a future without them, my chest hurt.
But Lorelei...

Each time the siren came to mind, I longed for the sea. Remembering her let me forget the pain of everything else. She was a world apart from reality. And, even for a moment, I needed to lose myself. I needed to be free.

I kicked off my sneakers and socks, tossing them at the foot of the steps. I sucked in a puff of air and dove from the platform. Spray flew around me as I splashed into the ocean, sinking to the sandy bottom. With my fear of drowning gone, my ability to swim had blown Victor away when we practiced at a hotel pool. It felt so natural to be in the water I couldn't believe I'd once been so scared of it.

I struck out, hands parting the waves as I cleaved through them.

Down here, deep in the turquoise ocean, I wasn't alone. Lorelei's very soul, if sirens had souls, was here.

I imagined Lorelei's strong scaled arm around me, remembered how it felt as we shot through the water, the safety and familiarity of her touch. She might be gone, and one day Viaii Nisi might disappear. But the memory of Lorelei would never fade from my mind.

We were one.

ACKNOWLEDGEMENTS

I t's taken me almost five years to write this Acknowledgement page. Well, not *this* page specifically. More like it has
taken me five years to publish *These Wicked Waters* so I
could write an Acknowledgement page in the first place. But
here I am—I can hardly believe it.

The last five years have been filled with amazing people
who have helped me along the way.

Thank you…

To my rockstar agent, Becky LeJeune, for believing
in *These Wicked Waters* even more than I did. Also to the amazing team at Owl Hollow Press who literally made my words into
a tangible book. I am so grateful.

To my many critique partners who read so many versions
of *These Wicked Waters*. Two of which involved puke. Specifically, Heather Cook who has helped edit my stories since we
first met in elementary school! Thank you all for your invalua-
ble insights.

To my friends Jeremy Bell and Natalie Myers who cele-
brated each milestone of publishing with me, usually by going
out to eat. No regrets.

An enormous thank you to my mom for her love and support and my dad for building me a desk from scratch so I had a
nice place to write. To my sisters Maddie (you finally got your
book dedication!), Becky, and Sarah who are always eager to
read my scribblings.

And to my husband, Jeff. The romance in my books pales to the life I have with you. Thank you for being my #1 fan, my tireless editor, and my best friend. I love you.

Finally, I thank God for the inspiration to write and for opening the right doors so this killer-siren story could be in your hands, Mysterious Reader. I hope you enjoyed reading this book as much as I enjoyed writing it.

EMILY LAYNE grew up a proud Army brat with an Anne Shirley-esque imagination. She loves reading, eating too many potato chips, and spending time with her husband—who loves books almost as much as she does.

When not writing fantastical stories, Emily acts a judge in an annual writing contest, explores the great outdoors, and spends way too much time at the library. Her debut novel was inspired by her experience on a cruise ship (which proved to be quite flammable, unfortunately).

Find Emily at emilylaynebooks.com

#THESEWICKEDWATERS